CONTENTS

A Christmas Ball

JENNIFER ASHLEY

"Enthralling and poignant . . . Ashley touches readers on many levels."

—RT Book Reviews (Top Pick) on
The Madness of Lord Ian Mackenzie

"A deliciously dark and delectably sexy story of love and romantic redemption that will captivate readers with its complex characters and suspenseful plot."

—Booklist on *The Madness of Lord Ian Mackenzie*

EMILY BRYAN

"Bryan has a great handle on the material and her characters, creating a charming, colorful story with an intricate, fast-paced story line."

—Publishers Weekly on *Distracting the Duchess*

"Wickedly witty writing and wonderfully entertaining characters are the key ingredients in Bryan's sinfully sexy historical romance."

—Booklist on *Distracting the Duchess*

ALISSA JOHNSON

"With its delightfully original characters and writing that sparkles with sharp humor, Johnson's debut historical romance is [a] triumph of wit and passion."

—John Charles, Chicago Tribune on
As Luck Would Have It

"Rapier wit and comedic timing lure readers into a romance that proves laughter is best shared with those you love."

—Kathe Robin, RT Book Reviews on *Tempting Fate*

A Christmas Ball

JENNIFER ASHLEY
EMILY BRYAN
ALISSA JOHNSON

LEISURE BOOKS NEW YORK CITY

A LEISURE BOOK®

October 2009

Published by

Dorchester Publishing Co., Inc.
200 Madison Avenue
New York, NY 10016

ISBN 10: 0-8439-6250-X
ISBN 13: 978-0-8439-6250-5
E-ISBN: 978-1-4285-0748-7

The name "Leisure Books" and the stylized "L" with design are trademarks of Dorchester Publishing Co., Inc.

Printed in the United States of America.

10 9 8 7 6 5 4 3 2 1

Visit us online at www.dorchesterpub.com.

A
Christmas Ball

My Lady Below Stairs

Emily Bryan

Thanks to my agent Vivian Beck, who first believed in my writing. And to my fabulous editor, Leah Hultenschmidt, who gave me my first chance. And most especially, I want to thank my parents who showed me what love that lasts looks like. They were married on Christmas Day (A three generation family tradition I did not feel called to continue when my DH and I tied the knot!). My parents will celebrate their 56th Merry Christmas together this year! Now that's a legacy of love!

Wishing you the same,
Emily
www.emilybryan.com

Chapter One

"Bastardy has its privileges," Jane Tate muttered. She slogged across the snowdrifted alley from Lord Somerville's grand townhouse to his not-so-grand henhouse. No one else wanted to gather eggs on this bitterly cold morning, so Jane had been pressed into service.

Which suited Jane better than a dollop of milk in her tea. Cook might get suspicious if she volunteered again.

She picked her way through the fresh snow. Even in this top-lofty London neighborhood, his lordship kept a dozen fat guineas and six red-capped Dorking hens. Their coop squatted next to the stable. An ill-tempered rooster strutted along its sagging peak, standing guard over his harem.

Cold lanced up Jane's shin. She had pulled on two pairs of woolen stockings that morning, but they were no match for the shilling-sized hole in her left shoe.

He's worth a touch of frostbite, she reminded herself.

Before she pushed through the henhouse door, a hand grasped her elbow and pulled her into the shadows of the stable. Even though she had hoped for this very thing, the man's mouth swallowed her cry of surprise. He smelled of fresh straw and oiled leather and warm horseflesh.

And tasted like heaven itself. Jane slid her arms into the warmth of his open jacket, pressing herself against him.

Ian Michael MacGregor. The sight of the head groom's

angular face was enough to give Jane shivers, even without a hole in her shoe. His kiss warmed her, sending hot urgent messages to secret places in her body. Places an unmarried scullery maid shouldn't be so achingly aware of.

"Janie, love." His voice tickled her ear and his lips set her skin dancing. She thought her name ordinary in the extreme, but when Ian said it, his soft Scottish burr caressed the sound with reverence, as if she were a grand lady.

His rough hands found her waist and tugged her closer. Even through the layers of wool, Jane felt the solid maleness of him. All the female kitchen help, even a few of the married ones, made an excuse to take a trip to the stable when the weather was warm enough for Ian Michael to remove his jacket and roll up his shirtsleeves. Dealing with the heavy team of horses that pulled his lordship's equipage made Ian's arms and chest ripple with strength.

"If the man's arms are that fine," Jane's friend Agnes had exclaimed the first time she watched Ian subdue a particularly mettlesome stallion, "just imagine what the rest of him must be like!"

Jane smiled. She had a good imagination. If Ian had his way, she wouldn't have to imagine much longer. She pushed against his chest and he drew back to look down at her, his peat-colored eyes hooded with wanting.

"Please, Ian. Someone might see us."

"There's none here but Tom and he's busy polishing the brass on the brougham. Come, lass, you're cold as a well-digger's knee." Ian rubbed her hands between his and blew on them, his breath puffing in the chilly air like a dragon's. Then he pressed a kiss on the skin of her exposed wrist. A wicked smile curved his lips. "I'm only after warming you a bit."

"If you think I believe that, you're the stupid, big Scot everyone takes you for."

Jane knew behind his rude upbringing, Ian's sharp mind bristled with intelligence. Their friendship had begun when he discovered she knew how to read and write. Ian had convinced her to teach him. Of course, the only reason *she* knew how was because of a well-kept secret.

Though Jane wasn't quite sure what to name it yet, her friendship with Ian Michael had blossomed from reading lessons into something much more.

"I brought you a copy of Locke and a warm tart." Jane handed him the precious book she'd pinched from his lordship's library. Lord Somerville would never miss it and she'd return the book after Ian read it, so it wasn't stealing. Not really. The neatly wrapped tart she'd made herself.

"Something for my mind *and* my body, eh? No one can fault ye for ignoring a man's appetites. Not all of them, in any case." He pocketed the book and unwrapped the fragrant pastry, waggling his dark brows at her. "Ye know how fond I am of . . . *tarts.*"

Jane smacked his chest. "I'm no tart, Ian Michael MacGregor."

"No, I can see you're not. But ye canna deny ye enjoy kissing me like one, can ye?" He bit into the plum tart with relish. "Och, Janie, this is almost as sweet as your kisses. Give me half a moment and we'll start again where we left off, so I can make a true comparison."

"I don't think that's a good idea," Jane said, even though the thought of Ian's kisses was what had had her tripping through the snow with a light heart this morning. "You know his lordship doesn't allow liaisons among the staff."

"Liaison," he repeated with a laugh, as he dusted the

last tart crumbs from his big workman's hands. "You've picked up some mighty fine airs, my Lady Jane."

"And you've some plum filling at the corner of your mouth, sir."

She reached up to wipe it away. Ian caught her hand, slipped her finger between his lips and sucked the jam off. Her knees threatened to buckle.

"Is that what we're after having? A liaison?" He planted a kiss on her knuckles and then pressed her hand against his chest so she could feel the great muscle of his heart pounding beneath her palm. Eyes closed, he leaned down and touched her forehead with his. Need hummed between them. "A liaison sounds like more than a stolen kiss or two. Sounds like verra much more."

For a few heartbeats, Jane thought of Ian's little room at the far end of the horse stalls. Of his string bed. Of what might happen if she let him lead her there. Her insides melted like a wax candle, but with effort, she pinched off the flame. Being an earl's bastard was bad enough. Being a scullery maid's bastard didn't bear contemplating. She wouldn't hang that label on an innocent child.

Jane stepped out of the circle of Ian's arms. "Don't you realize it's the sack for both of us if we're found out?"

"And I'm thinking that wouldn't be all bad." Ian tugged her close again. He was so warm, it was like a snuggling up to a roaring fire. Jane went willingly. "In fact, I just found out—"

"Jane! Where are you? I say! Janie, come quick!"

"That's Agnes," Jane said. "What's she doing out in this cold?"

As an upstairs maid, Agnes rarely ventured down into the kitchen unless it was mealtime, and never out to the stable, if she could help it.

Unless Ian Michael was in his shirtsleeves.

"After all," Agnes had explained, "this has nothing to do with our friendship, Janie. The day I fail to notice a fine-looking fellow is the day I turn up my toes."

"I must go." Jane pulled away from Ian.

"Stay, Jane. If we're caught together, we'll—"

"Ian, please."

He swept her up for a last kiss, an urgent play of lips, teeth, and tongue. The now-familiar ache *down there* made visions of Ian's string bed swim in her head.

Jane swayed unsteadily when he released her. "If I can," she said breathlessly, "I'll come again."

"Aye, lass, I'd make sure of that if you'd let me," he murmured as she ran off.

From the huskiness in his tone, Jane knew he'd said something vaguely naughty. Warmth glowed in her belly as she stumbled back toward the main house where Agnes was tiptoeing around the deeper drifts.

"Jane, where've you been? You'll make me ruin these slippers!" The outlandish beaded mules were Lady Sybil's last-season castoffs. They were a little small for Agnes, but she was wearing them as she worked, in the hope that they'd stretch a bit. "I have to keep them nice for the Ladies' Maids' Ball."

Once a year, all the footmen and maids from the city's great houses decked themselves in secondhand finery and "tripped the light fantastic" 'til dawn. The satin confections on Agnes's feet would be perfect for the coming event.

But they were not so handy in a snow-washed alley.

Jane suspected concern over her hand-me-down slippers wasn't the only thing making Agnes's brows nearly meet over her pert nose. "What's got your pantaloons in a bunch?"

Agnes glanced over her shoulder as if she feared someone might overhear their conversation. She grasped Jane's arm and hurried on in a whisper, "I can't say here, but you've got to come and quickly. And we can't let anyone see you."

"What on earth—"

"No more questions. Can't you see I'm freezing my bum off?" Since Agnes rarely strayed outside, she didn't have a cloak. The cold wind had her teeth chattering. "And for heaven's sake, do what they ask or I'm in for it."

They slipped into the scullery, where Jane hung her thin wrap on its peg. The girls dodged through the kitchen when Cook's back was turned. Then Agnes, a finger pressed to her lips for silence, led Jane up the back staircase to the family's floor.

"Agnes, I can't be caught here."

"Then you'd best keep quiet, hadn't you?"

Except for midnight raids on his lordship's library, Jane never set foot in the public or family portions of the great house.

When she was very young, she had served at table, carefully handling the fine porcelain and ladling out lavish portions. Then one fateful evening Lady Sybil had asked her mother and father why the soup girl had a face that looked just like hers.

Jane could have explained it to Sybil. Jane's mother was a pretty laundress who died in her birthing. The help at Somerville Manor undertook to raise Jane with benevolent negligence. But the folk who served below stairs made certain she learned young exactly what a bastard was.

The countess forbade Jane to be seen above stairs after that and even though several years had passed since her ladyship died of a lingering ague, the order was never rescinded.

Jane followed Agnes down the polished hall. The elegantly striped wallpaper made the corridor seem to stretch out far longer than it was. She forced herself not to run a fingertip along the gleaming oak wainscoting.

"Cook's going to be furious if I don't come back with the eggs soon," she murmured.

"Oh, Jane, forget the eggs. Hang the eggs. This is far more important than eggs!" Agnes's face squinched tight, as if she were trying to keep from bursting into tears.

"What—"

"I can't say more." She stopped before Lady Sybil's chamber. "Don't speak unless spoken to," Agnes ordered. "And for pity's sake, stand up straight. Oh, how I wish I had a comb about me."

Jane put a hand to her windblown hair. An unfashionable chestnut in a time when blonde was the color of choice, at least her hair was thick. Ian certainly never complained.

Except when she used too many pins.

Agnes opened the door and waved her in. Mr. Bottlesby, the stiff head butler, and Mr. Humphrey Roskin, Esq., his lordship's solicitor, were positioned at opposite ends of the room. The cold air in the chamber fairly shimmered with tension. A copper hip bath, the water crusted with a thin layer of ice, stood in the center of the room. One of the window sashes had been left halfway up, and a stiff wind had overpowered the shallow fireplace.

There was no sign of Lady Sybil.

Mr. Roskin raked his gaze over Jane like a wolf searching out the weakling of the flock.

"Bollocks, man! You can't mean to fool people with this!" Mr. Roskin punctuated his words with a flailing gesture.

"Sir, I humbly beg to disagree," Mr. Bottlesby said with downcast eyes.

Jane flinched in surprise. Below stairs, the butler was lord in all but name. Bottlesby wielded absolute power over the rest of the staff, swaggering with pride in the servants' quarters. Jane was taken aback by the change in his demeanor now that he was out of his element.

"If you look beyond this girl's disreputable clothing," Mr. Bottlesby said, "you'll see that they are as like as two peas. In fact, I've been assured that our Jane has presented herself as Lady Sybil many times in the past, with none the wiser."

Jane's gaze cut to Agnes, who was studying the tips of her beaded shoes with guilty absorption. Jane had sworn her to secrecy.

"Are you aware that not so long ago the penalty for impersonating a member of the aristocracy was branding?" Mr. Roskin's left eye twitched as he glared at her.

"Sir, there's no need to frighten the girl," Mr. Bottlesby said. "We are a civilized nation. Surely no one's been branded since—"

"No, you're right. Nowadays, they'll just pack her to off to Newgate, like as not."

Newgate! Jane's vision tunneled, and she forced herself to take a deep breath. If they sent her to prison, away from Ian Michael, it would be worse than branding.

Even though Agnes had warned her not to speak, she couldn't stop the words.

"Sir, my offense took place years ago. Lady Sybil simply asked me to sit for a few lessons in her stead. Her tutor never even knew the difference. Truly, no one was harmed by our childish prank."

She refrained from mentioning that she had learned enough to pick the lock of literacy. Some members of the upper class took exception to reading and writing among their inferiors.

"There, Mr. Roskin, you see," Mr. Bottlesby said.

"Well-spoken, for all that she's a scullery maid. Even their voices and inflections are similar. I tell you, she can do it."

"Do what?" Jane asked with a sinking feeling in her gut.

"Perpetrate fraud on the *ton* of London," Mr. Roskin said stonily, his already pasty complexion fading to the color of day-old suet. "And if you are discovered, I assure you, no one will dismiss it as a childish prank."

Chapter Two

"I'll not be party to fraud," the infuriating maid said with the primness of a bluestocking.

"It's rather too late for such scruples, don't you think? You've already committed the offense more than once," Humphrey Roskin said. If he could put a bit of fear into her before she agreed to do his bidding, so much the better. Terrified people were always so much easier to manipulate. "If I choose to report your activity, the fact that you were younger when you impersonated Lady Sybil will not matter to the magistrate."

Roskin had learned intimidation from a master—Lord Somerville himself.

The earl had threatened Roskin before he left for a season of leisurely hunting at his country estate.

"I want my daughter safely betrothed by Christmas to a gentleman of no small means," Somerville had demanded. "Do not fail me in this enterprise, sir, or I'll see you transported to New South Wales on the next packet on the charge of embezzlement!"

The earl suspected Roskin had helped himself to the Somerville coffers, but could prove nothing. Still, if a peer of the realm accused him, Roskin would stand condemned.

Justly, too, he admitted to himself. So far all Lord Somerville had was doubt and conjecture. Roskin was satisfied he'd covered his trail well enough that the missing funds would never be found. But he was in no hurry to be shuffled off to a wretched penal colony. So he had convinced Lord Somerville that a wealthy son-in-law was the answer to all his problems.

Then Lord Somerville had made finding that wealthy son-in-law *Roskin's* problem.

"Sir, I've no wish to be difficult," Jane said, calling Roskin back to his present predicament. "But what does Lady Sybil say to this?"

"We have no idea where she is," Mr. Bottlesby admitted softly.

"Or how much of a head start she has this time," Roskin added. *What does one wear in New South Wales this time of year?*

"Last one to see her was Agnes, very early this morning," Mr. Bottlesby said. "Lady Sybil rang you around six, didn't you say, girl?"

Agnes nodded mutely.

Roskin consulted his pocket watch. Half past ten. The little vixen had several hours on them.

"Milady called for a bath, then demanded privacy." Bottlesby mopped his brow with an impeccably white handkerchief. "Agnes said she wanted to take her time with her ablutions."

Roskin glared at the upstairs maid. Giving Agnes another tongue-lashing might ease his frustration, but it would accomplish nothing.

"A proposal of marriage is a special occasion, she said." Bottlesby popped his knuckles nervously. "Lady Sybil told Agnes she wished to make the most of it."

"Which she has obviously done." Roskin leaned out the open window and peered down again. A gnarly oak with sturdy limbs near the casements had provided an admirable ladder. Fresh footprints marred the snow at the tree's trunk, then dotted the white lawn in a beeline to the busy St. James Street. Lady Sybil could have hailed a hansom and might be anywhere by now.

Boil the wallaby stew! That passage to Australia was looking more certain by the minute.

"She left the betrothal portrait," Bottlesby said, waving a hand toward the shrouded canvas on an easel in the corner. "We may be getting ahead of ourselves here. Perhaps this is just a bit of high spirits, what? Lady Sybil must mean to return in time for the ball. Perhaps Jane won't actually be needed."

Roskin eyed the covered canvas. No one had seen the portrait on which Giovanni Brunello had labored in secret for the past six months.

"Art," the Italian master had declared with much *r*-rolling, "must bloom in seclusion before it is thrust into the cold light of the oh-so-critical world's eyes."

Six months. Personally, Mr. Roskin was impressed that the smooth-talking foreigner had managed to make Lady Sybil sit still that long.

He strode to the canvas and pulled off the sheeting.

Bottlesby and the two maids gasped.

The rendering was a perfect likeness of Lord Somerville's daughter, and if Roskin weren't so upset he'd have to admit it was also a dead ringer for the scullery maid. Chestnut hair framed her oval face in soft curls. Brunello had captured Sybil's laughing hazel eyes, and a sly grin tugged at her too-thin-for-fashion lips. There was no hint of artistic flattery in the representation of her features. Which meant Lady Sybil must also possess carnation-sized breasts with pert pink nipples, a slightly rounded belly and a tuft of curling dark hair at the juncture of her long legs.

"Oh, dear. Oh, dear," Bottlesby chanted.

That was not the first sentiment that sprang to Roskin's mind, but he bit his lip to keep the expletive from spewing out.

At least Australia's supposed to be warm this time of year.

There was a cream-colored envelope on the ledge of the easel.

Roskin ripped it open and read the missive silently. Bottlesby continued to murmur, "Oh, dear. Oh, dear."

Roskin felt his neck heating. By now it must be the same shade of scarlet as the sealing wax the blasted girl had used on the letter.

"It's official. She's run off with Brunello," Roskin said.

Bottlesby turned to go. "I'll form a search party."

Roskin caught him by the arm. "You'll do no such thing. We have no idea where to look, and we must proceed with discretion. If we raise a hue and cry, it will make no difference, even if we should find her in time. The damage will already be done in the minds of the *ton*."

"Oh, yes, quite. I take your meaning, sir."

Bottlesby bobbed his head like a sparrow, but truly, he had no idea. Scandal might be weathered if one were well connected, which Lord Somerville was. Or well moneyed, which he was not. But worse than scandal, the impending betrothal would certainly be called off. If that happened, Lord Somerville faced financial ruin.

And Humphrey Roskin would face ruin of his own.

It should have been so easy. When Lord Somerville had introduced him to Lady Sybil, Roskin had been quick to name her a marketable asset.

He revised his assessment in short order.

Lady Sybil might be fine to look upon, but her acerbic tongue and mettlesome temper quickly overbalanced her attributes. She belonged on the London stage, not before a gentleman's hearth.

Yet Roskin had managed to wangle a match for her with Viscount Eddleton. A wealthy young gentleman with excellent prospects, since his uncle, the Duke of Pemworthy, was languishing in the last stages of consumption and had no son to inherit his title. Eddleton might be called "His Grace" before the Season was out.

Arranging the match would smooth over Lord Somerville's suspicions and secure his enduring goodwill.

And his daughter's enduring wrath. Sybil despised having her fiancé chosen for her.

"We haven't much time." Roskin dragged a hand over his face, causing his jowls to droop more than usual. Lord Somerville was driving in from his country house to escort his daughter to the annual Christmas Ball hosted by the Marquess and Marchioness Hartwell. There'd be hell to pay when he discovered Roskin hadn't been able to keep Sybil from folly. "If the lady doesn't appear at Lord Hartwell's ball, she may as well not ever show her face in London society again."

"Then Lady Sybil must attend," the scullery maid declared. "I assume you wish me to go in her place."

"Splendid," Mr. Bottlesby said, a tight-lipped smile slicing his face like a spade mark across a potato. "Now it's only for tonight, you understand."

Roskin's head jerked at that. "Maybe not. Who knows when we'll find the real Lady Sybil? This pretty deception may stretch into weeks."

Or months. Or years. If Sybil really wanted to run off with her artistic lover to Italy or some other outlandish place, they might never find her.

And good riddance!

"You'll have to accept Lord Eddleton's suit," Roskin said. "He's planning to propose to Lady Sybil tonight."

The girl went pale as chalk. "I thought I'd only have to dance a few sets and make small talk. Then maybe plead a headache and leave early. I couldn't possibly fool Lady Sybil's fiancé."

"I don't see why not. They've never even spoken. This is an arranged match," Roskin explained. *His* arranged match, and no one, least of all a scullery maid, was going to muck things up. "The paperwork's been drawn up. The proposal is merely for form's sake."

"Still, a woman wants to accept her own proposal of marriage," Jane said. "I don't think—"

"We don't need you to think. Good God! It's a woman's featherheaded thinking that's got us into this mess!" Roskin said, mentally cursing the absent Sybil. "You only need do as you're told."

Jane stood straighter and looked him squarely in the eye.

Blast and damn! She did favor Lady Sybil out of all knowing. The resemblance was uncanny.

"No." Her voice was quiet but firm.

"No?" Roskin's brows shot skyward.

"No," she repeated, louder this time.

"If you don't do as I say, then I will make it my business to see that a certain head groom celebrates Christmas by losing his position." Jane Tate's face crumpled. The barb hit home, but Roskin might as well drive the nail in deeper. He glanced at the upstairs maid for confirmation. "MacGregor's the name you mentioned, wasn't it? Ian Michael MacGregor?"

Agnes nodded miserably.

"In his lordship's absence, I have the authority to release him from service without delay," Roskin threatened. "And without character."

A working man with no reference was branded a thief or a layabout in the minds of possible employers. MacGregor wouldn't find a position anywhere in the city. Not a reputable position anyway. A man might turn to anything if his stomach knocked against his backbone long enough.

"Well, girl, what's it to be?" Roskin demanded.

Jane's eyes blazed at him. "I'll do it. What choice do I have?"

"None at all," Roskin admitted. "See to it, then. You, girl." He pointed to Agnes. "Step lively and do what you can to turn this sow's ear into a silk purse."

He strode toward the door with Bottlesby dogging his steps like a Lancashire heeler after a ram. When he stopped suddenly, the butler hastily stepped back to keep from running into him.

"The only ones who know of this are we four in this room," Roskin said. "If the particulars of this little deception come to light, I shall know whom to blame. And whom to punish."

The door banged shut behind them.

"I think this will do, don't you?" Bottlesby said.

"Possibly. Flashes of genius strike the most unexpected of noggins. At least, we'll know tonight whether your scheme will work," Roskin growled. He really didn't want to have to develop a taste for boiled kangaroo.

Chapter Three

As soon as Mr. Bottlesby and that odious Mr. Roskin had left Lady Sybil's chamber, Jane rounded on Agnes.

"'Trust me, Janie. I'm your friend, Janie. The day I peach on you is the day the sun won't rise.'" Jane sing-songed an imitation of Agnes, her voice rising in pitch and quivering with fury. "How could you?"

Agnes dabbed her eyes with the corner of her apron. "How could I not? They blamed me for her ladyship running off. As if I could stop her from doing anything she jolly well pleased! But they were going to give me the sack anyway and at Christmastime, to boot! A manger might be well and good for the Lord Jesus, but I don't relish bedding down in one myself. Your secret was the only thing I could think of to save my skin."

Agnes sobbed in misery. Jane's anger sputtered out when her friend's slim shoulders began to shake. She put her arms around Agnes to comfort her.

"There, now. Don't take on so. *I'm* not going to sack you."

The waterworks dried up instantly.

Jane chuckled. "Agnes, you put the players on the London stage to shame."

The lady's maid grinned impishly and shrugged. "A girl has to use what the Good Lord gave her, don't she? You forgive me, Janie?"

Jane rolled her eyes. She might be exasperated by Agnes from time to time, but she could never stay mad at her for longer than a gnat's breath.

"Now, we need to figure out what to do next," Agnes began.

"No, *I* need to figure out what to do next, and I've had more than enough help from you today." Jane paced the sumptuous room. "What would Lady Sybil do?"

"That's easy." Agnes struck the same quasi-classical stance as Lady Sybil in her scandalous portrait. "Pose in the altogether like a light-heeled trollop for some foreign devil and then run off with him at a time most inconvenient for the rest of us."

"That's not very helpful." Jane slanted a sidelong look at Agnes.

"It certainly weren't," Agnes agreed, misunderstanding her completely. "Folk of quality have no consideration at all for them what work for a living, do they?"

Jane sighed. "No, they don't. Well, *this* Lady Sybil may as well follow suit. I'm going to have a bath," she decided.

"But I've already drawn a bath for her ladyship today," Agnes complained.

"Lady Sybil is feeling eccentric and wants another one," Jane said.

"Well, I suppose you will need one before the ball," Agnes admitted with a frown. A bath was the most back-breaking chore for an upstairs maid. "Come, then. You can help me haul out the cold water."

Jane laughed. "You seem to forget that you promoted me to Lady Sybil. I can't be seen doing anything that she wouldn't do at the ball tonight, so I may as well start right now." She flopped onto the bed and lay back on the cool, rumpled sheets. "It's terribly chilly in here, Agnes. Close the window and lay a small fire, there's a good girl.

Wouldn't want to catch my death taking a bath in a cold room."

Agnes stared at her as if she'd suddenly sprouted another head. Then, grumbling under her breath, she did as Jane bid. After she dipped out the first bucket of icy water, she bobbed a mock curtsey to Jane.

"Will there be anything else, *milady*?" she sneered.

"As a matter of fact, there will." Jane propped herself up on her elbows and grinned wickedly at her friend. "Cook sent me after the eggs, but no one's seen hide nor hair of me since I came back into the house with you. While *Lady Sybil's* having her second bath, be a love and fetch the eggs in my place, won't you? Cook is making meringue for dessert today. I'd hate to miss it."

Agnes glared at her.

"You know, you might be able to reheat the bathwater with the steam leaking from your ears," Jane said with a suppressed giggle.

"Now you've gone and made me miss the real Lady Sybil," Agnes said as she turned to go.

"Agnes, wait," Jane called after her. "This is serious. You have to treat me *exactly* as you would the real one. Even when it's just the two of us. This house has its own eyes and ears. You've told me that often enough. If we can't make the house staff believe I'm her ladyship, this will never work and Mr. Roskin will see you get your chance at that manger bed yet."

And Ian Michael will be dismissed without character.

Agnes studied the paisley carpet for a moment. "You're right."

"Thank you."

Agnes shook her head with a smirk. "Keep saying things like that and no one will take you for her ladyship."

Jane looked down her nose at her friend and waggled

her fingers in a dismissive gesture. "Off you go then, girl."

"Better. Still a little too friendly-like, but you'll do. We'll work on it when I get back. Strip out of those clothes and put on one of milady's shifts. I should be able to get some help hauling the water, please God. If Lady Sybil's seen lounging abed still, no one will think a thing of it."

"Really?"

"Some days, she don't rise till three or four of an afternoon."

Jane's day began before the sun showed its face in the tiny window of her attic cell. She settled back into the fine linens. "I think I'm going to enjoy being Sybil."

"Just don't get too used to it. Bad pennies always turn back up. And as pennies go, the real Lady Sybil's the baddest."

After Agnes left, Jane stared up into the festooned silk draperies hovering over the bed. In her garret room, there were bare rafters above her little straw-tick. Jane wondered how many times she could roll over in this luxurious bower before she tumbled out.

Five was the lucky number.

Jane undressed, stashing her threadbare clothing in the bottom of the wardrobe, neatly folded under Lady Sybil's riding boots. Then she found the drawer that held her half sister's unmentionables.

Half sister. Funny how she'd never thought of Lady Sybil in such familiar terms before.

Must come from rifling through someone's undies, Jane reasoned as she ran a finger along the lace trim at the neck of the fine lawn garment. *And planning to wear them.*

Even after Jane donned the shift, the drawer was still full. Sybil had left with nothing but the clothes on her back.

Surrounded by excess, servants at her beck and call, a doting father, a grand match in the offing—what on earth had possessed Lady Sybil? Why would anyone in her right mind run from such a life?

And where is Lady Sybil now?

Sybil arched her back and grasped the rungs in the iron headboard to steady herself. A large lump moved under the thin quilt and settled between her legs. With very little prodding, she raised her knees and spread them wide.

"*Che bella bambina!*" came a muffled voice, desire-roughened and throaty. "*Mi piace il tuo culo.*"

"English, Giovanni," Sybil reminded him with a sigh. "Otherwise you may as well talk to the washstand. What did you just say?"

Her lover's linguistic abilities were sadly lacking sometimes.

But his tongue more than makes up for it, Sybil decided. She gasped as shivers of pleasure licked her thighs.

He worked his way up her body, bypassing the part of her that most longed for his touch—*the wretch!* Giovanni dipped his tongue into her navel for a quick tease and then poked his head from under the covers between her breasts. He nipped each one gently and then turned his blinding smile on her.

"*Mi piace il tuo culo*, little one." Giovanni took a pink nipple between his teeth and bit down hard enough to make her squirm. "How you say . . . 'I like your bum.' "

Sybil smiled and reached under the covers to palm his firm buttocks. Perhaps she should try to learn his tongue. If they were going to live in Italy, she'd need to speak the language. "*Mi piace il . . .*"

"*Il tuo culo*," he prompted.

"*Mi piace il tuo culo*, too!" she said with triumph.

"*Bene*, very good. You are learning."

"But I can't imagine that phrase will be particularly useful in polite conversation. Not in Milan, at least."

"It had better not." His brows lowered slightly.

"Maybe Venice," she teased.

His dark scowl would have terrified most men. Sybil merely laughed.

"Only with you, Giovanni," she said, as she pushed a lock of hair behind his ear. "Yours is the only *culo* I *piace*."

His satisfied laugh resonated through her body as well. "*Eccellente, il mio cuore.*" He pressed his lips to her breastbone in a soft kiss. "My heart."

He raised himself on his elbows and looked down at her, his artist's eyes taking in every line and plane, highlight and shadow of her body. She was used to his scrutiny and she welcomed it. After sitting for the painting, she'd grown to love his hot gaze on her skin. Giovanni made her feel tinglingly alive. None of her pale English suitors had managed that, despite all their fine words and fair manners.

Giovanni was probably ten years or more her senior. His raven hair was shot with a few silver threads, his dark eyes touched at the edges with a fine line or two. Determined trenches ran from the corners of his mouth to his hawkish nose. His cheeks and chin were darkened by the shadow of a beard. Sybil ran her fingertips along the prickly jawline, remembering how delightfully wicked it had felt rubbing along the skin of her inner thighs.

Giovanni had a fascinating face. A mercurial face. A passionate face.

And one Sybil had decided she couldn't live without.

Now there was a hint of puzzlement playing on his features. He cocked his head at her.

"What is it?" she asked.

"I told you I am a man of no property, but—"

"Yes, that may be, but you *are* a man of amazing talent," she said, rocking her pelvis into him. Why did he insist on dwelling on the difference in their stations? It made no difference to her that she was a lady and he a commoner. The man was as well-hung as her father's Thoroughbred stallion and he was rock hard yet again. "You're even a fair-to-middling painter."

"Ah, for that outrage, you will pay!" Giovanni began tickling her ribs.

She squealed with mirth, trying in vain to free herself.

"Mercy, Giovanni," she gasped. "*Per piacere.*"

"Admit it! I am an outstanding painter."

Her laughter was growing desperate, but she managed to choke out her belief that yes, Giovanni Brunello was indeed a master with canvas and oil.

And a veritable wizard with his blessed hands and mouth and cock.

"That's better," he said, mollified. "And now you shall be rewarded."

His head disappeared under the blanket again. Bliss tickled along her ribs and over her belly. The small hairs between her legs swayed in the heat of his breath. She arched into his mouth. His tongue circled her sensitive spot, drawn tight and tender. A helpless moan escaped her lips as she clung to the bedstead for support.

Then suddenly Giovanni pulled back the covers so he could look at all of her. He replaced his mouth with his brilliantly talented hand and continued to massage her wanting into white-hot need.

"You were to be engaged this very night, *cara mia*," he said. "And yet you ran away with your Giovanni. Why did you do it, *Sybella*?"

She bit her lower lip. Her father would demand the

very same thing. And with more cause. Lord Somerville needed the money her future husband had agreed to funnel into his faltering estate. Lord Eddleton had promised to give up his shares in the *Pearl*, a whaler combing the Pacific, as Sybil's wedding portion. When the ship came to port, heavy with ambergris and oil, all her father's financial troubles would be over.

Sybil's conscience pricked over abandoning her sire, but at least she was saving Lord Eddleton the trouble of trying to shore up her father's debt-riddled estate. Lord Somerville had even had the gall to offer one of his unentailed properties as Sybil's dowry. Viscount Eddleton had no idea the bridal gift was mortgaged to the rafters.

Giovanni changed rhythm, stroking her harder. Thoughts of her father and his solicitor's schemes receded into a dark corner of her heart. The wanting was knife-edged now.

"Why, *cara mia*? Why did you agree to come with me?"

"Because I'm selfish!" Her voice was ragged with need. His touch threatened to unravel her, despite the niggling guilt. Her father would just have to think of some other way out of his predicament. "Because I want you and I must have you, devil take the hindermost. There. Are you satisfied?"

One corner of his mouth lifted. "Not yet."

He covered her body with his and she shattered into spasms as he entered her.

"Now, *il mio cuore*," Giovanni said as her inner walls fisted around him and her mouth hung slack with spent passion. "Now, I am satisfied."

Chapter Four

"'Be a love and fetch the eggs, there's a good girl,'" Agnes mimicked under her breath as she slipped Jane's woolsey cloak from the peg by the back door and wrapped the thin garment around her shoulders. "If Jane's lolling about in a tub like the bloody Queen of Sheba, *her lady-ship* ought not begrudge me the use of her wrap."

Agnes pulled the hood up and tied its rough tabs under her chin. She hated to admit it, but Jane was right about the eggs. If no one could find the real Sybil, no one must miss the real Jane.

No one had missed Jane yet. Her work kept her in out-of-the-way places about the massive residence.

So far, so good, Agnes thought as she slogged across the alley. She'd gather the eggs and leave the basket on the counter for Cook to find. But someone was bound to notice when the chamber pots went unemptied and the washing piled up.

Then Agnes would have to come up with some story to explain why Jane had gone missing, something people would accept without question.

Agnes lifted the latch and entered the dim, dusty chicken coop. She'd expected a terrible, acrid stink, but the stable lads must have changed the hens' bedding recently. It was no more unpleasant than beating a feather-bed during spring cleaning.

Agnes reached under the first biddy, darting her hand

in quickly to avoid a pecking. She came up with a warm brown egg to tuck into her small basket.

Can't use a sick grandmother for an excuse, she thought. Jane had no family on her mother's side that anyone knew of. Maybe Agnes could invent some for her. Not a grandparent. They would likely be dead already. *An uncle. A rich uncle. A rich uncle who'd just learned he had a niece and wanted to shower her with his wealth.*

"If a body's going to invent relations, they may as well have deep pockets and open hands." Agnes shrugged philosophically.

No, that'll never do, she mused. *Jane would never come into money and run off without sharing her good fortune. Maybe a* dying *uncle. A kindly old vicar with no one to tend to him and Jane drops everything to rush to his side.*

Yes, that was more believable.

"There ye are, love," a deep voice drawled behind her. "I knew ye couldn't stay away."

Agnes hadn't even heard the coop's door open. A pair of hands grasped her shoulders and spun her around.

"Ian Michael MacGregor!"

He'd bent to kiss her but caught himself just in the nick when he recognized her. He scuttled backward as though Agnes were a snake in the straw.

"Miss Agnes! What're you doing here? And wearing Jane's cloak? Where is she?"

There'd never be a better test of her fib, so Agnes launched into the tale of the dying vicar while she worked around each roost, scrupulously avoiding Ian's gaze. She could spin stories with the best of them, but the telling of them was an art she'd not quite mastered yet. Not if she had to look someone in the eye.

Who knew gathering eggs would be good for something besides making omelets?

"And after the sad passing, Jane says she'll be back,

quick as ever she can," Agnes said, trying not to sound too pleased with herself. Really, this story was ideal and she told it well, if she did say so, adding a neat little flourish at the last moment about how the unhappy illness had all begun with a toothache. Like Mr. Roskin, Agnes suspected Jane's stint as Sybil might be a long one while they searched for the real lady. This tale would serve them well. Who knew how long an old vicar with a rotting tooth might linger? "So it just goes to show, it don't pay a body to neglect his teeth."

Ian Michael's even brows lowered and he crossed his arms over his broad chest. "What's his name?"

"Who?"

"Jane's mysterious new uncle."

"Oh!" Agnes hadn't thought of that. Her gaze darted about the coop and fell on an old tin of snuff that had been wedged into a knothole to keep out the wind. She recognized the Rasp and Crown on the label that proclaimed the contents came from the tobacconists Friburg and Treyer.

"Treyer," she said, thinking Friburg sounded too foreign by half. "*Reverend* Treyer," she added for good measure.

"Och! And I suppose once the good reverend's gone on to his eternal reward, the care of his parish will fall to his faithful sexton, Mr. *Friburg*." Sarcasm made Ian's burr even more pronounced.

Drat the man! He'd noticed the snuff tin, too.

When guile failed, there was always the pecking order of the manor to fall back on and as an upstairs maid, she outranked a stable hand, even the head groom, by several rungs on the household ladder. Agnes made a dismissive little *hmph*-ing noise and tried to push past him.

Ian blocked her way with a long arm across the door.

"The true tale now, if ye please, Miss Agnes," he said,

pleasantly but firmly. "And take your time, lest ye forget any details of importance. Where is my Janie, and why are ye stooping to do her chores?"

Jane leaned back in the copper tub, luxuriating in the treat of a hot bath. She'd washed her hair and scrubbed her body with Pear's Transparent Soap. Once again, she doubted Lady Sybil's sanity for leaving this snug haven to run off with an itinerant painter.

Agnes burst back into the room, windblown and ruddy-cheeked.

"What? Not out yet?" Agnes demanded. "You'll have prunes for fingers, I shouldn't wonder."

"And I won't care a bit." Jane stood and let the soap slither down her clean skin in little runnels. She stepped out of the tub and began to towel herself off. "So far, being Lady Sybil is a slice of paradise."

"We'll see if you're of the same mind once I lace you into that ball gown this evening." Agnes busied herself tidying the already clean room. "Milady had it made on the smallish side and that corset will give you a tight squeeze."

But it was not yet time to dress for the ball and since Jane was playing at being a lady, she must dress according to the clock and expect to change her entire ensemble several times in a single day. It was too late for her to don a morning dress, but the casually elegant half-dress Agnes helped Jane into was deliciously comfortable. Jane had never worn such white linens and the silk Empire dress was so light and airy, it might have belonged to a nymph. The kid slippers looked as if they'd never touched the ground.

Since she had been a small child, Jane had imagined floating down the curved staircase to the dining room. She managed it with more grace than she expected. Descending steps was ever so much easier without a load of crockery or soiled laundry in one's arms. There was little to be done about the calluses at the base of her fingers, but the lotion Agnes had rubbed on her hands had left her skin so smooth, she couldn't bear the thought of donning gloves. Jane would have to wear them for the ball, but for now, she enjoyed the smooth wood of the showy banister beneath her palms.

Since Lord Somerville was not yet in residence, she'd dine alone, but just the thought of sitting on one of the mahogany chairs at the long table made her slightly giddy. Simple Jane Tate, the scullery maid who sat at the foot of the servants' table, was about to dine in the honored place as the daughter of the house.

"Don't look at any of the servants directly," Agnes had advised her. "Or speak to them other than to give an order. And for pity's sake, don't thank them. They'll think Lady Sybil's taken a knock on the head."

So Jane didn't spare more than a glance at the liveried footman who stood behind her seat. She bit her tongue to keep the "thank you" from her lips when he pulled the chair out for her.

Somerville Manor boasted two footmen. Was it Edward or Charles who ladled her white soup from the china tureen? It was difficult to tell when she'd only allowed her gaze to bounce over the man for a moment. All footmen were required to wear powdered wigs and frock coats, a stately, old-fashioned getup that made them all look rather the same.

Though this one seemed taller than she thought either of the Somerville footmen were.

In silence, Jane ate her soup and sliced her cold mutton. The white mushroom fricassee was especially tasty. Jane was unable to name one of the vegetable curries. The herbs and spices used to flavor the meal were richer and far more exotic than she was used to. Jane found herself longing for the friendly banter and plain fare she enjoyed in the kitchen with the rest of the help.

Was Lady Sybil lonely? Is that why she ran away? Jane wondered. She wouldn't have thought so. Not with all the comings and goings, the callers and their cards and—

"Oh!" Jane said aloud. She had just realized she might be called upon to play hostess if any members of the upper crust dropped by that afternoon.

"Is aught amiss, milady?" the footman behind her asked, his tone restrained, but his accent unmistakably Scottish.

"Ian!" she exclaimed, then sank to a furious whisper. "What are you doing here?"

"I'm thinking I might ask ye the same, my Lady Jane," he said, leaning down to pull out her chair. Instead of gently sliding the chair backward so she could stand, he whipped it around to face him and rested his hands on its gilt arms, pinning her in place. "Appears to me there's more than one person out of place in this fine dining room."

Chapter Five

"Ian, stop it. You're going to ruin everything."

"Which part is it you're most particular about me not ruining?"

He leaned down far enough that a little of the powder from his wig fell like snow on the tip of her nose. Jane stifled a sneeze.

"What is it you fancy most? Attending a snooty ball in a borrowed gown or accepting a proposal of marriage from some other blighter?"

"I notice you've not troubled yourself to offer for me," she said stonily.

"That's another matter altogether."

Jane arched a brow at him. If Ian wasn't prepared to marry her, why should he care if she accepted a suit on Lady Sybil's behalf?

"I'm not doing this for myself." She was doing it for him, blast the man! Mr. Roskin had threatened to sack Ian without character if she didn't cooperate. But she wouldn't tell him that. Knowing how much she'd dare for him might make him even more full of himself than he already was. She pressed herself against the padded back of the chair to put some distance between herself and the powder that still drifted from his wig. "I'm doing this for Lady Sybil and for Lord Somerville and for the good of the estate."

Ian narrowed his gaze. "And when has Lord Somerville ever done good for you?"

Jane knotted her fingers in her lap. Trust a stupid, big Scot to cut to the heart of the matter. As soon as she had agreed to the plan, she had realized this might be a chance to win approval from the man who had given her his chestnut hair and hazel eyes, but not his name. Was it so horrible to want Lord Somerville, at least once in her life, to look upon her as a father should look upon his daughter?

Even if he didn't know it was her.

The rice powder tickled her nose again and this time, she wasn't able to keep from sneezing. She caught the blow in one of Lady Sybil's fine lace handkerchiefs. Ian straightened to his full height and glared down at her.

"So ye still intend to go through with this farce, to let this Lord Eddleton paw ye and compromise your virtue—"

"Nothing of the sort. I'll simply attend the ball and accept his proposal in Lady Sybil's stead. *Gentlemen* don't try to ruin women they intend to marry," she said through clenched teeth.

"Ye know little enough of men. Ye've no idea what *gentlemen* are capable of."

"If anyone's trying to compromise me, it's you." There'd be no more fancies dancing in her head about his string bed. Not after this.

He shook his head. "Ye canna go, Jane. I'll not have it."

"You'll not have it? And just what makes you think you have any say in the matter?"

That settled it! The man was demanding a husband's due when he wasn't willing to submit to the yoke. If only he'd admit that he loved her . . . she shoved away that hope with force. Jane stood and struck a pose that was pure Lady Sybil at her haughty best.

"If you try to expose me, I'll denounce you," she promised. "Who will people believe, you think? A stable hand in a borrowed wig or the daughter of the house? Mr. Bottlesby and Mr. Roskin will back me up, if needs be."

"Janie, love—"

"Don't think to sweet-talk me out of this."

Ian's lips drew together in a grim line, but he stepped back a pace. Then he made a less-than-elegant leg to her. Hostling did not lend itself to mastering the finer points of etiquette, after all.

"Verra well. Will there be anything else, *milady*?" His demeanor was deferential in case another servant entered the room, but when he lowered his voice, his whispered tone bristled with fury. "You've had me heart for luncheon, Janie. Mayhap ye'd like me manhood for dessert."

Jane's eyes flared in surprise. A true gentleman was never vulgar to a lady. She flashed a deceptively sweet smile at him. "Only if you let Cook roast it on a spit first."

Jane turned on her heel and flounced out of the dining room before he could speak another word.

The brass knocker on Lord Eddleton's town house banged against the English oak as if an invading army were trying to batter down the portal. Wigram, the last of Eddleton's remaining servants, started for the door.

"Hold a moment." Eddleton slid a finger between the thick damask curtains and chanced a glance down on his front stoop. "No point in answering if it's only a bill collector."

"Milord, I don't think any of them would be so bold as to accost you at your home," Wigram said. "Not by day, at any rate. And chances are very good the word hasn't gotten 'round to all of them yet."

"Thank heaven for small blessings, Wigram. Who knew the randy old goat still had it in him?"

Viscount Eddleton had been heir apparent to Lord Pemworthy for years. Then, less than a fortnight ago, his ailing uncle had felt well enough to wed his pregnant nurse. If the child she carried turned out to be a boy, Eddleton would be cut off without a shilling. The impending disaster—he couldn't view the imminent birth as anything less—wasn't public knowledge yet, but his creditors seemed to have caught wind of it through the back channels of his uncle's staff. Eddleton's credit had been pinched off like an overripe pimple.

Wigram loosed a long-suffering sigh. "Lord Pemworthy has led a retired life for some years—"

"Evidently not retired enough." Eddleton closed one eye and peeped through the small slit in the curtain, again trying to see who was pounding on his door.

"What I mean to say, milord, is His Grace, your uncle, did not often show himself in public. It will surely be some time before the change in your disposition with regard to the inheritance becomes common knowledge among the beau monde."

Eddleton nodded grimly. Not all the upper crust had as open a relationship with their servants as he had with Wigram. Their loss. Servants in the great houses knew everything.

"Let us hope, Wigram," he said. "Gambling debts are deucedly inconvenient to a gentleman. Last time I ventured into White's, the blighters I owed there were almost impossible to shake off."

"If I may suggest, milord, perhaps you might offer your shares in the *Pearl* to settle—"

"I tried, but unfortunately they knew as well as I that the *Pearl* was reported lost in a typhoon off Sumatra." Eddleton smiled sardonically. "Besides, I've already pledged the *Pearl* shares to my soon-to-be-betrothed's father."

Fortunately, Lord Somerville was not as well informed as Lord Eddleton's creditors. The earl's solicitor had agreed to give Eddleton exclusive rights to his unentailed property in Kent in exchange for shares in the whaler as part of the betrothal arrangement between Eddleton and his lordship's harridan of a daughter.

"Sally? Cecily? Hang it all, what is that chit's name?"

"That would be the Lady Sybil," Wigram supplied in a monotone.

"No matter," Eddleton said, with a wave of his hand. "Our salvation lies between her thighs. The girl is Lord Somerville's sole heir and that old graybeard must be pushing seventy. All I need do is get a son on her—a chore I will happily devote all my energies to!—and the succession will continue."

With Eddleton in control of the considerable land-rich Somerville estate until the snot-nosed brat came of age. That left plenty of time for him to enjoy the fruits of his future father-in-law's rank.

He parted the curtains another finger-width and caught sight of a frill of yellow lace.

"Ah! A parasol. Very well, Wigram." Eddleton let the curtain fall back into place. Women were always more taken with his blond Byronic curls than his finances in any case. "Show the lady in."

The rest of the town house was entirely bare of furnishings, but Eddleton had been careful to keep his parlor appointed in the first state of fashion for just such an eventuality. His sorry financial state was still a secret to the *ton*, and he intended to keep it that way.

He settled into a red leather wing chair flanking the fireplace and opened a dog-eared copy of Keats. He rarely read poetry, but *appearing* to read poetry was every bit as effective when it came to impressing members of the fair sex. Women found Keats's work sensitive and endearing, qualities Eddleton could not claim in his own right but was happy to borrow for short periods of time. He might be intending to plight his troth at Lord Hartwell's ball later that evening amid much pomp and general well-wishing, but a prudent man always kept a few tender morsels on the string.

He didn't look up immediately when the delicate patter of feminine steps came to a stop at his threshold. Whoever his caller was, she'd no doubt think him enthralled by the poet's fine words. He forced himself not to turn his head when he heard the faint rustle of silk.

"Ahem!" the woman finally said.

Eddleton looked up with what he hoped was a dreamily distracted expression. Then he recognized his caller. He snapped the book shut.

"Lady Darvish." He rose to greet the last woman in all London he'd wish to find in his parlor.

"Good afternoon, Lord Eddleton," she said with a wry smile. "Your man said you were at home and receiving callers. The way you've kept me standing, I must say, it doesn't seem as if you've much talent for hospitality."

"Forgive me." He rose to his feet, trying desperately to think of some way to be rid of her quickly. "I wasn't expecting company today."

"Of course you weren't. That's why you were trying to read Keats upside down. Thinking of your coming betrothal to the lovely Lady Sybil Somerville, no doubt. No, don't bother to deny it. The *ton* talks of nothing but who intends to do what to whom."

He choked out a startled laugh. "Still, I apologize for making you wait."

"Think nothing of it, my dear boy. I will forget it in a trice if you ring for tea and do your best to entertain me forthwith." She floated across the room with grace and settled into the chair Eddleton had just vacated.

"Of course," he said, jangling the bell that called Wigram to the doorway. He sent his butler a look of alarm over Lady Darvish's ornately decorated bonnet.

Good Lord! Is that a stuffed pigeon wedged amid the lace and other folderol?

"Wigram will be right back with our refreshments, Madam." And, he hoped, a manufactured emergency that required Eddleton's immediate presence elsewhere.

"Oh, that will never do! 'Madam' sounds so old." Lady Darvish laughed gaily as she removed her hat, signaling that the visit would be an extended one. "You must call me Leticia for I predict we will be great friends. May I call you Bertram?"

Eddleton's mouth opened and closed wordlessly several times before he managed to sputter, "But my name is George."

"Oh! How deplorably dull and unimaginative of your parents."

He blinked in surprise. "May I remind you George happens to be the Christian name of our king?"

"And I can't imagine why anyone would want to share a name with a halfwit or his pudgy son. Besides, George is far too ordinary to stick in my head. Every other titled gent in London is called George these days! Bertram suits you, so Bertram you shall be." Leticia flashed a toothy smile. "Sit down, Bertie. You're wobbling a bit."

Eddleton sank into the other wing chair and said the first bland pleasantry that came to his mind. "You're looking fit. I trust you're well."

If he bored her with polite tedium, perhaps she'd leave sooner.

"Coming out of mourning will do that for a body," she said, spreading her bright yellow skirt across the red leather to good effect.

Lady Darvish's smart ensemble must have come in on the latest boat from Paris. The baroness was well moneyed and, if Eddleton were being honest, he'd have to admit he found her surprisingly easy on his eyes for a woman of her age. The high-waisted fashion of the day suited her. She was attractive in a long-toothed, too-thin-for-comfort sort of way.

"I'm ever so glad to be wearing color again," she said. "Black is rarely becoming to anyone and that pale lavender makes even the hardiest miss appear lifeless."

"My condolences on your loss."

Lady Darvish had buried four husbands. Burying one husband might be chalked up to bad luck. Burying four smacked of skullduggery.

"Water under the bridge," she said with a wave of her ringed hand. "Bert was never the robust sort."

"Bert? Your husband's name was Bert?"

"I called all my husbands Bertram. It kept things uncomplicated."

So, the rumors were true. Lady Darvish, the Black Widow of Wembley Street, was on the prowl once again. Eddleton had no desire to be Bert Number Five.

"Lady Dar—"

"Leticia," she corrected.

"Leticia," he repeated. Bugger him, if the woman didn't dimple almost prettily when he said her name. "I confess myself at a loss as to the point of your visit today. Of course, we know each other in the most oblique manner, but you and I rarely move in the same circles—"

"Ah, but we do have common acquaintances," she all but purred. "And my particular friend Lady Martin-Featherwight assures me that, unlike my dear departed Bert, you *are* the robust sort."

He stifled a groan. His ill-considered affair with the wealthy matron was coming back to bite him on the arse.

The lady had been very generous, but it was the hardest work he'd ever done with his breeches round his ankles.

"Um, Lady—I mean, Leticia, well, I . . ." He groped for the right words as a drowning man might clutch at flotsam. "I'm to be married." There! He'd grasped a promising straw.

"Oh, I know," she said brightly, leaning forward to pat his knee. "And I wish you much joy, Bert. Marriage is a wonderful thing. I loved all my husbands, you know. In my way."

"Then, what . . ."

Leticia giggled like a much younger woman. "Oh, this *is* the fun part. Don't you just love the chase?"

His brow furrowed in puzzlement.

"Don't be coy, my dear," she said. "Your impending nuptials needn't impinge upon us. I'm sure we can come to a mutually satisfactory arrangement."

"Good God! I believe you are offering me carte blanche." Eddleton reached for indignation and found a shred still buried deep in his soul. He sheltered behind it like an invisible shield as he stood. "Madam, you have mistaken me for another sort of man altogether. I must ask you to leave."

Her smile faded. "Very well, if that's the way you want it." Lady Darvish rose and strode to the doorway. Then she stopped and looked back at him, a feline smile lifting her lips. "But we aren't finished yet, Bert. You are a young man in a great deal of debt."

"My financial state is none of your concern."

"That's where you're wrong," she said, with an arch of her painted brow. "You see, I bought your vowels. All of them."

Eddleton felt himself blanch white as paper. His creditors had sold his IOUs to Lady Darvish.

"You owe me a considerable sum. A staggering sum,

actually. I imagine that's something you'd rather your future father-in-law not discover," Leticia said, as she adjusted her bonnet, making sure the dead pigeon faced forward. "But don't fret, dearie. One way or another, we'll work out a repayment plan. I expect I'll see you at Lord Hartwell's ball tonight. Everyone who's anyone will be there. I'll save a waltz for you. Perhaps several of them. Good day, Bert."

Eddleton sank back into his chair. He had never thought he'd envy a dead man, but he was sick with resentment toward the four already-dead Berts.

He might even trade places with the pigeon.

Chapter Six

Night fell over the city, a heavy black mantle. The few stars that managed to pierce the gloom glittered like shards of glass, hard-edged and cold. Ian Michael was still wearing the footman's powder blue knee breeches and frock coat when he helped Tom Peckham hitch up the beautifully matched ebony mares to Lord Somerville's elegant brougham. In the yellow light of the lantern, Tom cast a sideways glance at Ian.

"Where's Charlie?"

"I'm filling in for him," Ian said. "He's a touch under the weather."

What Charlie was actually under was a pile of hay. Ian had shelled out tuppence for some gin. A one-penny tot was enough to lay most men low, and Charlie had no head for drink at all. The footman was peacefully snoring off his snootful above the snug stable.

"Any sign of his lordship?" Ian asked.

Tom shook his head.

"Then maybe Lady Sybil won't be off to the ball." Ian swatted one of the mares on the rump. She startled, but moved into the traces with an irritated whicker. "Surely milady won't go without proper escort."

"No chance of that." Tom jerked his head toward the back door of the manor house. Edward, the other footman, was heading toward them. "Willful as that young lady is, I suspect she figures *we're* all the escort she needs.

Glad she'll be spoken for this night. Reckon a husband will settle her proper."

"I doubt it," Ian said, knowing they were talking about two different young ladies. But Jane and Sybil shared more than a father and a disturbingly similar face. Single-mindedness bred true in the Somerville line on both sides of the blanket.

Ian climbed onto the back rail of the carriage with the other footman. He'd already squared matters with Edward. For a tin of pipe tobacco next payday, Ed had agreed to look the other way no matter what befell this night. Tom mounted the driver's seat and chirruped the team down the snow-clogged alleyway. Once they spilled out into the wider street, he drove the equipage up smartly in front of Somerville House, so her ladyship could trip lightly down the shoveled walk.

Jane appeared, silhouetted in the grand doorway, decked out like a queen. Ian's chest constricted. This was the life she should have had. In a kinder world, she would have known the love and approval of her father without having to go to such ridiculous lengths to earn them.

And Lord Somerville couldn't even bother to show up in time to squire his daughter—his real daughter, so far as his lordship knew—to meet her future husband.

Who's the real bastard in this little play?

"Hope Lord Somerville hasn't met with difficulty getting back into town," Edward said, as he hopped down to open the door for the approaching lady.

Funny. Ian hoped his lordship was tail-over-teakettle in a ditch someplace. *Anything that would explain his absence besides just not giving a damn.*

Ian tried not to look directly at Jane as Edward handed her into the brougham. A real footman would keep his eyes in his head instead of ogling the lady, hoping to see a slender wrist or a neatly turned ankle. But Ian's peripheral vision had always been keen. Her lovely face was tight and drawn.

With nerves over what she was about to do? Or disappointment that she wouldn't spend the short drive over to Hartwell House in the company of the man whose carelessness with his seed had given her life? Other than seeing to it that Jane had a roof of sorts over her head, the earl had never troubled himself with his by-blow. Yet Ian knew without being told that if Lord Somerville had been there to escort her, those private moments with her father would have been the highlight of Jane's evening.

His fingers itched to strangle the old bugger for disappointing her.

The brougham lurched forward, the harness bells tinkling a merry tune. His Janie was off to the ball and all Ian could do was hang on to the coach rail and try not to fall off.

Or was it?

"Hold a moment, friend," Ian said to the other footman. "I'll be right back."

Gripping the carriage rail, he worked his way along the bouncing rig to the right side door, finding what toeholds he might, swinging by his arms alone when he couldn't locate a resting place for his feet. Then just as they neared a corner, he pulled open the door and swung his body into the moving carriage, feetfirst.

Jane yelped, but he covered her mouth with his hand.

"Easy, girl. It's only me," he said with the same soothing tone he'd use for a spooked mare. "If ye cry out, Tom will stop the carriage and Lady Sybil will be found in a compromising position with a mere stable hand."

Her eyes widened in the soft carriage lamplight and then she bit his finger as hard as she could.

"Ow!"

She leaned forward and clamped *her* palm over *his*

mouth. "Guess you don't like being surprised either." Jane withdrew her hand and crossed her arms. "Now, what are you doing here, Ian?"

"Trying to talk sense into ye while there's still time to stop this foolishness."

Her mouth set in a firm line. "You know I won't listen."

"Then I won't talk."

He pulled her across the narrow space onto his lap. She smelled of rose petals and her cheek was as soft as one beneath his palm.

Her eyes were enormous in the dim light. "Ian, I—"

"Ye don't need to talk either, love."

He caressed her jawline and lowered his mouth to hers, stopping a finger-width from his goal. Her breath feathered across his lips, warm and sweet. A rough roustabout like him, he knew he didn't deserve her, but he couldn't help himself. He looked into her eyes, hoping to see invitation, fearing he might not, and wondering what he might do if he didn't.

Her eyelids fluttered closed.

There is a God in heaven!

He covered her mouth with his. They'd played at kisses before, teasing and nipping, and all the while, his mind had wandered to what might come next. Should he try to touch her breast? Was she wearing lacy drawers? Was there any chance she'd lay her sweet body down beside him on his little string bed?

This time, the kiss was all he wanted. Some sign that despite all the luxury into which Jane had suddenly been thrust, she still held a place in her heart for him. The wonder of her lips beneath his, her breath filling his lungs, her cunning little tongue tangled up with his, it was enough joy to flood his whole body.

He poured his heart into the kiss. If he could just show her how much she meant to him, how much he'd dare for her, maybe he could turn her from this path that led her away from him.

She moaned softly into his mouth and tugged his lapels, urging him closer. He wrapped both arms around her, his hand slipping beneath the ermine cloak to the unbearably soft silk of her gown. So thin, this shield of fabric that separated them. He savored the weight of her on him, her softness against his hardness.

He longed to pull the pins from her hair, but he knew she wouldn't thank him. Ian settled for kissing his way along her jaw and nuzzling her ear. An earbob dangled from her soft lobe, a filigreed fancy of diamonds and emeralds. He pulled back and looked away.

Another reminder of what he couldn't give her.

Maybe . . . the thought took a while to form because just the thinking of it stabbed his brain . . . maybe it was wrong of him to hold her back.

"Ian?" Jane palmed his cheek and turned his face toward hers.

She was so lovely, all decked out like a lady. If they never found Sybil—and they probably wouldn't if she didn't wish to be found—Jane could keep up this pretense for the rest of her life. She'd never want for anything ever again.

Ian couldn't even promise her a full belly. Unless a body counted filling it with a brat every year. What could he offer Jane but a life of hard labor at the side of a workingman? He'd hoped to dazzle her with that new position he'd been offered only this morning. A wee cottage on a country estate didn't seem so grand a thing now. And if he somehow lost that post, the thought that she might know hunger because of him made his gut roil.

"Keep kissing me like that," she said softly, her hand massaging his chest, "and I'll be of a mind to listen to whatever sort of sense you want to talk into me. But believe me when I tell you, I have to do this. For a little while, at least."

He clasped her hand and held it still over his heart.

"Why?" He hated himself for not leaving the bouncing carriage the same way he had come, but she was the finest thing he'd ever seen, let alone had sitting on his lap. He couldn't bear the thought of leaving her until they rounded the last corner before Lord Hartwell's grand estate. "Why must ye, Janie?"

She drew a deep breath. "Because Mr. Roskin threatened to give you the sack if I didn't."

Anger burned in his chest. "And ye think I'm not man enough to take care of meself?"

"No, Ian, it's not like that—"

"Then what is it like?" She didn't trust him to fend for his own neck, let alone hers. "By heaven, woman, ye've no faith in me at all."

And maybe she was right. He ground his teeth together and lifted her off his lap and across the narrow space to the opposite seat. The carriage made a sharp turn and began to slow. Ian caught a glimpse of Hartwell House at the end of the block, every window ablaze with light. Lady Sybil's future husband waited inside that festive manor.

Maybe his Lady Jane's future husband.

"Happy Christmas, love," Ian said as he swung open the carriage door. "Do what ye think ye must, but I'll be leaving Somerville House after the first of the year."

"Ian, wait."

"I'm not a man to be hiding behind a woman's skirts." In truth, he couldn't bear the thought of tending the stable while Jane slipped deeper into her role as Sybil, spiraling farther and farther out of his reach. "I wish ye well of your choice, Janie."

Ian Michael vaulted out the open door and jogged

alongside the slowing carriage. He hauled himself up beside Edward on the rear rail as the brougham came to a halt before the columned, arched front of Lord Hartwell's imposing edifice.

Edward hopped down and opened the carriage door with a flourish. He extended his hand to help her alight and Jane emerged from the enclosed carriage. From her graceful movement to her elegant costume, her transformation into Lady Sybil was flawless.

Only Ian noticed that her expression was strained and the tip of her nose was redder than the cold should have made it. She was fighting back tears.

Keep fighting, Jane, he thought fiercely. If he saw a tear fall, he'd disgrace them both by swooping her up and carrying her away.

Instead he fell into step with Edward behind her as she walked up to the tall double doors. Liveried porters swung them open at her approach, and light and heat spilled out into the frosty air. Strains of a string quartet pierced the night.

The massive doors thudded closed behind her, swallowing Jane up and shutting Ian out.

Ian cleared his throat before he trusted his voice. "Now what do we do?" he asked Edward. Normally his work ended once the horses left his master's stable.

"Now's when we nip round to the kitchen. There'll be food and drink aplenty on a night like this." Edward nudged him with a sharp elbow. "Bound to be a comely maid or two hereabouts, if you can catch one what ain't busy serving at table."

Ian's gaze shot back to the closed doors.

His Jane belonged to the glittering world behind them now. And she was as far above the likes of a stable hand, or even a Man-of-All-Work, as the waxing moon over his head.

Chapter Seven

Ian dogged Edward around the massive residence, past the spots where long shafts of light spilled down onto sparkling snow. They passed a spreading oak with a heavy branch stretching near one of the tall windows on the second story. Before he thought better of it, Ian put his foot in a low crotch of the tree and shimmied up the rest of the way to peer through the wavy glass at the revelry inside.

"What are you doing?" Edward said, hugging himself and hopping from one foot to the other against the cold. "If you're caught playing peep-Tom, we'll both be in for it."

"No one's looking this way. I'll only be a moment. Just remember that tin of tobacco I promised ye." Ian leaned in to improve his view.

The dancing had begun, stately and elegant. The fine ladies and gentlemen moved through the prescribed steps with grace and refinement. Along one greenery-festooned wall, seated matrons gossiped behind their fans. A few young bucks were gathered around a steaming wassail bowl, sipping from silver cups and eyeing the row of wallflowers in speculation. One of them screwed up his courage and approached a slender miss in a pink gown so pale it seemed only a ghost of the color.

In stark contrast, Janie was a splash of red silk, making a dipping curtsey to a man and woman Ian decided must be the host and hostess of the affair, the Marquess and Marchioness Hartwell.

"What do you see?"

Ian couldn't very well admit he was watching Jane. "I think I see Lord and Lady Hartwell."

"Good man, that. So they say."

"Aye," Ian agreed as he took the marquess's measure. Robert Braithwaite, Lord Hartwell, was a tall man, powerfully built, his dark hair shot with silver. "He wants to put an end to child labor, ye know."

Ian had read some of his lordship's impassioned speeches on the subject in the tabloids. *A formidable man with a good heart, despite his lack of understanding,* he decided.

"Mayhap someone should remind his lordship that poor families will be even poorer for the lack of their children's wages," Edward pointed out with practicality.

Ian nodded. He couldn't remember a time when he hadn't worked, mucking stables or polishing saddles for one fine lord or another.

"The poor work, and the rich play," Edward said, blowing on his hands to warm them. "It's the way of the world."

The marchioness was leaning forward to kiss both of his Janie's cheeks in greeting now. The smiling lady had no idea she was welcoming a scullery maid, someone who would normally be beneath her touch, to her grand fete.

Ian had advanced himself through hard labor. He'd struggled to learn to read in the hope of a better life. The position waiting for him in Wiltshire was as high as he could aspire. Being Man-of-All-Work was heavy responsibility, to be sure, but it came with a decent salary and a private cottage. It was every workingman's dream.

But Janie could dream higher. She could be a lady in

truth. She was smiling and nodding to the marchioness now. Jane fit seamlessly into the picture of elegance.

He was right to let her go.

A stiff wind whistled past.

"Come on, man," Edward urged. "There's Christmas pudding waiting, I shouldn't wonder."

Bitter cold settled on Ian's heart. He swung himself down from the branch, dropped into the snow, and trudged after the other footman. As they neared the corner of Hartwell House, Edward raised a hand to signal a halt.

"What—"

"Shh!" Edward hissed, and pointed toward one of the porticoes opening onto Lord Hartwell's frozen garden. There in the shadows, Ian could make out the forms of a man and a woman. The woman was pinned against the gray stone, her skirt hiked to her waist while the man pumped vigorously against her. The woman moaned.

Ian started forward, thinking the cad was using her against her will, but Edward stopped him with an arm across his chest. "It's all right. Give 'em a moment. Won't be long now. Not in this weather."

The man stiffened with a groan and the woman gasped in pleasure. Feigned or real, Ian couldn't tell, but it was obvious the woman was a willing party to this cold tryst.

The man stepped back, and moonlight struck them full on. The woman was wearing a mobcap and apron, but the man was a dandy with a high collar, mutton-sleeved jacket and slim dark trousers.

"He's decked out like a lord," Ian whispered.

"That's because he is," Edward whispered back.

The man tucked himself back into his trousers, without so much as a glance at his partner.

The woman leaned toward him. "Oh, I never dreamed it'd be so grand with a titled gent." She giggled. "Just imagine. Me, taking a tumble with a viscount."

"Yes, well, don't allow yourself to become accustomed to the idea," the man said coldly. "It was not so grand an occasion from this end. Rather ordinary, actually."

He turned on his heel and strode away, leaving the woman gaping after him. Then she loosed a sob, covered her mouth with her hand and broke into a stumbling run toward the scullery door.

"Right-o," Edward said, as if this sort of thing were hardly surprising. "Now for the kitchen."

Anger burned in Ian's belly. It was bad enough the rich had all the good food and drink and fine things. Did they have to despoil the help as well? "Who is that gobble-cock anyway?"

"That," Edward said with a shrug, "is the Lady Sybil's future husband, Lord Eddleton."

"The devil ye say!"

"Almost, according to the rumors." Edward crunched through the snow toward the fragrant kitchen door. "But a well-connected devil by all accounts, and that, my young friend, covers a multitude of sins." Edward sniffed the air. "I think I smell beef. Can't remember the last time I wrapped my choppers around a good brisket. We'll make out like a pair o' brigands tonight."

Edward slapped Ian on the back companionably and strode forward. When Ian didn't follow, he stopped and looked back. "Coming?"

"Go ye ahead," Ian said. "I'll be along."

"More beef for me then." Edward shrugged and followed his nose toward the source of the delightful smell.

Ian tromped back around the corner and climbed the oak to peer through the window of the ballroom once more. After a few moments, he found Jane. And in another heartbeat or two, so did Viscount Eddleton.

That worthless piece of dung was fawning over his Janie's white-gloved hand.

Perhaps there was more to life than the promise of a full belly. Mayhap Jane would put more stock in a true heart than a title. And a true heart, Ian was confident, he could offer in abundance. All he wanted in this life was his Janie. If Eddleton had been a decent sort, Ian would have let her go, figuring it would be for the best. But Eddleton wasn't, and that settled the matter. Ian decided to press his suit.

If she rejected him, well, he'd deal with that if he had to. Though he didn't intend to go down without a fight.

"No thank ye, Edward," he muttered. "Enjoy your beef. I'd rather make out like a lord than a brigand this night." He narrowed his gaze at Eddleton's poker-stiff back. "Though I may have to turn brigand to do it."

"Lady Sybil, I presume," the blond, cherub-faced gentleman said with a slight bow. When Jane extended a hand, he straightened to his full height, which was about half a head taller than she. He favored her with a dazzling smile and lifted her knuckles to his lips. "*Enchanté, mademoiselle. Vous êtes plus jolie que je me suis attendu.*"

Blast! Why hadn't Sybil ever skipped out of her French lessons? Well, whatever the man had said sounded perfectly delightful, so she smiled at him while she tugged her hand free. "Likewise, I'm sure."

"So I'm prettier than you expected, too! How droll. No one warned me of your wit." He laughed and clicked his heels together. "From the furrow on your lovely brow, I can tell you don't know who I am. I don't see Lord Somerville anywhere to do the honors, so allow me to introduce myself. Viscount Eddleton, at your service." Then he relaxed his rigid posture and leaned toward her conspiratorially. "But by the end of the evening, I hope you'll be calling me George."

Jane's belly roiled. So this was the stranger whose proposal she'd have to accept before the end of the ball. Even though the marriage agreement was all but signed, his manner was so forward, so blatantly confident, Jane was irritated on Sybil's behalf. Even an arranged bride deserved a little courtship.

What would Lady Sybil do?

"Perhaps, milord, I'll find another name for you." Jane arched one brow in perfect imitation of the knowing expression on Lady Sybil's nude portrait. "But it may not be George."

That knocked the smugness off his face. It would do the man good to have to work a bit for this engagement. He cocked his head at her, clearly reassessing.

"Lovely, but stubborn," he said. "My informant wasn't all wrong then. I was warned of your temperament."

Jane flipped open her gilded fan and fluttered it before her. It was a small shield, but it was all she had. "You have me at a disadvantage, sir, if you have been spying on me."

"Spying on you? What a charming notion!"

Jane didn't have much experience with men, but she recognized a rakish grin when she saw one.

"I'm curious, milady. What sort of activities of yours do you think I'd most enjoy from a clandestine vantage point?"

"I think perhaps a view of me walking away." She turned and glided from him.

He caught up with her in short order. "Please, I meant no harm. Surely a jest between those whom the fates have thrown together is no cause for offense."

Jane kept walking as the string ensemble began the stately, somber tones of a quadrille.

"I fear we've started on the wrong foot," Eddleton said, clearly dismayed. "Allow me to make amends. May I have this dance?"

"If you tend to start on the wrong foot, do you think dancing the wisest course?"

He chuckled, nervously this time. "Touché, mademoiselle. Once again, I am wounded."

"Rest easy, sir. It doesn't appear mortal."

"You think not?" He splayed a hand over his chest, careful not to crush his cravat's waterfall. "Cupid's dart carries quite a sting."

"So you are well acquainted with the boy with the arrows?"

"I would have thought so," he admitted. "Before I met you. Now I see that my other amours were mere flesh wounds. You, mademoiselle, fairly pierce my heart."

What a bag of moonshine! Jane narrowly resisted rolling her eyes. For whatever reason, it was obvious Lord Eddleton wanted the betrothal to go forward. Wanted it quite desperately if he resorted to such overblown declarations within a minute of their meeting.

Well, accepting Lord Eddleton's proposal was why she was here. But if she could start the relationship between Lady Sybil and her betrothed on a more equal footing she would consider that her gift to her half sister. She rested her palm on his offered arm.

"By all means, if indeed the fates have thrown us together, we should dance," she said, tossing his words back at him. "Let us see if at least our feet can find an accord."

Jane and Viscount Eddleton formed up with another couple for the quadrille. She caught a fleeting reflection of herself in the dark windows, her scarlet gown wavering in the soft light. She didn't recognize the stranger who stared back at her.

How long could she keep up this charade without losing herself?

Bless Agnes for making me learn to dance, she thought as she answered the viscount's bow with a deep curtsey. Dancing was a welcome respite. Since the quadrille involved another couple, no one spoke. Lord Eddleton was on his best behavior, smiling politely and executing the dance with grace.

Jane moved through the prescribed turns and steps, surprised by how easily she was accepted as Lady Sybil. She'd been both disappointed and relieved when Lord Somerville failed to arrive in time to escort her to Lord Hartwell's ball. Surely he'd have been difficult to fool. Once here, she had expected to have to bluff her way through a dozen conversations with Sybil's friends, but other than the marchioness, no one had greeted her with more than a slight nod.

Could Sybil really have so few friends?

They reached the last turn in the quadrille and Lord Eddleton escorted her from the floor.

"I'm sure your dance card will fill quickly, my dear," he said, reaching for the gilt booklet that dangled from one of her wrists. "I'll not presume upon your company, but I'll pencil myself in for the last dance. After all, we do have business to conclude this evening."

Business! Was that what he thought of his coming betrothal? If she were acting as herself instead of Sybil, she'd have put a knee to his groin right there.

Lord Eddleton scribbled his name and then handed the dance card back. His gaze focused on something over her right shoulder. She could have sworn he blanched whiter than a toad's belly.

"Right, then," he said. "I'll see you soon. Have a lovely evening."

He rushed his obeisance over her hand and then practically ran from her, glancing back over his shoulder. Jane turned slowly, to see if she could determine the reason for her soon-to-be-betrothed's quick departure, but she could spot no danger. There was only a small woman in a canary yellow ball gown. The lady didn't appear at all threatening, but her sharp eyes did seem to be marking Eddleton's progress across the crowded ballroom.

Jane didn't have time to puzzle over why the viscount had fled like a harried fox. Or why the lady in yellow trailed him like a hound on the scent. True to Eddleton's prediction, Jane's dance card filled quickly. Lady Sybil obviously didn't have many female friends, but she was undeniably popular with the men in attendance.

Sybil's cunning embroidered slippers might be all the crack for fashion, but Jane's feet ached by the time the musicians laid aside their bows for a short break. The quartet of matrons playing whist at a table in the corner gave her directions to the ladies' retiring room and she started toward one of the doors that led away from the ballroom. She hoped with her whole heart that real ladies were sensible enough to take off their pinching slippers for a good foot rub.

She somehow doubted it.

But before she made good her escape, she noticed someone lounging by the doorway who made her forget she even possessed feet.

He was leaning against the thick mahogany panels, his manner completely at ease. But his dark eyes watched her with the intensity of a cat before a mouse hole.

His slim dark trousers, gray cutaway jacket, and waistcoat embroidered with silver threads looked like they'd leapt from a fashion plate. Barring the indifferently tied cravat tumbling from his high collar, he was as well turned out as the marquess himself.

He smiled slowly at Jane. As she walked toward him, his crooked grin fisted her heart. She tamped down the flutter in her belly.

"Ian Michael MacGregor," she hissed. "What do you think you're doing here?"

Chapter Eight

"For a bright girl, Janie, ye're a bit daft this evening. It's plain as the nose on your face what I'm doing here. I'm looking at you, of course." Ian's hot gaze traveled down her form and back to meet her eyes again. "Ye're well worth looking at, lassie, all flushed and rosy. Ye should wear red all the time."

"Never mind that." Her voiced rasped with irritation, even though his admiration sent a tingle spiraling down her belly. She stepped closer to him so no one would overhear them. Ian didn't smell of fresh stable straw now. A solid whiff of sandalwood emanated from his fine clothes, along with his own masculine scent. "How did you get that suit?"

"Same way you got what you're wearing." He folded his arms across his broad chest and leaned toward her to whisper, "I borrowed it."

"That much I figured," she whispered back, so she had to move even closer. Or was he drawing her in? "From whom?"

"Well, it was more trouble than I expected, I'll grant ye. I counted on being able to waylay one of these dandies hereabouts. These fancy gents make frequent trips out to the garden to smoke and . . . other things, but most of them are on the puny side and for the longest time I didn't see any whose clothes I thought I could fit into," he said, clearly enjoying stringing out the tale. "Then I remembered that Lord Hartwell is a goodly-sized fellow—"

"Oh, Ian!" Jane's stomach turned a backflip. "Tell me you did not steal from the marquess."

"Borrow," he corrected. "Borrow from the marquess."

"Borrow then, you stupid, big Scot." Jane suppressed the desire to pound her fist on his chest beneath the messily tied cravat. That sort of violence might be frowned upon in polite society, though if any would dare flout society's rules, it would undoubtedly be Sybil. Jane struggled with the urge for another couple of heartbeats, then continued in a furious whisper, "Why would you do such a thing?"

The musicians started a softly yearning tune in three-quarter time. Ian's eyes darkened as he looked at her.

"Maybe I wanted to dance with ye, love."

His husky voice sent a shiver over her. Her heart pounded as if she'd run up three flights of stairs with an armload of washing. With infinite slowness, he slid a hand along the side of her waist, the silk of her gown rustling, almost purring, beneath his touch. Ian took her hand and the fight sizzled out of her.

"Waltz with me, Jane."

She didn't speak. She didn't need to. Her body answered for her. Jane found herself swirling around the dance floor. Ian pulled her closer so their bodies brushed each other on the dipping first beat of each measure.

The rest of the ball guests whisked by in a colorful blur at the edge of her vision. They blended with the greenery and scarlet bows and the blaze of tapers, but she couldn't tear her gaze from Ian's face. When the waltz slowed to a stop, Jane realized that he'd danced her out one of the large double doors and down the hallway that ran alongside the ballroom. The next man on her dance card was unlikely to find her. Not that that troubled her at all at the moment.

They came to a stop with a final slow turn before one of the tall Palladian windows that overlooked the ice-spangled garden. Snow had drifted onto the lower right corner of each pane of glass, a sparkling frozen triangle in every little rectangle.

Ian made no move to release her, even though the music had stopped. Jane couldn't bear to pull away.

"I didn't know you could dance, Ian."

A smile crinkled his eyes. "Even a stupid, big Scot can count to three."

His words reminded her she was angry with him. "But a stupid, big Scot apparently can't tell whose wardrobe he shouldn't be raiding."

"This is no raid," he said. "I don't even intend to take his lordship's fine things out of his house. If it's a raid we're talking of, I could tell ye of some beauties! Me ol' grandsire once made off with thirty head of the neighboring clan's best Angus beeves. Now *that* was a raid."

"You know what I mean."

"Aye, lass, I ken your meaning. But a real raid means taking something of value with no intention of giving it back. I fully intend to return his lordship's fancy getup." He leaned down, his dark eyes searching her face. "But I do mean to take ye, Jane. And I have no intention of giving ye back."

There was no mistaking the tilt of his head as he bent toward her. She forced herself not to stand tiptoe to meet him halfway.

"No." She splayed her fingers across his chest but couldn't bring herself to push against him very hard. "Lady Sybil is supposed to be accepting a proposal of marriage this night. How would it look if she were found kissing someone else?"

"Like she'd been caught under the mistletoe," he said, pointing upward to the clump of greenery Jane had missed. "A perfectly innocent situation. None can fault Lady Sybil for a bit of Christmas spirit."

"But—"

"Besides," Ian said, as he tugged her closer. Her body melted against him, her softness conforming to his hardness. "What if my Lady Jane were offered a proposal this night for herself?"

She gasped a quick breath. Did he mean it? The soft gleam in his eyes said he did. Still, it was a backhanded way to ask her to marry him.

"I guess," she said slowly, "it would depend on who was doing the offering."

"Let me show you."

His lips brushed hers, a teasing kiss. Then he covered her mouth with his. Jane's lips parted and he accepted her welcome, sweeping in with his tongue.

Jane arched against him. His warmth penetrated the silk as if she were naked. Heat settled low in her belly and the strange dull ache she always felt when Ian kissed her began afresh. It wasn't painful exactly. But it was an odd sensation, a wanting, hollow feeling, a craving more potent than hunger, more urgent than thirst.

She was certain Ian could make it better, if she let him.

But she didn't dare. There was too much at stake. She had to fulfill her role as Sybil this night and that meant she had to stop needing Ian so desperately.

She pushed against his chest until he released her mouth, but Jane didn't have enough willpower to pull out of his arms. She laid her head against his chest and felt his heart pounding beneath her cheek.

"Why must everything be so hard?" she whispered.

"I don't know, lass," he said, stroking her spine. "But there are some things that come easily if we let them."

Her body throbbed an *Amen*.

A group of gentlemen suddenly spilled out one of the doors from the ballroom, talking in low murmurs.

"Oh, no!" Jane spotted Lord Hartwell at the center of the moving circle. "If the marquess recognizes that suit of clothes you're wearing, you're done as a Christmas goose."

Jane grabbed Ian's shoulders and turned with him to face the tall windows. He slipped an arm around her waist, and she leaned into him. Maybe if they stood still, Lord Hartwell and his entourage would overlook them.

"If you'd only consider the plight of these children," the marquess was saying, "you'd not think twice about voting with me."

"But what of the factory owners? Who'll compensate them for loss of laborers?" another man asked. "I can't see raising taxes on account of these snot-nosed ragamuffins."

"Come, Richland." Lord Hartwell's tone was still calm and reasonable, as though Lord Richland had agreed with him already. "I've discovered an exceptionally fine case of Spanish port. Let's discuss this further down in my study, shall we?"

Jane held her breath until the last click of their heels on the hardwood faded in the distance.

"That's it, Ian," she hissed. "You must get out of those clothes right now."

"I thought ye'd never ask," he said with a chuckle. "Only if ye help me."

"His lordship might come back at any moment."

"Then we'd best hurry." He took her elbow and started leading her down the hall.

"Ian!"

"Those are me terms, love." He stopped and looked down at her. "I canna leave ye to the like of Lord Eddleton."

Jane laughed mirthlessly. "My sham betrothed. I can't think why you're bothered about this little farce."

"I know ye think this is some sort of game ye're playin', but if Lady Sybil never comes back, his lordship's proposal is as good as real. Ye'll be a lady in truth, Janie." He settled his big hands on her shoulders and leaned to touch his forehead to hers, their breaths mingling. "I'm mindful that it's a big choice I give ye now. But I do give it. Choose."

She closed her eyes, scrunching her brows together in thought. The string quartet started up a stately sarabande and Jane mentally ticked off the remaining dances on her card. There were at least twelve or thirteen until the final slow waltz she'd promised Lord Eddleton. And maybe a break or two for the musicians. She doubted it was enough time to talk sense into Ian's thick Scottish skull, but she ought to at least be able to see him safely back into his footman's livery.

She opened her eyes. "Let's go."

Sybil peered through the grimy window to the snow-rutted street below. A fancy equipage rattled past, throwing slush on the foot traffic that scurried out of its way. Was it someone she knew riding inside that gilded coach? Lord Hartwell's grand Christmas Ball was almost worth staying in London for. No one of quality left in the city would think of missing it.

Cold seeped through a crack in the glass and reached its icy fingers toward her. With a shiver, she drew the woolen blanket she was using in place of a bedshawl tighter around her shoulders.

"I must go for a little while." Giovanni came up behind her, lifted her hair, and planted his lips on her nape. Pleasure and warmth spread down her spine. She arched, catlike, into him.

"Go? Where?"

"To bespeak passage for us, *cara mia*," he said. "We cannot hide here forever."

She turned and twined her arms around his neck. "It would be nice."

"But we must come out sometime, and I would have us make for someplace safe, before your father catches up to us." He pecked her cheek and turned away to tug on a heavy jacket. "The mode of travel, she will not be in the style you are accustomed to, I fear. It's steerage class for a poor painter and his lady."

"I brought some jewelry." Sybil turned away from the window and rifled through her small satchel. "We can sell these earbobs and travel in style."

She pressed the pair of sapphire and pearl studs into his open palm. He studied them so intently, she wondered if he was considering adding them to a still life composition.

"No, my *selfish* little heart," he said with a laugh as he returned them to her. "Your trinkets you must keep. Giovanni will take care of you. Perhaps I will sell a painting on the way to the wharf and we can move up to a second-class berth. Would you like that?"

"I don't care," she said fiercely as she hugged him, hooking one leg around his and rocking against him. *Selfish?* Well, it was what she'd called herself, wasn't it? "As long as I'm with you, it doesn't matter where we are."

He kissed her long and deeply, cupping her bottom to lift her against him. Sybil moaned into his mouth. Just when she thought she'd persuaded him to stay, he pulled away.

"If I do not go now, we miss the morning sailing." He wound a thick muffler around his neck. His southern blood had never thinned enough for England's cold, damp winters. "Go back to bed and keep warm. I will join you soon."

Once he had latched the door behind him, Sybil slumped on the edge of the bed. Over the last six months, she and Giovanni had made love in his little garret apartment so many times, she'd lost count. Fear of being caught stealing away from her father's house had added spice to the adventure. The tiny space was magical when Giovanni was with her, a fleshly pleasure garden.

Now, looking around the sorry collection of cast-off furniture and half-finished canvases, she could only see its seediness. And the neighborhood was so dicey he even had to lock the much-dented trunk that held his spare clothes. She wondered how Giovanni could bear this place alone.

Sybil drew the blanket up to her chin. When he had left, he'd taken the only source of heat with him—his body. Once he returned, she wouldn't give his pitiful room another thought. She could live anywhere, so long as Giovanni was with her.

But what about Father?

Her conscience hadn't troubled her in so long, Sybil was surprised when she heard its small voice in her mind.

"He'll be fine," she said aloud.

She replayed their last, crockery-smashing argument in her head. His angry tirade hadn't moved her, but when her indomitable father finally sank into his leather desk chair and held his gray head in his hands, his shoulders shaking with suppressed sobs, Sybil had been completely overcome.

Only the threat of her father's utter ruin had made her agree to let Mr. Roskin arrange a lucrative match for her. But then the earl had left for a season of hunting, as if her sacrifice were nothing.

It had been easy to climb out the window this morning without a backward glance.

What will happen to Father?

The small voice began chanting the question. A snippet of memory rose up to torment her.

"Oh, Father, you remembered!" An eight-year-old Sybil squealed with delight as the earl lifted her onto the back of a fat pony. She'd hounded her father for months about a mount of her own and now, he took as much pleasure in it as she did. Her father's eyes lost that look of carefully guarded emptiness for a few moments as he watched her trot around the small pen.

Mother's fever was better that day, so she watched, too. Small and frail in her wheeled chair, she was so obscured in the dark shade of a broad sycamore, it was almost as if she watched from some other realm already.

Sybil's father had seemed to shrink into himself when her mother died not a fortnight later.

Guilt, Sybil suspected.

She knew men of her class thought nothing of keeping a mistress, and most of their wives maintained a state of willful ignorance about that "other one." But when her mother had discovered her father had sired a bastard on one of the help right under her own roof, her health, never robust, began its steep decline. Lord Somerville blamed himself.

Now, her father faced his own decline—a financial one. And might not his health follow his fortunes?

Sybil sighed. Had the earl passed guilt on to her along with his eyes and the soup girl's face?

She stood and paced the small room. Giovanni was bohemian enough in his lifestyle not to ask her to marry him. He was content with warming her bed and that was fine with her. It kept their relationship blissfully uncomplicated.

Emphasis on bliss.

Then an idea struck her.

Why not go ahead and marry Lord Eddleton?

She swallowed a shudder of distaste at the idea of coupling with someone other than Giovanni, but she supposed she'd have to in order to make the contract valid. Then, once the *Pearl* made port and her father's finances were settled, she and Giovanni could run away together and live in delicious sin beneath a blue Tuscan sky.

It was only a matter of a quick wedding and a few months of pretended wedded harmony. She wouldn't even need to give up Giovanni, so long as they were discreet.

But that meant Sybil had to appear at Lord Hartwell's Christmas Ball this night to accept Lord Eddleton's proposal.

She dressed quickly and then sat down to write Giovanni a short note. Yes, this would be best for all concerned. It would give her time to plan and pull together some traveling money as well. She'd go with Giovanni in any case, but why not go in style?

"I wonder if I can convince my fiancé to hire Giovanni to paint our wedding portrait," she said with a laugh. She sealed the note with a glob of candle wax, then dashed down the rickety stairs and into the snowy night.

Chapter Nine

Ian led Jane down the corridor and into the staircase hall. One floor below them, more guests were being admitted at the front door with loud announcements of Lord and Lady Somesuch-or-Other ringing in the grand foyer. The porter was minding his position. But at the second-story landing, Ian and Jane tiptoed past a liveried servant who nodded at his post, like a tired cart horse, snoring softly. The scent of gin wafted about him.

Too much Christmas spirit, Ian thought thankfully as they climbed the gracious main staircase, their steps silent as the snow falling outside.

Halfway up to the next landing, Jane tugged his hand and whispered, "This leads to the family's floor. Someone's bound to see us there."

Ian shook his head. "His lordship is playing politics and Lady Hartwell is busy with her guests. All the servants are either running up and down the back staircase in service or in the kitchen, enjoying their own Christmas feast."

He hoped Edward was enjoying his beef.

Ian had a feast of his own in mind, if only she'd start up the stairs once again. "Come, love."

Jane pushed around him, lifted her skirts, and took the steps two at a time, her slippers making a soft swish against the polished oak. Ian hurried to catch up to her. When he threw a sidelong glance at Jane, her face was set in a frown. He'd smooth that away in short order if she'd give him his way just this once.

Ian ducked into the marquess's chamber. The gas lamp had been left burning low, softening the dark edges of the masculine room with a golden glow.

Jane was still scowling at him as she followed him in. "Well, what are you waiting for?"

He started to embrace her but she straight-armed him.

"Not now." She spoke softly, but her determination was unmistakable, a spine of steel wrapped in silk. He wondered if she knew how fetching she was when blood heated her cheeks and spread down her neck to the tops of her breasts. "Out of those clothes, Ian. And I mean it."

"Willingly." Even though she was angry with him for dragging her up here, his body roused to her with an aching cockstand. A smile tugged at his mouth. "But remember your bargain. You're here to help me out of them."

"You'll have to tell me what to do, since I've never undressed a man before." She cocked her head at him and arched a not-so-innocent brow. "What do you want?"

You, Janie love, up against the wall with your gown bunched around your waist. His mouth went dry. Damn, he was as randy a he-goat as that blasted Lord Eddleton. But unlike the viscount, Ian loved this lady. Surely that counted for something.

"I . . ." He tugged at his cravat and hopelessly fouled the knot. "I want to be rid of this bloody bit of rubbish about my neck."

Tugging off her long white gloves, she floated toward him. Her kid-soled slippers skimmed across the floor as if she possessed invisible wings.

"Let me see about it, then." She dropped the gloves

and her fingers grazed his neck in teasing touches. "Oh, you've tugged the wrong end of the waterfall. There."

She held both ends of the neck cloth and pulled his head down so there was hardly a hand's span between them. Her breath was moist and sweet. The remembered taste of her mouth made his cock twitch.

"Next time," she said in a husky whisper, "steal a cravat with less starch."

Then she yanked the cravat off his neck, the stiff cloth raking his flesh.

"Ow!" He clapped a hand to the back of his neck and rubbed vigorously.

"Less starch would smart less, I expect," she said with a poisonous smile.

"You did that of a purpose."

"Of course."

"I thought ye agreed to—"

"Help you out of those clothes? So I did." She poked out her bottom lip in a wickedly seductive pout. "You wanted to be rid of your cravat and I've rid you of it."

"But that's not—"

"Not what you asked for? Or not what you expected?" She poked his chest with her forefinger. "Ian Michael, this is no game. Do you not understand what will happen to you if you're caught in his lordship's clothes?"

"Aye, but—"

"But nothing." She reached up and started to push the gray wool jacket off his shoulders. He turned a slow circle and slid out of it before he knew what was happening. "We don't have time to waste. I'm only here to make sure you get back into that footman's livery, you stupid, big Scot."

He decided silence was his best defense.

She dipped to retrieve her gloves and spread them and the jacket neatly across the foot of his lordship's tall bed.

He followed close behind so that when she turned around there was only a hand's span between them.

"And don't think you'll be sidetracking me with kisses," she went on, as her fingers flew down the row of silver buttons marching down his waistcoat.

The sweet lilac smell of her hair made his mouth water, but he wisely kept it shut. She folded the waistcoat and laid it beside the jacket before turning back to him.

"Do you really think Lord Hartwell won't notice that someone else has been wearing his shirt?" Her hands slowed as she undid the buttons on the fine white lawn, exposing more and more of his chest as the fabric parted.

He balled his fingers into fists to keep from reaching out to her.

"Turn around." Her voice trembled a bit, enough to let him know she was losing steam.

He forced himself not to smile until he'd presented his back to her. She tugged the shirttail out of his trousers and peeled it slowly off him, baring his back. Her breath hitched.

"You're not wearing any small clothes at all," she said softly.

Ian shrugged. "Charlie's livery is a snug fit. It's easier to fasten up wearing nothing but me skin beneath. Then once here, I figured it was bad enough to help myself to Lord Hartwell's wardrobe. I didn't think I should press his hospitality so far as borrowing his drawers."

A giggle slipped from Jane's lips.

So lightly he almost thought he was imagining it, she ran her fingertips along the tops of his shoulders and then down the sensitive indentation of his spine. It took every ounce of will he possessed to remain still.

"You shouldn't have come." Her breathless tone belied her words. "Honestly, Ian, what were you thinking?"

He turned to face her. "I was thinking I couldn't bear for ye to belong to someone else."

Something softened behind her eyes. The hazel seemed to darken to indigo in the dim light.

"Do ye not ken that I want ye only for myself?" He cupped her face and was grateful beyond words when she leaned her cheek into his rough palm. Her skin was smoother than her silk gown. He ached to press his lips against her cheek. "I couldn't bear the thought of another man touching ye the way I long to."

Slowly, as if she were a spooked mare, he leaned down and kissed her on the sweet hollow beneath her cheekbone. She didn't stop him, so he moved down to the corner of her mouth, the spot that was half warm skin, half intimate moistness. With a low moan, Jane turned her head. Her lips parted in unmistakable invitation.

He took her mouth, gently at first, then because he couldn't help it, with bruising passion. His tongue played a lovers' game with hers, a darting chase of capture and release. Jane proved his equal, stealing the breath from his lungs and replacing it sweetly with her own.

While he slanted his mouth over hers, Ian slid his hand down to the top of her gown where the line of pearl buttons began down the front. He fiddled with the top one and it popped open. She broke their kiss off.

"I thought we were here to undress *you*," she said with an impish grin, but she made no move to stop him when he moved down to the next pearl.

"Perhaps we could take it turn and turnabout," he suggested, as he circled the button with his finger.

"Perhaps we could."

With a rustle of silk, her gown parted on either side of her bosom, revealing a thin chemise and beribboned corset beneath. He could make out the dark shadows of her nipples through the chemise. Her breasts rose and fell slightly with each breath. She was so lovely. Without conscious volition, his hand claimed her softness. He pulled back immediately. He knew he didn't deserve her.

"Oh, Janie." His gaze shifted from her breasts back up to her wide eyes.

"Do you love me, Ian?"

"Aye, lass, more than me next breath."

She took his big, rough hand and placed it back over her right breast. "Then show me."

Jane splayed her hand on his chest, palm over his galloping heart, then slid down to the buttons at his waist.

"If you . . ." Even through the marquess's thick wool trousers, when her hand brushed against his hard cock, he thought his eyes might roll back in his head for a moment. He wanted her so badly, he didn't know how many teasing strokes he could take before he disgraced himself. His tongue felt suddenly thick in his mouth. "If you want, I can do that."

"And ruin my fun?" Jane leaned forward.

The tips of her breasts brushed against his chest through the thin fabric of her chemise. The light touch sent his groin into spasms.

Pressing honeyed kisses across his chest, she tackled the buttons at his waist by feel alone. The flap front fell away and she delved in to follow the narrow strip of hair that led downward from his navel to spread over his groin.

The trousers sagged down his hips. Jane avoided contact with his throbbing cock as she tugged them down the rest of the way. He toed off his shoes. A few chestnut curls that had escaped her neat bun brushed over him as she bent over.

Ian gritted his teeth.

Jane paused, crouching before him, her eyes widening as she looked him over.

He tipped her chin up to meet his gaze. Her red lips were mere inches from his cock. A tiny pearl of fluid formed at the tip of him.

Take me in, love, he wanted to say.

But when she drew a timid finger down the full length of him, a shock of need coursed through his body and the power of speech deserted him completely.

He raised her to her feet, pressing flush against her. Jane's curves molded to his hardness. He ran his hands down her spine and stayed to dally with the crevice of her buttocks through the thin silk.

When he heard her breath catch, he pulled back. Her eyes were heavy-lidded, her mouth kiss-swollen. He'd made her want him. There wasn't a no left in her.

Dear God, he hoped not. Else he was a dead man.

Ian lowered his mouth to her breasts, dampening her lace-trimmed chemise with wet kisses. He suckled her through the cloth and bit down on her nipple enough to send a wicked streak of pleasurable pain knifing through her. What would it be like without the thin layer of muslin?

As if he'd heard her thoughts, he tugged at the lace tie, the anticipation on his face like that of a boy unwrapping a Christmas present. Her skin shivered in excitement. Ian bared her breasts above the stiff fabric lip of her corset. He nuzzled the hollow between them and then suckled one nipple while he strummed the other with his thumb. Jane's whole body sang.

How many nights had she lain awake wishing for this? A spurt of warmth moistened the folds between her legs. She imagined their bodies entwined on his lordship's bed, writhing on the brocade counterpane. Her body throbbed with pulsing life.

But when he started to unbutton her gown further,

sanity gripped her. "Please, no. What if someone should come and catch us here?"

He stopped, but he fretted against her no as if it were an invisible tether and he Lord Somerville's stallion when the mares were in heat. "Janie, do ye love me or no?"

She took his face in both her hands and pressed a kiss on him. "I love you, Ian Michael. More than *my* next breath."

"Then trust me, lass. I'll never see ye shamed."

He covered her with kisses as she tumbled with him willingly onto the marquess's fine featherbed.

Chapter Ten

Lord Eddleton mopped his brow with his last good hand-kerchief. He'd been skulking from one clump of revelers to the next, trying to hide among Lord Hartwell's guests. He hadn't spotted Lady Darvish for the past quarter hour. His sense of gratitude nearly led him to reconsider his opinion on the existence of God.

Of course, he hadn't seen his soon-to-be betrothed either, but he wasn't overly concerned. Lady Sybil was probably gossiping in the lady's retiring room about her trousseau and whatnot with the other hens.

Thank God, he thought, forgetting for a moment he was still entertaining doubts about the deity's existence. *Somerville's daughter isn't the horse-faced drudge I feared she'd be. A tempting armful with a father who has deep pockets! I couldn't have arranged matters better!*

Eddleton decided to celebrate his good fortune and reward himself with a smoke on the marquess's veranda.

After all, when a man marries for money, he expects to have to do more than look the gift-horse in the mouth, he thought as he pushed through the double doors that led out to the frigid garden.

The wind had died, but brittle stars shivered in the clear night sky.

"Cold as a witch's tit." He lit a cheroot and puffed a trio of smoke rings into the frosty air.

A *tsk*ing sound came from behind him and he turned to find the woman he'd been avoiding.

"Cold as that, is it, Bertram?" Lady Darvish strode up to him, bold as any bit of muslin in Haymarket, and leaned forward. Her bosom threatened to spill over the bodice of her canary gown. "Perhaps you'd rather try a widow's tit, dear boy. Guaranteed to warm you right up."

Her creamy breasts thrust up toward him, pert as a girl's, and he nearly reached for them out of habit.

Probably some clever trick of whalebone and padding, he told himself, as he shoved his free hand into his pocket and took a pull on the cigar with the other. Soon he'd be engaged to a lovely young lady and her even lovelier dowry. No need to throw a rub into his own carefully laid plans by following his cock into trouble.

"Tempting as your offer is, madam—"

"Leticia," she corrected.

"*Lady Darvish,*" he said pointedly. "I'm very nearly engaged to be married."

"But you're not very nearly dead, are you?" She rested her gloved palm on his chest and then walked her fingers down to his groin.

Despite his better judgment, his body roused to her.

"No, I can tell you're not dead." Lady Darvish caressed his trouser front lightly. She made another pass, running her hand directly over his erection this time, and frowned. "You're also not as gifted as Lady Martin-Featherwight led me to believe."

Eddleton grabbed her wrist and pulled her hand away. "In case it's escaped your notice, madam, it's deucedly cold out. No man is at his best when his jewels are frosted over."

"Well then, Bertie, we'd best get you inside where it's warm and I'll give you an opportunity to prove yourself," she said, rubbing herself against him like some fawning tabby cat.

"I have nothing to prove to you."

"Ah! As I thought. You have nothing. My condolences. I don't blame you, Bert. It must be difficult for a man to be so cruelly underequipped." She cocked her head and pursed her lips. "However, I will have a few choice words for Lady Martin-Featherwright when I see her next for feeding me such a load of twaddle about you." She turned to go. "Hmm. I wonder if she's in attendance tonight?"

"That settles it, madam!" he said through clenched teeth. Eddleton grasped her arm and swung her back around to face him. "Kindly accompany me to his lordship's library and you'll see for yourself just how 'gifted' I am. Then, by Jove, I shall swive you 'til your teeth rattle." He flared his nostrils at her in what he thought was a sufficiently masculine display of contempt. "And after that, you may tell Lady Martin-Feather-whatever anything you damn well please!"

Lady Darvish's mouth curved in a feline smile. "Ah, Bert, when a gentleman asks that prettily, how can a lady say no?"

She grabbed his hand and nearly dragged him back through the double doors, through the festively draped corridor and down the main staircase in search of Lord Hartwell's library.

Sybil paid the cabby and clambered down without any help from the rude fellow. In fact, he pulled away so quickly, the hansom threw a fresh dusting of snow on her half sister's threadbare cloak. As she made her way up the walk to Lord and Lady Hartwell's gaily lit front door, she promised to see that Jane got a new one after this night's work. Heaven knew, she'd earned it.

"Sorry, miss," the porter said. "Servants' entrance in the back."

Sybil's spine stiffened and she bit back the urge to blister the man with a stinging set-down. Then she remembered that in Jane's clothes, she must appear the meanest sort of house drudge. She turned away.

"Go you on the south side, ducks," the porter said in a kindlier tone, "and you'll be out of the wind."

She followed his advice.

After Sybil had sneaked away from Giovanni's garret, she'd made her way home, hoping to don her ball gown and arrive at Hartwell House in fashionably late style. A tongue-tied Agnes had explained that Jane was already wearing the red gown, acting in Sybil's stead so the betrothal could go forward. Sybil had decided the best way for her to switch places at the ball was to wear Jane's rags there.

The idea had made sense at the time.

Now Sybil shivered against the cold as she tromped around to the back of Lord Hartwell's grand manor.

"Suppose I'll have to go through the kitchens," she muttered irritably. "God knows what sort of greasy mess that'll make of these slippers."

She'd steadfastly refused to don Jane's holey ones. At least she'd be able to give her half sister a decent pair of shoes when they made the trade.

Once she rounded the last corner, a pair of footmen in rose-colored livery came through a door, sending a long shaft of light dancing across the snowy ground. The aroma of braised beef and spiced rum wafted out the opening. One of the footmen held the door for her, not with the sweeping leg she was used to receiving, but with an appreciative wink and leering grin. Footmen were the comeliest male servants in any household, and this fellow was no exception.

But his dark hair and eyes only reminded her of Giovanni.

Now she wasn't so sure how he'd take her change of

plans. She imagined him ripping up her note in a glorious Italianate rage. She wished she could've seen it!

"Jane, I say, Jane Tate!"

Sybil realized with a start that someone was calling the name she should answer to. She turned to see one of her own footmen working his way around the crowded table toward her.

Charles or Edward? She never could keep them straight. Now that she'd walked a bit in a servant's shoes, she was determined to pay more attention to the people who filled her life with comfort from now on.

"Oh, er, hello!"

"Come now, Jane. You can do better than that for old Ed! Happy Christmas, girl." Edward gave her a quick kiss on the cheek and pointed up at the sprig of mistletoe dangling between the hanging pots and meat hooks above her. Then he presented his cheek to her.

"Happy Christmas." She returned his peck. "Have you seen Ja—Lady Sybil?"

Edward raised a quizzical brow. "Not since we escorted her to the front door. Ladies don't make a habit of celebrating Christmas with us salt-of-the-earth folk, you know."

"I've got to find her."

"Why?"

"I . . . I've a message for her."

Edward sighed. "No rest for the weary, I see. Well, let's have it and I'll see she gets it."

Drat! How could she have forgotten that delivering messages was part of a footman's duties?

"No, it's a . . . a private message. One they didn't want to commit to paper."

"Nothing amiss, I hope," Edward said, now far too interested for her comfort. "His lordship made it back to town, didn't he?"

"I . . . don't know," she said, swallowing her surprise. Father wasn't back from the country? She'd dressed in Jane's clothes so quickly, Agnes evidently hadn't thought to share this little tidbit with her. What would keep Lord Somerville from being present at her betrothal?

"Well, it's probably nothing," Edward said, with a comforting pat on her shoulder. She must not have schooled her face as well as she'd thought. "Reckon he's doing something important. You know how folk of quality are. Everything they do is important, from an audience with His Majesty to an audience with their chamber pot." He laughed hugely at his own wit, then sobered when she didn't join him. Edward had obviously enjoyed the rum punch. "This is a mighty big house to find Lady Sybil in. Shall I go with you then?"

"No, no, I'll be fine," she said quickly as she turned away. Sybil had been a guest at Hartwell House countless times for soirees, interminable recitals, and sumptuous dinners. She'd be able to find her way easily enough once she reached the public areas.

She pushed her way out of the crowded kitchen and down the dark hall toward a better lit T, where the hall ran perpendicularly in both directions. Now, if she could avoid being seen in Jane's horrible homespun by anyone she knew, she just might make it through the evening.

Jane stared at the gilt ceiling, her vision going in and out of focus. A fresco of nude little cupids cavorted above Lord Hartwell's bed. She'd convinced Ian to let her remain more or less fully clothed, but her soul was stripped bare as the naughty cherubs.

Ian's naked body was stretched out beside her, his hardness rocking a slow knock against her hip. He'd parted the thin chemise enough to free her breasts and was doing totally wicked things to them with his mouth.

A small voice in her head whispered that this was madness, but Jane wouldn't stop him. Couldn't. No more than she could fly.

"Janie, love, have ye any notion how fine ye are?" He drew a slow circle around one of her aching nipples with the tip of this tongue.

She gasped at the zing of pleasure that streaked from her breast to her womb. He rolled her nipple between his thumb and forefinger and she arched her back reflexively. The man knew how to make her want.

"Say ye're mine," Ian prodded.

With what she knew she still must do this evening, Jane couldn't bring herself to lie. "I belong to myself," she said between gasps.

"Do ye? Perhaps I'll have to persuade ye different." To prove his point, he trailed his fingertips down past her ribs, over the mound of her belly, and hiked up her gown. His thick fingers found the lacy slit in her pantaloons and played with the curls between her legs.

The ache grew deeper. She bit the inside of her cheek to keep from crying out as she crossed her ankles and clamped her thighs together, trapping his hand. He didn't try to free it, but he couldn't torment her with it either.

"Not fair," he said.

"Not fair? You're the one who forced me to come up here with you."

"I'll not force you now. But open to me, love. I'll make you glad you did."

When she didn't budge, he bent to nuzzle her nipple, sending another jolt of longing to her core. Her legs parted of their own accord.

His fingers slid deep into her wetness. Equal parts delight and despair shivered through her. He stroked her, teasing, featherlight touches. She raised her hips to meet him.

His blessed hand stopped moving and settled over her hot mound, just holding her. She throbbed in an agony of need. Someone whimpered. She was too far gone to feel shame when she realized it was her.

His hand moved again, his fingers circling and stroking, whipping her into aching fury. "Admit ye're mine, girl."

His lips closed over her nipple, suckling in rhythm with his hand. His fingers danced over her flesh. Helpless little sounds escaped her throat. Jane's breath hissed over her teeth. The wanting was so sharp-edged, she fisted Lord Hartwell's fancy counterpane with both hands, her eyes squeezed shut.

Then Ian stopped. Her eyes flew open. Her body screamed in frustration, but he left her throbbing with heat. He withdrew his hand and sat up.

"Say it."

She shook her head, not trusting her voice. If she spoke at all it would lead to pleading and she couldn't bear that.

"Can ye not? Then I'll try again," he said, lowering his head to nip again at her breast. "Do ye not love me?"

"You know I do."

"I belong to you, love. I'll not deny it." He kissed her neck, teasing her earlobe with his tongue, while his fingers found that special spot that threatened to unravel her again. Her body shuddered with anticipation.

"Try again. Are ye mine?"

Only all I am. He moved down between her legs and kissed her, open-mouthed. His tongue took over for his talented fingers.

"I . . . have mercy!" she gasped, propping herself on her elbows.

"There's none in me." Ian looked up to meet her gaze

for a moment, then returned to savaging her with his lips, teeth, and tongue.

She was losing herself. Bit by bit, little pieces of her were breaking off and floating away. Ian, too. With each of his growls of need, she sensed him letting go, releasing his tight rein on himself and joining her in this madness.

They were creating a special place together where there was no right or wrong, where there was only the dance of light and insanity of sensation, of need and heat and blessed friction. Of warm skin gliding on silk and fevered kisses. Of—

Ian moved up and slid his full length home.

A pinch of pain lanced her, then disintegrated in the bliss of holding him inside her. "Oh, Ian."

Jane had led such a controlled existence 'til now. *Do this. Don't go there. Touch not.* She accepted that the circumstances of her birth had denied her certain things. Now unbridled life roared in her veins and she welcomed it.

No one would deny her here. There was no one else in this place apart, none but they two. She wrapped her legs around him, drawing him farther into their private world of push and pull, rise and fall.

"Say ye are mine, love," he urged, thrusting deep with each word. Then he stopped and raised himself on his elbows to look down at her. "Say it. Even if it's a lie."

She was so close to some unseen edge. One more time, just one, and she'd unravel completely, like a spindle of yarn tossed across the floor, whipping free.

"I am yours, Ian Michael MacGregor." She rocked her pelvis, pressing her sensitive spot hard against him. The contractions began. She convulsed around him, urging him to join her. He moved with her. She bucked beneath him, holding him tight and wishing she'd never have to let him go.

"I'm yours," she repeated. She didn't care if he used her words against her later. "Body and soul, bone and breath."

A groan escaped his lips. Ian's body stiffened and he poured his seed into her, hot and steady, shuddering with the force of his release. Then he settled his cheek between her breasts and lay still as a dead man, except that his breath feathered warmly over her tight nipple.

"I am yours." She pressed a kiss on the crown of his tousled head. "And it is no lie."

Chapter Eleven

Jane slid her fingertips along the indentation of Ian's spine. His breathing was so slow and even, she began to suspect he'd fallen asleep. She didn't care. Their bodies were no longer joined, but she still reveled in his weight on her.

She sighed in contentment. All her joints felt loose and she suspected she'd be a little sore in the morning. It didn't matter. She wouldn't trade this moment for—

The strains of a waltz drifted up to her ear.

"Oh, no!" She squirmed and Ian rolled off her. Jane scrambled from the bed, pulling her chemise top closed and knotting the lace tie. She fastened the buttons marching down the front of her gown and toed on her slippers. Thank God she'd insisted on remaining more or less clothed.

Ian sat up on the bed, his legs thrown over the side. "What the—"

"I must go."

One look at him almost broke her resolve. Broad shouldered, deep-chested with the slightest dusting of dark hair whorled around his brown nipples—Jane sighed and yanked her gaze from him. There was no help for it. The last waltz was playing. Jane ran to the mirror in the corner of Lord Hartwell's chamber, trying to finger-comb her coiffure back into some semblance of order.

She could hear the music more clearly now. How many bars was that? Eight? Sixteen already gone?

"Where do ye think ye're going?"

"To accept Lord Eddleton's proposal." She strode toward the door.

He beat her there and splatted a thick palm against the English oak. "Jane, I beg ye. Don't do this."

"I gave my word." She tugged on the handle but Ian held the door fast.

"And what of your word to me? Does that mean nothing?" Barely bridled anger rolled off him in scalding waves.

"I'm still yours. Now more than ever." She put a palm to his cheek and his black scowl softened. "But this is something I must do for—"

"For Lord Somerville," he finished.

"Yes, and for Sybil, too. Don't forget. If not for her needing to run off from time to time, neither of us would be able to read or write."

"Sybil was a selfish, spoiled b—" He caught himself, drawing his lips tight. The joy of literacy was obviously the last thing on Ian's mind. "She didn't do it out of the kindness of her heart."

"So you won't let me do this for her out of the kindness of mine?" She slid her palm down to his bare chest. The warmth of his flesh called to her and she almost gave answer.

"If Eddleton lays a hand on ye—"

"He won't," she assured him. "A gentleman doesn't compromise a woman he intends to marry."

"Hmph!" Ian's mouth turned up in a wicked grin. "Guess that makes me no gentleman."

"No, thank heaven!" She arched a brow at him. There was another backhanded marriage proposal in there somewhere, but she didn't have time to fish for it now. She stood on tiptoe to peck his cheek. "Now let me go.

And get yourself back into Charlie's livery before someone catches you here in the altogether."

"Don't want me to frighten the upstairs maid?"

"Don't want you to *anything* the upstairs maid," Jane
said with mock sternness, before she slipped out the door
and down the dim hallway.

"Is that a waltz?" Eddleton asked between gasping
breaths.

"Why? Do you need music to keep the rhythm going?" Lady Darvish asked, grasping his buttocks and
pulling him in deeper. "I'll hire a quartet full-time then,
Bert! One-two-three, one-two-three . . ."

Jane was running now. It was like a nightmare! Hartwell
House was so huge and the hallways so convoluted, she
couldn't find the head of the staircase they had come up.
She couldn't even hear the music any longer. She skittered to the end of the hall and started trying doors. Finally one opened onto a dimly lit back staircase and she
dove down it at breakneck speed.

"There's no door," she said in despair when she reached
what should have been the second floor, the level of the
ballroom. This staircase was obviously reserved solely
for the use of those who served on the family's floor, so
there was no need for another exit. She put an ear to the
wall. Faintly, she heard the whine of violins. "There's
still time."

She turned and continued downward. "This staircase
has to end somewhere."

"Careful with that, my good man," Giovanni said as he
handed his top hat to Lord Hartwell's porter. "The bea-
ver, she does not like to be crushed."

"Of course, milord," the servant said, bowing deeply. "Lord Hartwell is in his study with several other members of the House of Lords. Whom shall I tell him is calling?"

"The Count of Montferrat." Giovanni flared his nostrils with aristocratic disdain, as if noticing for the first time that a grand fete was in progress. "But do not trouble his lordship. I can hear he has a small entertainment under way. Perhaps I should return at a later time."

"Oh, no, milord, he'd not want a gentleman of quality such as yourself turned away. Not one who came all the way from . . ."

"Tuscany," Giovanni supplied helpfully.

"That near Wales, is it?" the porter asked.

"Near enough."

Giovanni spied Sybil out of the corner of his eye. The little minx was scurrying toward the main staircase as if her knickers were on fire. She was tugging on her second glove. When she reached the foot of the steps, she cast a furtive glance each way, her gaze bouncing over Giovanni as if she didn't recognize him.

Did fine clothes really change a man that much?

She started in the direction of the music, nearly taking the steps two at a time. Then she seemed to catch herself and slowed to a more sedate pace. She looked like sin with feet swaying in that scarlet gown.

"I believe I see someone with whom I am . . . well acquainted," Giovanni said. "Tell his lordship I am at his disposal after he has finished with his other guests."

He didn't wait for the porter's murmured "Yes, milord" as he hurried after his wayward lover. He caught up to Sybil before she reached the first landing.

"Well met, my Lady Sybil," he said, snatching up her hand and bowing over it correctly, when he wanted nothing more than to scrape his teeth against her perfumed knuckles. "I hope you have saved a dance for me." Then he lowered his voice to a furious whisper, because the porter was gawking up at them with deep interest. "Why not cut out my heart with my own palette knife, *cara mia*? It would be less cruel."

Her hazel eyes registered shock.

"*Si*, it is me." Sybil had never suspected his locked trunk held velvets and gold brocade. Giovanni turned back to the porter. "The lady and I are old friends and have much to . . . how you say . . . catch down on? Is there such a place where we may not be disturbed?"

"His lordship's library. Back down on this level. Round that corner. Second door on the right," the porter said. "If it please you, milord, I could have a bit o' rum punch sent in for you and the lady's refreshment."

"No need," Giovanni said, as he grasped Sybil's elbow and was pleased by her little squeaking gasp. "The Lady Sybil's company is refreshment enough."

The real Sybil picked her way through the labyrinthine corridors leading from the kitchen to the showier parts of Lord Hartwell's grand manor. Jane's homespun was scratchy against her skin as she walked.

The halls were better lit in this part of the house, but dark doorways led off on either side. For a moment, Sybil fancied she was creeping past the open maws of slumbering beasts.

"That's what I get for bedding an artist," she muttered. "More imagination than a body needs."

She could hear the sound of music one floor above. In the ballroom, the string quartet would be competing with the low rumble of myriad conversations, clinking crystal, and the swish of silk.

There was the grand foyer ahead, with the porter leaning indolently against the wall. She quickened her pace.

A footman was coming down the grand staircase, moving quietly as a cat, his gaze focused on the porter.

He doesn't want to be seen, Sybil thought, wondering if the man was making off with a pair of Lord Hartwell's diamond studs. She squinted at him. There was something vaguely familiar about him.

He's wearing Somerville livery, but he's not Edward or Charles, Sybil realized suddenly. Even though all footmen tended to look alike, surely she'd have remembered that handsome face and broad-shouldered frame.

The floor creaked under her step and his gaze shot to her. A smile lit the man's face like a sunrise.

"Jane!" He abandoned stealth and bounded down the rest of the stairs in a couple of leaps. "Janie, me love, I know ye enjoyed wearing that borrowed finery, but believe me, ye shine everyone else down in your own sweet things. I knew ye'd see reason, lass."

Suddenly Sybil was in the large man's embrace. His lips covered hers in a deep kiss. She put up a token struggle, but his kiss was far from unpleasant, so she decided to relax and enjoy it.

He'll have to come up for air sometime.

When he did, she ran her tongue over her bottom lip and said, "Well, that was interesting, but I think you should know I'm *not* Jane."

"What are you two doing here?" the porter demanded, leaving his post to close the distance between them. "If you're not in service, get you back to the kitchen. No, no. We can't have you wandering the halls. Take the back way."

The porter pulled open a low-slung door along the side of the staircase to reveal a dim, narrow route disappearing beneath it. "And don't let me catch you in the public areas again or I'll toss you both into the snow myself."

Sybil grasped the handsome footman's hand and pulled him into the small space after her. Once, when she was ten, she had managed to sneak out of the most boring piano recital in human history and discovered the door beneath these main stairs. She'd spent the entire evening wandering the secret places of Hartwell House and no one was ever the wiser.

"This might be just the thing for finding your Jane without being seen," she whispered.

The door closed behind them, casting them into dimness, broken only by thin shafts of light knifing through the cracks in hidden doors.

"Then you must be Lady Sybil."

"Brilliant deduction," she said as she moved down the narrow space. "Never let it be said Somerville doesn't hire the brightest and best. Come. There's a dumbwaiter hidden in the library. We can use it to get up to the ballroom level."

A man's voice carried through the thick library door, his tone angry and growling. Eddleton couldn't make out all the words and he suspected some of them were foreign. Pity he hadn't paid more attention while he was on his grand tour. Once he had picked up the best way to invite himself into a lady's boudoir, his interest in other languages waned.

"Someone's coming," he whispered, pulling back and adjusting his small clothes.

"But we're not done yet, Bert," Lady Darvish complained. "Leastways I'm not."

The crystal doorknob jiggled and began to turn.

"Quick! Through there." Eddleton picked Lady Darvish up, clamping a hand over her mouth, and scuttled toward the curtained alcove where French doors led out onto a terrace. The last thing he needed was to be caught in flagrante delicto with the Black Widow of Wembley Street on the night he plighted his troth to Sybil Somerville.

Just as he yanked the draperies closed, a man and woman stormed into the room. Eddleton peeked through a slit in the curtain.

And recognized the red gown. His nearly betrothed, b'Gad! With another man. Why, he ought—

Lady Darvish squirmed in his arms and grabbed one of his hands. After she slid it into the top of her bodice, she settled and gave him a wink and a shrug.

Eddleton sighed and began toying with her tight little nipple. Anything to keep the woman quiet . . .

"Well?" the man demanded. His ensemble was cut in fashion of the first stare, Eddleton noted. But he wore the fine clothing carelessly, with none of the English stiffness, as though the trappings of success were nothing.

"Well, what?" Sybil demanded with a quaver in her voice. "You're the one who dragged me in here. What do you want?"

"Wait." In the hidden passage, Ian set his feet and pulled the real Lady Sybil up short. "I hear Jane. On the other side of this wall."

Sybil scrunched down and peered through the narrow slit around the hidden servants' door. A slice of the library and its occupants came into sharp focus.

"No wonder servants always know everything that goes on in a great house," she muttered. Then she blinked hard. "That's Giovanni. He's only a poor painter. Where did he get those clothes?"

Ian braced himself behind her to peek through the

same slit at a higher level. "A resourceful man will use whatever he must to get close to the woman he loves." He frowned. "But that's not the woman he loves. That's my Janie."

"Are you not surprised to see me like this?" Giovanni spread his arms and did a slow turn. "Allow me to introduce myself to you properly." He executed a sweeping bow with careless elegance. "I am Giovanni Baptiste Salvatore Brunello, Count of Montferrat. I posed as a starving artist in your country so I could find a woman who would love me for myself, not my station."

Sybil gasped. Jane only stared at him in puzzlement.

"And I thought I had found her, but now I know that money is all you care for, *crudele*."

"No—" Sybil began, but Ian clamped a hand over her mouth to keep her quiet.

"If I have caused you pain, milord, I'm truly sorry, but I really must go," Jane said, two frown marks drawing her brows toward each other. "I'm determined to accept a proposal of marriage from Viscount Eddleton during the last waltz and nothing you can say will make me change my mind."

"Stubborn as a rock," Ian muttered.

Sybil dug her elbow into his ribs. "Have a care what you say," she whispered furiously. "That's my sister you're talking about."

"Words will not move you?" Giovanni closed the distance between him and Jane with the grace of a great cat. "Then I shall not speak."

He crushed Jane to his chest and kissed her.

"No way in bloody hell," Ian shouted and gave the secret door a kick that knocked the portal off its hidden hinges.

Chapter Twelve

"Ian!" Jane couldn't decide if she was relieved to see him or upset that he was about to destroy her disguise. She still had a promise to keep.

"What is wrong with this cursed country?" Giovanni bellowed. "Can I not make love to the woman I intend to wed without the walls erupting with peeping-Thomases?"

"That's not the woman you intend to wed." Ian stepped between Jane and the Italian count, a fist drawn back at the ready. "She's mine."

"I should say not!" The draperies parted at the far end of the room and Viscount Eddleton stalked out. "Lady Sybil is promised to me. Her father and I have all but shaken hands upon the matter. I tell you, Lord Somerville shall hear of this!"

The library door flew open and a tall, white-haired gent strode in.

"Someone has been taking my name in vain." Lord Somerville's frosty manner thawed when he looked at Jane. "My apologies, Sybil dear. I so wished to escort you to the ball this evening, but once you hear my news, you'll agree my time has been well spent."

Lord Somerville's gaze darted from Viscount Eddleton to Ian, to the Italian, and then back to Jane. This time, his brows tented in a puzzled frown.

"The porter told me I'd find you in Lord Hartwell's library with a gentleman. Apparently, he miscounted how *many* gentlemen by a goodly number." He lifted a silver brow and the chill returned to his tone as he eyed the viscount. "Was that you, Eddleton, bandying my name about?"

"Lord Somerville." Eddleton bowed stiffly. "I'm gratified you're here to see for yourself what a shameless wanton your daughter is—consorting with foreigners and common footmen! It would have pained me deeply to bring the matter to your attention. I fear this means I must insist upon an alteration of our arrangement. I shall require additional incentives to take her as my bride."

Lord Somerville's lip curled. "You miserable little worm. As if I'd give you a farthing for the privilege of marrying my daughter. That arrangement you speak of was drawn up by Humphrey Roskin, the man who bilked my estate of thousands of pounds. And now I have proof of it. I finally tracked down the funds and Mr. Roskin is even now boarding ship for the penal colony of Australia—and lucky to get away that lightly. Consider our agreement null and void."

Lord Somerville turned back to Jane and his features softened. "My dear, you needn't marry anyone against your wishes." He took both of Jane's hands in his. "Can you forgive an old fool for trying to barter your happiness?"

"But I'm not—"

"In that case," Giovanni interrupted with a courtly bow to Lord Somerville and an evil glare at Ian, "may I present myself? You have known me aforetimes as Giovanni Brunello, artistic genius. You shall know me hereafter as the Count of Montferrat."

He bowed and bussed his lips over Jane's fingertips. She restrained Ian with a frantic look. He limited himself to the Scottish version of a growl—a low "Hmph!"

"I have reason to hope the lady will find happiness with me," the count said, tossing Jane a wink. "Please consider me a suitor for your daughter's hand, *signore*."

"Well spoken, Giovanni." Sybil's voice came from the

darkened space behind the wall. She stepped into the light of the room, hands fisted at her waist. "But you're asking for the wrong daughter."

"*Cara mia*?"

She nodded and the count lost no time in scooping her into a twirling hug, their laughter filling the library. Giovanni swept Sybil into a deep kiss, oblivious to the open-mouthed stares from the others. Then he lifted her in his arms and carried her out of the library. Sybil peered over his shoulder and mouthed "Good-bye" to her father and Jane.

"I suppose that settles the matter of my consent," Lord Somerville said with a chuckle. He turned back to face his other daughter. "Then you must be . . . Jane."

"Yes, milord."

"Ah, my dear, I think the time for formality between us is past. I held you at a distance because of my sins, not yours. It is time I rectified matters."

He squeezed her hands. Jane's vision blurred. How many times had she dreamt of this?

"Nearly losing everything has made me consider carefully those things which remain to me," Lord Somerville said. "I let my wife keep me from showing kindness to you. Even after she was gone, guilt kept me from doing the right thing. Now, nothing will stop me."

Jane swallowed hard.

"I cannot legitimize you. The law does not permit it. But I can acknowledge you as mine." Lord Somerville leaned down and kissed her cheek. "Will you allow me to treat you as a daughter in my house?"

The power of speech deserted her and she could only nod.

From the corner of her eye, Jane noticed a shadow pass over Ian's face and he took a step back.

"But what about me?" Viscount Eddleton demanded.

"Oh, you'll think of something, Bert." A feminine

voice came from behind the curtained alcove and the slight lady in the eye-straining yellow gown joined them. "Your choice is obvious. You've enough cat in you to land on your feet, I think."

The viscount gritted his teeth and then knelt stiffly before the woman. "Lady Darvish, will you do me the honor of becoming my wife?"

Her laughter tinkled merrily. "Of course *not*, Bert. Leastways not until you show more promise. But I'm not without hope. I believe you can be trained. You and I will put our . . . heads together and think of another way you might settle your debts. Come now, dear boy. You look ridiculous on your knees." She motioned for him to stand and then whispered, "But you might try that position again once you get me home."

She grasped Eddleton's arm and led him out the door.

"Now then, Jane," Lord Somerville said. "That waltz won't last forever. Will you dance with your father?"

She glanced at Ian, but he was studying the inlaid wood at his feet. If he were going to speak for her, now was the time. When he didn't do anything, something inside her wilted. Heartsick, she placed her palm on Lord Somerville's offered arm and let him lead her from the room and up the stairs.

They were only steps from the ballroom when she heard footfalls pounding behind them. Her chest constricted.

"Lord Somerville," Ian said. "I wish to tender my resignation as your head groom."

"This is hardly the appropriate time." Somerville narrowed his eyes, taking Ian's measure. "Besides, it appears to me you're a footman, not a groom."

"Aye, milord, appearances are deceiving this night. But this is no deception. Ye see, I wish to be a *bride*groom." Ian dropped to one knee. "Janie, I cannot give ye silks and a life of ease as Lord Somerville can, but I've been offered the post of Man-of-All-Work on a Wiltshire estate. The pay is well enough and the position comes with a wee cottage—"

"And you think to tempt me with a wee country cottage?" she asked.

"No, lass," he said with a sad smile as he stood. "I hoped to tempt ye with me heart. I love ye, Jane Tate. And all that I am is all I have to offer."

"Oh, Ian!" She threw her arms around his neck, hugging him fiercely. "That's all I'll ever need."

His lips found hers and she lost herself in the wonder of his mouth.

Until Lord Somerville cleared his throat.

"I believe we've missed the waltz," her father said. "My fault. We've missed too many things over the years, you and I. But perhaps you'll allow me to give the two of you the grandest wedding a head groom and a scullery maid have ever had, as a belated Christmas present?"

"Oh!" Jane's hand went involuntarily to her heart.

"I'll see you wed like a lady, my dear," Lord Somerville promised. "Perhaps you'll save a waltz for an old man next Christmas. But for now, might I recommend the two of you find some mistletoe?"

His hazel eyes crinkled with amusement as he inclined in a slight bow and headed toward the crowded ballroom.

Ian and Jane ran to the window where they'd found mistletoe earlier. Moonlight fractured the frosty panes into thousands of diamonds. Winter howled outside, but Jane was too warmed by Ian's love to feel the least chill. Ian bent to her and she stood on tiptoe to meet his lips.

"His lordship was wrong about one thing," Ian breathed into her ear when he finally released her mouth.

"What's that?"

"He can't see ye wed *like* a lady because you're already a lady." Ian pressed a kiss to her forehead. "My lady. My Lady Below Stairs."

The Longest Night

Jennifer Ashley

For my readers, who loved the Nvengarian tales.
Thank you.

Chapter One

"You will sort it out, Aunt Mary, won't you? *Please?*"

Seventeen-year-old Julia Lincolnbury pirouetted in front of the mirror while Mary tried to make sense of the chaos of Julia's bedchamber. Julia expected her "Aunt" Mary Cameron to sort out her bonnets, her gowns, her invitations, her maids, her tutors, and her mind. If Mary had been the young woman's governess or even her true aunt, she'd feel obligated to do so, but she'd offered to chaperone Julia these past few weeks as a favor to her father.

Mary had arrived two weeks ago, planning to spend Christmas with her son. She'd happened upon Julia's father, a sad baronet named Sir John Lincolnbury, outside a bookshop on a gray London street.

"Stuck in London for the winter," he'd said mournfully. His northern accent pronounced it *Loondon*. "I like th' quiet, but Julia is driving me mad. She made her bow in the spring, but no one's offered for her, poor gel. She's been invited to a Christmas ball at the Hartwells', the best invitation, but of course she can't attend unchaperoned. If her poor, dear mother had lived . . ."

Julia's poor, dear mother had been Mary's closest childhood friend. When she'd died, Sir John had gotten through his grief by spoiling Julia rotten.

"You are allowed to escort her to a ball, Sir John," Mary pointed out. "You are her father, after all."

"But a gel needs a wooman's hand, doesn't she? I can

do nowt with her. And here we are in the South at an unfashionable time of year." Sir John eyed Mary speculatively. "I say, Mrs. Cameron, if you're stuck here like a lump as well . . ."

"I'd be happy to chaperone her."

Mary cut off what was sure to be a long, rather wet appeal to Mary's charitable instincts. She had come to London early to wait for her son, Dougal, because back home in Scotland, the castle was preparing for another warm, happy, overflowing celebration, which had only reminded her of her acute loneliness. "For Allison's sake."

By the time the day of the ball rolled around, the nineteenth of December, Mary was reflecting that even Allison wouldn't have asked her to take on such an onerous task as looking after Julia. But it was a distraction, and Mary needed distractions these days.

Julia held a new gown of pale yellow muslin against her body and admired herself. "Lord Sheffley is certain to be at the Hartwell Ball. We must think of ways to keep him from dancing with that horrid Miss Hamilton. Aunt Mary, do think of something clever."

"The best way to attract a gentleman is to do nothing," Mary said. "If Lord Sheffley dances with Miss Hamilton, you pretend you care nothing for it."

"But I *do* care. I want to scratch her eyes out."

"You'll do nothing of the sort." Just as with Julia's father, Mary had discovered that a firm tone did wonders on this girl. "Remember what I said about manners."

"Yes, Aunt Mary."

Mary hid a sigh. The girl was naive and feckless, but she meant well.

A bell rang downstairs. Julia dropped her new dress to the floor and dashed out of the room. "The post has come!"

In the hall below, Julia snatched the handful of letters out of the footman's gloved hands and sorted through them, squealing every time she found one addressed to her.

"So much correspondence one has when one's friends are away in the country. Oh, Aunt Mary, here's one for you." She tossed it carelessly at her.

The missive was from a Lady Stoke, a friend of Mary's brother. Mary had made the acquaintance of the lady when she'd come to London. It was whispered that the lady's husband had once been a pirate, and Mary admitted that he looked the part.

"I was pleased to see that you would be attending Lady Hartwell's ball tomorrow evening," Lady Stoke wrote. "It might interest you to learn that the ambassador from Nvengaria and his wife will be there. Having met your brother in Nvengaria, they are eager to make your acquaintance. His aide, one Baron Valentin, indicated that he previously met you at your family's house in Scotland; indeed, that he stayed with your family for a number of months. I am certain you will enjoy the unlooked-for reunion."

Mary's fingers went numb and the letter fell to the floor.

"Aunt Mary?" Julia asked in concern. "Is it bad news? Your son?"

"No." Mary retrieved the letter and crumpled it in her fist. "Not bad news. But I will not be able to attend the Hartwell Ball."

She turned and marched up the steps to her chamber, ignoring Julia's shrieks of dismay.

The man needed to be watched.

Baron Valentin glided after the Nvengarian ambassador and his wife as they entered Hartwell House the night of the Christmas ball. The house overflowed with ladies in glittering jewels, gentlemen in dark finery. Garlands of greenery threaded the rooms, and balls of mistletoe dangled from every doorway and chandelier.

The English had a bizarre custom that if a person paused beneath a clump of mistletoe, it was an invitation to be kissed. In Nvengaria, the parasitic mistletoe was a symbol of death, used in funeral wreaths. But Valentin had learned during his previous visit to the British Isles just how odd the English could be.

He had no interest in attending balls, even those in the most lavish houses in London. Crowds unnerved him, English chatter unnerved him, acres of bared female shoulders and promising smiles unnerved him. But he couldn't afford to let Rudolfo out of his sight. Much as he chafed at this assignment, Valentin was not about to fail it.

He walked a pace and a half behind Rudolfo, watching the much-ribboned hem of Duchess Wilhelmina's dress flow across the marble tiles. If the Hartwells' servants hadn't dusted the floor today, it would be well dusted now.

They entered the ballroom, a lavish chamber with a mosaic-patterned ceiling that spoke of Near Eastern luxury. Lines of colorful ladies and monochromatic gentlemen met and parted in an English country dance, making the room seem to move.

Valentin couldn't help glancing through the throng, searching, seeking. He did not really expect to see the red-lipped, dark-haired Scottish lady he'd met last year, though he'd fallen into the habit of looking for her everywhere. She'd tended him when he'd been hurt, and her lilting voice had twined around his heart and pulled him back to life.

She wasn't here. Of course she wasn't. Mary would be in Scotland at her brother's castle, preparing for Christmas and Hogmanay. She'd be helping the housekeeper stir the black bun, perspiring in the warm kitchen while firelight glistened on her hair. She'd smile her slow smile, which had made his blood heat the first time he'd seen it.

He'd kissed her, touched her, asked her to come to him in Nvengaria. He'd gone home and waited for her through a brief, golden summer and a colder-than-usual autumn.

She had never come. As the weather worsened, so did his hopes of opening the door of his run-down manor house to find Mary Cameron smiling on his threshold.

Why should she bother? The journey to Nvengaria, a tiny country wedged between the Austrian empire and the Ottoman one, was long and dangerous, and Mary had every reason to stay in her brother's castle. Her new sister-in-law was having a baby, and Mary had a son of her own to look after, even if he was seventeen.

As an added complication, Valentin was logosh. Mary knew. She'd seen him shift to his animal form—a black wolf—and she'd not been upset by it. But perhaps after Valentin had gone, she'd had second thoughts about promising herself to a man who was part demon, part animal. That fact made even Nvengarian women think twice.

Ambassador Rudolfo, however, *didn't* know that Valentin was logosh, which was one reason Grand Duke Alexander had given Valentin the task of spying on him. Valentin, in fact, was only half logosh. He could pass for human very well.

A commotion behind him made him turn. At the head of the receiving line, a young woman crowed to Lady Hartwell at the top of her voice.

"What a *privilege* to be here, my lady. What an *honor*. Mrs. Cameron and I were so pleased by your *kind* invitation."

And there stood Mary, his Highland lady, just behind the girl, her face set in tired patience. Valentin had no idea who the young woman was, nor the plump gentleman behind Mary, nor why Mary should be with them. He only saw her. Here.

A year fell away. Memories poured at him—Valentin lying in a stone chamber in a drafty Scottish castle, Mary leaning over him. Her bodice had been damp with the water she'd used to sponge his wound, her face beaded with perspiration. A tendril of hair had escaped her bun and stuck to her cheek, and he'd reached up to touch her.

She'd gasped, eyes widening. Then Valentin had slid his hand behind her neck and pulled her down to him. Her breath had swirled into his mouth, and her lips touched his. He'd tasted her sweetness—Scottish honey and heady wine.

Later, he'd revealed all his secrets to her. Valentin had kissed her again, held her supple body against his. Now his heart beat in slow painful throbs as Mary stood in stillness across the Hartwell House ballroom.

As her companions effused over Lord and Lady Hartwell, Mary turned to sweep the crowd with her gaze. Her eyes met Valentin's.

Everything stopped. Mary did not move, and neither did he. Her hair was still brown, shining in the candlelight, and her dark blue bodice slid seductively from her shoulders. A man privileged to touch her could slide his arms around her waist, pull her against him, press his mouth to her bare throat.

Valentin's heart thundered in his ears. After months

of waiting and planning, torn by anger, impatience, and need, he at last stood in the same room with her.

Loud female laughter interrupted. The young lady with whom Mary had arrived had moved to a knot of gentlemen, where she waved her fan and sashayed her hips. Mary pressed her mouth closed and glided away, graceful as a doe, to fetch her. She took the young lady by the elbow and steered her out of the ballroom, the girl arguing every step.

Valentin let out the breath he hadn't realized he'd been holding. Mary, here—why? Who were those people, and why did Mary behave like a mother would to the young lady? Too much time had passed, so much had happened in her life, and Valentin was no longer part of it. The thought burned through him like a slow match.

Someone bumped him. Lines of dancing had formed around Valentin, and he stood like a rock against the tide. The guests eyed him askance, wondering what the strange foreigner was doing. Valentin took himself out of the way.

Then he cursed. Ambassador Rudolfo, the possible traitor whose every move Valentin was supposed to watch, was nowhere in sight.

"There you are, my boy," Ambassador Rudolfo said in Nvengarian. After searching the confusing house, Valentin had finally found the duke and duchess in a room full of card tables. Gentlemen and ladies clumped around the tables, gazing at cards in rapt concentration, while paintings of stiff English men, women, and horses watched from the walls.

Duke Rudolfo clapped Valentin on the back, a habit Valentin already abhorred. "This is where our work is done in England, Valentin. Over their games of whist and piquet and vingt-et-un. You lose gracefully at cards, and they eat from your hands. This is what Prince Damien tells me."

Rudolfo's mouth pulled into a sneer as he spoke Damien's name. Rudolfo thought he was safe showing his disapproval of Nvengaria's Imperial Prince to Valentin, which was another reason Alexander had given Valentin the assignment to watch him.

Before Valentin could think of an answer, Duchess Wilhelmina swept into the card room, leading Mary, Mary's young charge, and the plump man Valentin had seen with them earlier.

"Rudolfo," Duchess Wilhelmina said, "This is Mary Cameron, sister of the most honorable Egan Macdonald of Scotland."

Rudolfo swiveled an admiring gaze to Mary's bosom and bowed over her hand. "Charmed, my lady."

Valentin fought his logosh instinct to rip out Rudolfo's throat. Rudolfo liked to look at ladies, the more comely the better.

Mary raised a brow. "You are kind, Your Grace."

"Do not be so formal," the ambassador boomed in painfully accented English. "Address me as Rudolfo, and my wife as Mina. You are friend to Nvengaria, no?"

Valentin expected Mary to say no, very firmly. Through his anger, he wanted to laugh. Rudolfo would never take in Mary.

"My brother has said nothing but good things about Nvengaria," Mary replied. "And of course, I met Zarabeth, the prince's cousin."

No mention of Valentin. His temper flared. Any thought of letting Mary go fled. He would get an explanation out of her, make her tell him why she'd shunned him. Why she continued to shun him.

The girl was bouncing on her toes. Mary introduced

her to the ambassador and his wife as Julia Lincolnbury and her father, Sir John. Rudolfo at least did not slide his lecherous gaze over Miss Lincolnbury. He had enough sense to leave virginal daughters alone; besides which, virgins bored him.

"Nvengarians, eh?" Sir John Lincolnbury said. "Funny, Nvengarians came up when I was looking over some of my investments in the City today. You buy much braid, you lot do. By the bucketful." He pointed at the gold trim adorning the ambassador's uniform coat. "You dress like soldiers, but there ain't no more war in Europe, now that we gave old Boney a kicking, eh?"

The ambassador looked polite but uninterested. The duchess suggested that they sit down for cards. The so-charming Miss Lincolnbury could assist her, she said, and Mary could stay with Lord Valentin and explain the games to him.

At last Mary came to life. "I am sorry, but Miss Lincolnbury has come to dance. We should return to the ballroom."

Miss Lincolnbury dug her fingers into Mary's arm and glared. Apparently playing cards with a duchess trumped dancing with young gentlemen. Mary conceded reluctantly, and the duchess smiled and led Miss Lincolnbury and her father away. Her husband followed, leaving Mary alone with Valentin.

Valentin pulled out a chair and placed it in front of her. "Sit, please."

For a moment, he thought she'd refuse. But Mary was ever one for rigid politeness, whatever the circumstance. She plopped down in the chair, snapped open her fan, and flapped it vigorously.

Valentin seated himself across from her and reached for a card box in the middle of the table. It held three packs of cards, ready for any game.

"You will teach me." Valentin extracted a deck and laid it in front of Mary. "Perhaps this English game of whist?"

Mary continued to wave her fan. "You need four people for whist."

"There is a game for two, then?"

"Piquet. But you need a piquet deck."

"And this is not a piquet deck?"

Mary slammed her closed fan to the table and turned the pack over, her slender fingers separating the cards. "For piquet you use only seven through king, and aces."

He leaned over the table and lowered his voice. "Mary, why did you not come to me?"

Mary's hand stilled, but she did not look up. "You have just betrayed how un-English you are, my lord. In this country, a gentleman would not dream of asking a lady an awkward question in so forthright a manner."

"But I am not English. Nvengarians do not cloak feelings behind a mask of words."

Mary's gaze flicked to his at last. Her eyes were cold, tight with anger. "No, I hear you take out knives and go at each other in your Council at the slightest provocation. Debating tax bills must be dreadfully exciting."

"That violence is a thing of the past now that Prince Damien rules."

"Thank heavens for Prince Damien. I am sure Nvengarian wives feel much better about sending their husbands off to a day in government."

"Is that what you fear? The violent nature of Nvengarians? I am not in any of the ruling councils, in any case."

Mary continued to extract cards. "No, but Prince Damien sends you on missions where you get yourself shot."

Which he had while being bodyguard to Prince

Damien's cousin at remote Castle Macdonald. "It was my duty to protect Zarabeth."

Mary glanced at Rudolfo and his wife, now absorbed in a game with Miss Lincolnbury and her father. "At least this time your duty is no more dangerous than following about an ambassador who has a roving eye."

Valentin said nothing. He slid the cards Mary had discarded to his side and started to straighten them.

"Oh, dear," Mary said. "It *is* dangerous, isn't it? That is why you were sent and not some mindless lackey."

Mary was an intelligent woman, one of the things Valentin loved about her. "I watch him," he said. "It may come to nothing."

"But if it comes to something . . . ?"

"Then I will do what I must."

"Which is?"

Valentin shook his head. "Too many ears."

"I understand." Mary heaved a sigh and began to shuffle what was left of the deck. A lock of hair curved like a streak of midnight across her cheek. "Nvengarian secrets."

Valentine laid a heavy hand over hers. The words grated and hurt, but he had to say them. "Why did you not come? Tell me."

"Back to forthright questions, are you? Please, do not ask me."

"I do ask you. I deserve to ask you."

Her fingers moved beneath his. "Nvengaria is quite far away."

"Yes."

"My son is here. At Cambridge."

"Yes."

Mary finally stopped trying to toy with the pack. She looked up at him, her brown eyes troubled. "When we were in Scotland, you made me feel like a girl again. Full of hope, when I'd known nothing but disappointment for so long."

"And for this, you decided to stay home?"

She gave him an anguished look. "How could I go? Should I travel halfway across the Continent to find that you'd forgotten about me? That you meant nothing by your invitation? How could I risk that sort of humiliation?"

"Why did you not write me? I would have reassured you."

"Why did *you* not write?" Mary countered. "You ask a woman to travel a thousand miles to see you, but you cannot be bothered to mention whether you made it home safely yourself?"

"Princess Penelope and the Grand Duchess would have told you this."

Mary rolled her eyes and slid her hand from his. "I suppose I shouldn't be surprised that you behave like a man."

"I am a man. Or half man." Valentin paused. "Is the fact that I am logosh what deterred you?"

She gave him an indignant look. "You think I hesitated because you are logosh?"

"You did not believe in logosh when I first came to Scotland. You believed in no magic at all. Nvengaria is a heavily magical place."

Mary laughed a little. "After what happened at my brother's castle I believe in magic, thank you very much."

Valentin's heart beat rapidly, and his hands sweated inside his gloves. "Then may we begin again? I am whole and well now, and can be a fine lover to you."

Her dark eyes widened. "Lover?"

"You are a beautiful woman, and I wish to offer you the pleasures of my bed."

"*Valentin.*" Mary leaned forward, the soft round of her bosom swelling against the table's edge. "You really must reread your book on English customs. A gentleman doesn't say such things to a lady in a room full of people. Not at all, in fact. Not if she's a lady."

"The people in this room are playing cards and not listening. The ambassador has their attention, not I."

"Do not believe it. I have already overheard several bold ladies of the *ton* speculating on what you look like out of your clothes."

Valentin smiled, thinking of how he'd stood with Mary outdoors on a cold Scottish night. "And did you tell them?"

Mary flushed. "No. Good heavens, Valentin. What am I to do with you?"

Valentin stood. Before Mary could protest, he took her hand and pulled her with him to another door. Opening it, he slipped through, tugged her after him, closed the door, and pinned her against it.

"You will do this with me," he said, and kissed her.

Chapter Two

Valentin's strong body held her in place against the door. His tongue swept into her mouth without permission, his hands finding the curve of her waist. He kissed like he meant it, not like he wanted to impress Mary with his tenderness. He wanted her; she could taste it. No man had ever kissed her like Valentin.

He eased his mouth away, but the panels of the door still dug into her back, her thighs tight against his. When he'd left Scotland a year ago, he'd been wan from his wound, but he'd grown strong and sun-bronzed in the intervening months. Tonight he wore a formal black military uniform of Nvengaria, complete with gold braid, colorful medals, and slanting sash.

Mary couldn't help remembering the power of the body beneath that uniform, the muscle under his tight, warm skin. She'd seen all of Valentin's flesh, first when she'd nursed him, then again when she'd led him stealthily from the castle to the dark heath. He'd thrown off his clothes until he'd stood bare, his body gleaming in the moonlight.

Valentin nuzzled the line of her hair, as he'd done that night in Scotland, as though he learned and memorized her scent.

"Do you propose to kiss me until I come with you to Nvengaria?" she whispered.

He smiled into her skin. "This does not seem so terrible a thing."

It did not seem terrible to Mary, either. "If it were as simple as kisses, I would have left Scotland long ago. But it is not that easy."

Valentin's blue eyes flickered as he drew back. He'd shaved that evening, leaving his hard jaw smooth, rather than sanded with whiskers as she remembered it. He'd grown strong again, like the rock cliffs on which Castle Macdonald was built.

"It is easy," he said. "But perhaps I want too much."

Valentin's voice had always been mesmerizing. Mary had forgotten in the intervening months how full and deep was his timbre, how rich his accent, how he pronounced each word as though he did not want to make a mistake. She'd been praising herself for escorting Julia to the ball despite knowing he'd be here, but now she wondered if she shouldn't have ignored Julia's pleas and stayed home.

"I barely know you," she said. "I'd only learned who and what you were, and then you were gone." Taking Mary's peace of mind, what little she'd had, with him.

Valentin closed his hands on her shoulders. She loved the hard heat of him against her, his breath on her lips. "Then you will learn more of me, as I stay to watch my ambassador."

A trickle of unease moved down her spine. "Is he so dangerous? Is that why you're watching him?"

"The Grand Duke is suspicious. That is enough for me."

"Yes, I remember Grand Duke Alexander. A formidable man. Icy and precise." Tall and eagle-eyed, Grand Duke Alexander was reputed to be the iron hand inside charming Prince Damien's velvet glove. So Mary had heard, and she believed it.

"The Grand Duke is the most dangerous man in Europe," Valentin said. "So if he worries that a man wishes to destroy Nvengaria, I, too, worry."

Mary touched his face, seeking the lines she'd tried so hard to forget. "It is not fair that they always send you to face their troubles."

"I am good at it."

"If I asked you to tell them no, you will not endanger yourself for them, would you?"

He didn't hesitate long. "No."

There it was, then. Valentin would not unbend for her, nor she for him. And Mary was no longer the bending sort.

He brushed a tendril of hair from her face, his touch so warm her knees nearly buckled. "The ambassador's wife wishes to be friends with you. It would help me if you let her."

"Help you?"

"In my task."

Mary smiled to mask her hurt. "Ah, you mean will I cultivate her friendship and give you any juicy gossip she spills about her husband?"

"I would not ask, were it not important. The safety of Nvengaria, and perhaps England, might depend on it."

"That important, is it? You know that as a Scotswoman I would cheerfully watch England sink into the sea, as long as the Stone of Destiny washed up again on our shores. But then I have many English friends I would not like to see hurt. Nvengarians, as well. I will help you for their sake."

"Thank you." He sounded relieved.

Mary kissed him lightly on the chin, pretending his warm skin under her lips didn't make her heart hammer. "You could have convinced me without the kiss. Not that it wasn't pleasant."

Valentin continued to trace her cheek, his other hand still on her waist. "My feelings for you have nothing to do with the ambassador. I would stay here with you all night, showing you what I want with you, but I should not leave him for long."

"Now I know why the Grand Duke sent you. You are good at flattering others to help you."

"I would never flatter to gain help. That smacks of deceit, and I tired of that long ago."

Mary wondered what he meant by that, and realized she knew so little about Valentin. He was younger than she was, but she wasn't certain how much younger. She knew nothing at all of his life in Nvengaria, and her Nvengarian friends had surprisingly little information about him.

She softened her voice and let her hand drift to the medals pinned to his broad chest. "Of course I will help. I will befriend Mina, as she wants me to call her, and report all she tells me. As the ambassador says, I am a good friend to Nvengaria. Perhaps we should return to them, now, before they plot any assassinations."

"It is not a laughing matter. The ambassador might do just that."

Mary felt a qualm. "You're right. Nvengarian politics, from what I have seen, are exciting and deadly. I've promised to help. We should go now."

Instead of releasing her, Valentin cupped her face in his hands, his thumbs warm on her cheeks. His eyes held concern, wariness, and a vast watchfulness that she'd noticed in him before. He could be as volatile as any of his countrymen; she'd seen that when he'd hunted for kidnappers last year. But he was also very good at containing his violence, honing it until it became as quiet and deadly as a sword.

Valentin kissed her lips again, his touch almost gentle. "Thank you," he said, and finally let her go.

The next day Mary, Julia, and Sir John rolled from the Lincolnbury house in Curzon Street to a Grosvenor

Square mansion by invitation of the Nvengarian ambassador and his wife. Julia was excited, reasoning that acquaintanceship with a duchess, even a foreign duchess, would carry much weight when she entered her second Season. She had fussed over what to wear until Mary had nearly gone mad, but as they traveled the short distance to the ambassador's residence, Mary found herself as nervous as Julia.

Mary worried over her own appearance, but for a different reason. She'd peered anxiously into her mirror for a good half hour before they left, wondering if the fine lines at the corners of her eyes were entirely noticeable. Should she cover them with powder? Was she that vain?

She was, if a little powder meant Valentin would not notice how elderly she was. But he would discover the lines sooner or later, especially if he kissed her again like he had in the anteroom. He likely had already noticed them. In the end, Mary left off the powder, but dared to touch her cheeks with the tiniest bit of rouge.

As Mary suspected, this was not to be an intimate visit with Duke Rudolfo and his wife. When they entered the ambassador's mansion, two other English gentlemen Mary did not know, along with their wives, strolled the drawing room. Julia looked dismayed until she realized she was the only young, unmarried lady present.

The gentlemen retired to the billiards room, leaving the ladies to tea and the pianoforte in the high-ceilinged drawing room. Long windows brought in winter light to touch gold highlights into the French chairs, delicate tea tables, and ladies' gowns. Mary sat at the satinwood Sheraton pianoforte at Duchess Mina's insistence, the ambassador's wife having heard that Mary played well.

Mary let her fingers take her through the Mozart minuet while her gaze strayed to the doors to the adjoining billiards room, which stood ajar. The click of balls and male voices drifted out, but Mary was aware only of Valentin, who'd discarded his coat to play in shirtsleeves. The half-open doors gave Mary tantalizing and maddening glimpses of him leaning over the table to shoot.

Mary turned back to the keyboard for a difficult passage, pleased at the way the notes rippled from her hands. Mary had excelled at music as a girl and had mourned when her husband's gambling debts had taken away her beloved pianoforte. She'd practiced some at the Lincolnburys' these past weeks, but this was a fine instrument, well tuned.

When she lifted her head again, Valentin was standing in the doorway of the billiards room, his cue upright beside him. Without his coat, his tight shirt clung to his torso, his Nvengarian uniform having no waistcoat. Mary fumbled a chord, her heart racing.

Valentin watched until she reached the end of the piece. The ladies clapped, Julia with enthusiasm. Valentin said nothing at all. He gave Mary a long look, then turned silently and went back to the game.

Julia came to the pianoforte, still clapping, and slid onto the bench beside Mary. "Tell me what I should play, Aunt Mary. Something the duchess will like."

She meant something she would not mangle too embarrassingly. Mary sorted through the music on top of the instrument until she found an easy piece Julia already knew. She laid it out for her, then rose and left Julia to it.

Duchess Mina smiled at Mary and patted the cushions on the sofa next to her. Julia launched into her piece rather loudly, and Mary sat down, her hands hurting for some reason. She must have held them too stiffly on the keys.

Duchess Mina leaned toward Mary and spoke into her ear. "I saw him watching you. Valentin, I mean. It is difficult for him."

Mary glanced at the other ladies, but they sat together on another sofa listening to Julia, not the ambassador's wife. "Difficult?"

"That piece you played. It was a favorite of his sister's."

"Valentin has a sister?" Mary asked in amazement. She'd never heard anything about a sister.

"No more, my dear," Duchess Mina said. "Her name was Sophie. She died, poor thing, when Valentin was about twenty."

"Oh." Mary's heart squeezed. "How sad."

"It was more than sad. It was terrible." The duchess leaned closer. "Our old Imperial Prince came to call one day when Valentin was not at home. Valentin had been sent away by the Imperial Prince himself, on 'official' business. The prince found Sophie alone and expected her to show him *hospitality*." Duchess Mina lowered her voice. "If you know what I mean."

"I'm not certain I do."

"Ah, my dear, you English are so innocent."

"I'm Scottish," Mary murmured.

"I mean he wished to seduce her. Valentin's sister resisted, as you might expect, so the old prince, he took what he wanted. No one refused the Imperial Prince anything." Duchess Mina shook her head. "Then he let his manservant have her, to punish her for being so stubborn. Sophie could not live with the shame. Not many days later, she took her life. I do not blame her for this."

Mary put her hand to her throat. "Dear heaven. He never told me."

"He does not talk about it, no. But his need for revenge is great." Duchess Mina put her open fan between the two of them and the rest of the room. "His hatred for the Imperial family of Nvengaria is great also. It is said he will stop at nothing to destroy every last one of them."

This was news to Mary. "I know he once tried to kill Prince Damien. But he has reconciled with Damien, hasn't he? He escorted Damien's cousin Zarabeth to Scotland last year, where she married my brother. Zarabeth has only high praise for Valentin."

"He bides his time, my dear. My husband Rudolfo, he so worries about Valentin. Of all the men the Grand Duke could have sent with us to England, he chose Valentin. To remove him from Nvengaria perhaps? Was he plotting something against Damien again?"

Mary thought carefully before she replied. She had learned enough about Nvengarian politics to know they were never straightforward. People could have a dozen different loyalties and choose which one best suited the moment without thinking themselves inconsistent. Gossip and whispers were effective campaigns to destroy a rival. Valentin had warned her to watch the ambassador; now the ambassador's wife told her to watch Valentin.

"Valentin must miss his sister very much," Mary ventured.

The duchess shrugged. "He keeps much to himself."

Julia's piece came to an end. Duchess Mina dropped her fan and applauded, and Mary followed suit.

"Most excellent, my dear," Duchess Mina crooned to Julia. "Your playing, it is so delightful. Now, you must sit next to me and tell me all about your English Christmas customs. I have been given the use of a house in Hertfordshire, and I intend to celebrate a very English Christmas this year. I want to know everything about the Yule log and the bowl of wassail and maids stealing the footmen's trousers."

Julia went off into a peal of laughter, and Mary raised her brows.

"But is this not so?" the duchess asked, not the least bit embarrassed. "I read that if the footman does not fill the house with holly on the day of Christmas, the maids may take his trousers."

Mary fought the urge to laugh as loudly as Julia. "I am afraid we never practiced such a thing at Castle Macdonald."

"But Aunt Mary is Scottish," Julia said, popping her head up. "Men there don't wear trousers. They wear skirts."

"Kilts," Mary said.

The duchess smiled a sly smile. "Yes, I have seen these Scottish men. Your brother, Mrs. Cameron, he wears the kilt, no? And Lord Valentin has told us about your customs—the black bun, and the first-foot man, and other intriguing things."

"Not all of which is practiced in England."

"No matter. Miss Lincolnbury, you must come to my house in Hertfordshire and show me how to be very English. We will have some Scottish things, too, and on Twelfth Night have the—how do you call him?—the Lord of Un-rule?"

"Misrule," Julia said. "You put a bean in a cake, and whoever gets it in his piece is the lord that night. Everyone must obey him for the night."

"Excellent. We have a similar custom in Nvengaria, but our Lord of Misrule commands that all ladies must kiss him."

Julia giggled. "Oh, I think I should like Nvengarian customs."

"Then it is settled. You will come. I go tomorrow to be ready for Christmas Day."

Julia's face fell. "Oh, but I cannot. Papa has many meetings in the City, to do with his importing business, I think. We are staying in London for Christmas."

"Mrs. Cameron could accompany you, could she not? My husband, he stays in London as well, to do business with your king, but he will join us when he can. He will speak to your father. I'm sure all will be well."

Mary glanced at the billiards room again. Framed in the half-open door, Valentin bent over the table to take a shot, his body like a taut spring. He lined up his cue with the precision of a hunter, then made a sudden, tight shot. Balls clacked and rolled into pockets, and the other men groaned.

Mary's heart squeezed as Valentin turned away, lost to her sight. If the ambassador stayed in London, so would Valentin. That meant Mary would see little of him for the rest of her visit to England. At New Year's she would return to Scotland, leaving London and Valentin behind.

Which was what she wanted. Wasn't it?

She waffled. "I expect my son from Cambridge any day now. He will look for me in London."

Duchess Mina waved that aside. "Send him a letter and invite him to Hertfordshire. He can attend us ladies."

Julia gave Mary an imploring look. "*Please*, Aunt Mary? Hertfordshire is ever so much closer to Cambridge anyway. Just think how it will be if I can tell everyone I spent Christmas with a *duchess*."

It would be a social feather in plain Miss Lincolnbury's cap. The visit would also enable Mary to watch the duchess and learn what she could about the ambassador. She sighed.

"Very well. I will ask your father."

Julia flung herself to her knees and hugged Mary's lap. "Thank you, thank you. You are the best aunt in the entire world. Even if you aren't really my aunt."

Mary looked up to see Valentin at the door again, his blue eyes quiet but his body tense. He nodded once at her, as though she'd made the correct choice, and turned away.

Later, when Mary departed with Julia and Sir John, Valentin, coat restored, saw them into the coach. He said nothing to Mary, but she felt the rough edges of a paper press against her gloved palm as he handed her in. He stepped back to let a footman slam the door, while Duchess Mina waved them off like an excited schoolgirl.

Mary kept the note hidden until they reached home, treasuring it as though it were a diamond he'd bought specially for her.

Chapter Three

Valentin's heart beat faster when he saw Mary coming toward him through the lowering fog in Hyde Park. The hour was late, and it was cold, but she walked steadily in her sensible cloak and hood. Practical Mary. The cloak would hide her identity from the casual passerby as well as warm her.

A prim-looking woman walked several yards behind her. Her maid, he guessed. A respectable Scottish widow could not be seen walking about alone, especially near dark.

"Can she be trusted?" Valentin asked in a low voice as Mary stopped beside him.

"A good evening to you, too." Mary took his offered arm and strolled away with him on a path that led across a wide green. The park spread out to their left, offering a view of horses and carriages on the Rotten Row at the south edge.

Valentin liked the feel of Mary's slim hand on his arm, liked her body warming his side. Her plaid skirt rippled out from her cloak as she walked—Macdonald plaid, the tartan of her clan.

"Yes, I trust her," Mary answered. "She's Scots and loyal to my family. She might disapprove of my behavior and tell me so bluntly, but she would never spread tales outside the family. I read your note. What is this clandestine meeting all about?"

"Where is Hertfordshire?" he asked.

"You bade me meet you in secret to ask where Hertfordshire is? Would it not have been simpler to consult a map?"

He let the ridicule flow past him, liking the sound of her voice no matter what she said. "I need to know all about it. The duchess mentioned her plans for her English Christmas, but I have not seen this house she speaks of. Is Hertfordshire far from London?"

"No, it is only a few hours north, and quite picturesque, as I recall. The duchess longs to skate on a pond and savor English country Christmas traditions."

"You will go with her?"

"Julia wants to. And I admit, it would be good for her. She is not wrong that making friends with an ambassador's wife will raise her worth on the marriage market."

Valentin watched the horses and riders fade behind them into the fog. "You speak of marriage so coldly."

Mary shrugged. "I made the mistake of marrying for love—passion, rather. I hope Julia never does the same."

"It is not your fault that your husband turned out to be a fool."

Mary looked up at him, her eyes tight. "You are blunt."

"He hurt you and left you destitute. You had to beg for help from your brother."

Mary's glance turned cool. "Egan was happy to have me live again at Castle Macdonald. And I never begged."

Valentin smiled. "No. Not you." He imagined Mary standing ramrod straight in front of her brother as she explained that her husband had died penniless and that Egan was stuck with her. It must have shattered her spirit to do even that.

"In Nvengaria it is considered honorable to marry for passion," he said. "We prize love over riches. If a marriage must be arranged for political reasons, it is agreed that both parties can fulfill their desires with whomever they wish outside of the marriage, without retribution."

"How very convenient."

"I would not know. I never married."

"Why not?" She sounded curious. "Did you never find anyone who ignited your passion?"

"Not until I went to Scotland."

Mary flushed. "You tease me. I am a widow of five-and-thirty and have a son who has started at Cambridge."

They took a turn into a damp, narrow walk screened by hedges, where light fog wove ghostly fingers through bare branches.

"These things, they are part of who you are," he said.

"How old are you, Valentin? I never asked."

Valentin had to calculate; he so little thought about such things. "Seven-and-twenty as the English would say it. But I am logosh."

"What has that to do with anything?"

"Full logosh are considered men at fifteen, ready to take a mate and produce offspring. Here your son does not even begin university until he is seventeen or reach his—how do you say it?—majority—until he is one-and-twenty."

"And then he goes on his grand tour." Mary's smile was strained. "Before he even considers taking a wife. My husband was seven-and-twenty when he married me, the same age you are now. Only I was seventeen, making my first bow. And now here I am, a widow walking alone with a young, dashing ambassador's aide. What a scandal."

Valentin leaned to look under her hood, inhaling in her scent trapped by her cloak. "Nvengarians would not consider us a scandal at all. They would celebrate it."

"Well, I am not Nvengarian. And I have a son to consider."

Valentin stopped, pulling her around to face him. They stood alone on the path, the cold wind blocked by the tall hedges. "Do you think I would shame you by creating scandal for you? That I value you so little?"

By the pain in her eyes, she did think that. "Duchess Mina told me what happened to your sister."

The words were not ones Valentin expected to hear, and he wondered why Mary spoke of it now, without preamble.

"Why did the duchess tell you this?"

"I'm not certain, really. She wanted to explain that you lived to 'take your revenge' and nothing more."

An image of Sophie rose in Valentin's mind, the one he always saw. Her eyes sparkled with laughter, with her vibrant love of life. She'd remained lighthearted even as they'd watched their money dwindle and the house grow colder and shabbier each year. It didn't matter, she'd said. They still had each other. Remembering her still hurt, but he never tried to push thoughts of her away.

"She was lovely," Valentin said. "You would have liked her."

"If she was like you, yes, I think I would have." Mary put a gentle hand on his arm. "I am so sorry, Valentin."

Valentin swallowed the ache in his throat. "The ambassador's wife is correct only in part. I tried to kill Prince Damien in vengeance for my sister. As I was not given the opportunity to kill his father, I thought to destroy his son. In Nvengaria, we are willing to take one family member in payment for another."

"But Damien talked you out of it."

Valentin nodded, remembering the day he'd crept into the palace, knife hard under his coat, ready to both kill and die. He'd managed to get all the way into the Imperial Prince's private rooms, to take the place of one of the servers at his dinner table, to stand behind Damien's chair. He'd lifted his dagger to drive it into Damien's neck. Damien's wife Penelope, a young Englishwoman, had seen and screamed, and Damien dove aside just in time. Valentin's blade had slashed Damien's coat, missing the prince by a hairsbreadth. And then Damien's bodyguards had piled on Valentin and dragged him away.

Valentin had woken up in a cell. They'd known somehow that he was half logosh, and had reinforced the cell against his unnatural strength. They'd let him stew a few days, and then Prince Damien himself had come to talk to him. Every day.

Valentin had been sullen at first, refusing to speak, but gradually he'd opened up. Valentin found himself telling Damien about Sophie, what the now-dead Imperial Prince had done to his family, and all about his rage. Eventually he'd come to understand that Damien was an intelligent, shrewd, generous-hearted, and wise man, very different from his horrible father. Valentin had grown to respect and even to like Damien.

"Prince Damien can talk very well," Valentin said with a touch of amusement. "He is, as you say, a raconteur. But it was his wife's love for him that convinced me I had it wrong. She is pure of heart and could not love a monster."

"Then your quest for vengeance is over? And the duchess is mistaken?"

"My quest is of a different kind now."

"To catch the ambassador doing something illegal?"

Valentin slid his arms around Mary's waist. They were alone on the path; even the maid had dropped out of sight. "To find a woman with eyes the color of chocolate." The soft of her breasts pressed his coat, and he lowered his head to lick the hollow of her throat. Her skin was salty, warm from their walk.

"Valentin."

"I do not ask lightly." Valentin pushed back her hood, let his lips skim the line of her hair. "I want you as my lover. To give you all that the word means."

"While you are in London, fulfilling your task of spying on the ambassador?"

"For as long as you'll have me."

"Now we're speaking again of me traveling to Nvengaria, a land of which I know nothing. I've never been farther from home than Brighton, and I didn't think much of that." Mary tried to keep her voice light, but Valentin heard the strain in it, the fear.

"Do you wait for me to offer marriage?" he asked.

Mary shook her head. She broke his hold and walked away.

He quickly caught up to her. "The reason I do not offer marriage is because I have nothing to offer. My estate is bankrupt. I lost everything even before my sister died. It was one reason the Imperial Prince could not understand why Sophie resisted him. He offered to clear our debts."

Anger flared on Mary's face, and Valentin liked that anger. She understood. "What a loathsome man. I hope he died painfully?"

"Rumors say that Grand Duke Alexander poisoned him, but no one has proved it. No one wants to."

"I can believe it of the ruthlessly efficient Grand Duke Alexander. But surely Alexander can help restore your estate. As could Prince Damien, if he has become so pleased with you."

"The Grand Duke pays for my services, but not enough to keep a wife." Valentin took Mary's hand and turned her to him again. "I know that your husband left you destitute. I would never saddle you with another penniless husband."

"Mr. Cameron wasn't so much penniless as profligate. You seem the frugal sort."

"Mary." He lifted her hand to his lips. "I can offer you nothing."

"That's not true, you know. You can offer yourself."

He wished she understood that he wanted to give her everything a beautiful woman should have—gowns, jewels, horses, carriages. He wanted her to be the envy of every lady in Nvengaria. He wanted himself to be the envy of every gentleman.

"I do offer myself." Valentin pressed firm kisses on each of her fingers, then lifted her hand to his cheek. "My friends would think you prudent for not tying yourself to me. You would be free to leave at any time, free to live your own life, with your own money."

"Let me understand you. You are saying that people in Nvengaria live together openly, without marriage, and consider it *prudent*?"

"If a woman risked beggaring herself by marrying, yes."

"This Nvengaria is a strange place."

"It is a beautiful place." Mary would love it: its knife-sharp mountains, deep blue lakes, emerald meadows, brilliant flowers. "Also, Nvengarians would think you prudent because I am logosh. They are still not comfortable with wild creatures in their midst."

"Neither am I, to tell you the truth."

"Then it would be wise for you not to marry me."

Mary disengaged her hand from his. "I think you've run mad. You wish me to travel with you to Nvengaria—whenever your duty here has ended—and live with you as your mistress. So that the allowance my brother gives me will keep me well in your drafty house, and if your ability to change into a wolf becomes too much for me, I can leave without impunity."

Valentin nodded. "Yes. To all of that."

She gave him a wry smile. "You do realize that most Englishwomen would consider your offer shocking and a grave insult?"

"Would they?" The English never ceased to amaze him.

Mary's mouth curved, and her eyes filled with wicked beauty. "How fortunate for you that I am Scottish."

Hope flared in his heart. "Then you will agree?"

"I mean that I will give it careful consideration." She turned from him again. This time Valentin let her walk away, liking how her cloak flowed over the curve of her hips.

After a few yards, Mary turned back. "I refuse to believe that you arranged this assignation simply to make your shocking proposal. Why did you wish to meet?"

Valentin no longer wanted to talk about business, but he forced himself back to the matter at hand. "To ask you about Miss Lincolnbury's father."

Mary's brows rose. "Sir John? What about him?"

"Who is he? What sort of business does he conduct, and why is he here over Christmas?"

"Goodness, is that all? Why do you want to know?"

"Because the ambassador seems interested in him, more so than a Nvengarian duke should be interested in a plain English baronet."

Mary gave him a thoughtful look. "Duchess Mina, too, seems quite interested in Julia. I am fond of Julia and Sir John, for my old friend's sake, but they are not among the great and titled. Though Sir John is very rich."

"How did he make all this money? Is he in employ of your government?"

"My friend Allison told me his wealth came from family money and good investments. He is forever going to the City and the Corn Exchange, and Julia will become a very wealthy young lady on her majority. I'm certain the gentlemen will come out of the woodwork for Julia then."

"I wondered whether Sir John was a liaison for the ambassador to some English spy. So the ambassador can betray Nvengarian secrets."

"If so, I think the ambassador could have chosen a better conspirator. Sir John is a kind man, and Allison loved him, but he's not very bright."

"Perhaps that is the exact kind of man the ambassador needs. A man known to be slow-witted and innocent. Who would suspect him?"

"Goodness, you see plots everywhere. Perhaps the ambassador and his wife simply like Sir John and Julia. The duke and duchess are a bit slow-witted themselves."

"When Nvengaria is involved there *are* plots everywhere," Valentin said. "And conspirators and spies."

"Like you." Mary smiled.

Her smile could stop his breath. It made him want to be the best man in the world—honest, pure of heart, rich. He was none of those things.

If he could hold Mary in his arms, bury his face in her neck, breathe her scent all night, he was certain he would be all right. His wounds might heal, and he might forget, for just a little while, how much he'd failed.

"Like me," he agreed in a quiet voice.

He'd kissed her at the ball last night in a fever of longing. His longing was no less today, but he wanted to take her slowly this time. He leaned down, and she readily lifted her face, letting their lips meet.

I need you to make me whole, he wanted to say. Did he have the right to ask that of her? Of anyone?

Mary slid her arms around his neck. Her lips were warm in the cold December air, the heat in her mouth a haven. He loved her sharp taste, like cinnamon and exotic spices.

"Be with me, Mary," he said against her lips. *"Please."*

She eased away. "I am Julia's chaperone. I could compromise her chances."

"In Scotland, you were tied to no one. You were ready to leave the castle to your brother and Zarabeth. Now I find you with these people you do not even respect. When will you free yourself to be Mary?"

She flushed. "Julia is the daughter of my best friend, who died some years ago. Julia needs help, and I will not let her drift. I owe it to Allison."

"You like to tie yourself to needy people. They take advantage of you."

"That might be true. But it's nice to be needed."

"I need you."

Mary clasped Valentin's arms, fingers sinking into his flesh. "You are the strongest person I know. You take care of everyone—Zarabeth, the ambassador, Prince Damien. When will you release yourself to be Valentin?"

"It is not the same thing. I am atoning for my past."

"For trying to stab Prince Damien? You've been forgiven that, I thought."

"Not for Damien," he said impatiently. "For Sophie."

"We have already discussed this."

Valentin shook his head, eyes stinging. "I was not there to defend her. I'd gone off and left her alone."

"Not alone, surely. You had servants and bodyguards, I imagine. Every Nvengarian nobleman and -woman has bodyguards, I've been given to understand."

"If they'd stood against the Imperial Prince, he'd have

had them shot. Sophie knew that. She wouldn't let them stop him."

Tears trickled down his face, hot on his cold skin. Englishmen avoided showing emotion, Valentin had noted, but Nvengarians were not ashamed to weep.

He saw Mary's anguished face before her arms were around him. Her embrace held heat against the winter day, the fur of her cloak tickled his cheek, and her body against his comforted him, as though he floated without care in a warm sea.

The feel of her heart beating between her breasts soothed his hurt a little. Valentin pressed his lips to her neck, absorbed the warmth trapped inside her cloak. If he could stay in Mary's arms forever, all would be well. He was certain of it.

Chapter Four

Mary's head spun with conflicting thoughts the rest of the evening, through the long winter night, and on into morning as she finished sorting Julia's things for the visit to Hertfordshire.

She and Julia rode with Duchess Mina in a traveling coach that was a decadence of cushions and velvet upholstery. Ingenious fold-down cabinets contained food and drink and books, everything the well-heeled traveler could want, with punched tin boxes of glowing coals to warm their feet. The duchess even had a hand-warmer—a small metal box wrapped in cloth—inside her muff. She generously let Julia use it when Julia complained of cold fingers.

The morning was cold and crisp, the sky bright blue, the air dry and clear. Perfect for a carriage journey out of the metropolis. Pristine English countryside unfolded around them as the four horses in gleaming harness jogged along. Hedge-lined lanes led through a patchwork quilt of small farms; woods and gentle hills flowed to the horizon.

Julia and the duchess exclaimed at the prettiness. Mary, used to rugged mountains that dropped to churning seas, found the scenery tame and dull.

The house in Hertfordshire was anything but dull. Good King George must have wished to keep the Nvengarians happy, because he'd given them an enormous Palladian mansion that rose, escarpment-like, from a vast snow-covered lawn. The extensive park ran to a wood in the east, and a frozen pond glimmered like a fallen mirror across the ground.

The grounds even had a ha-ha, a green bank, now dusted with snow, which rose gently to end in an abrupt drop. A trespasser dashing across the great English lord's land in the middle of the night would suddenly find himself flat on his face in the mud, five feet down. Ha-ha.

Mary disapproved. English country houses always repelled her. Scottish castles were open to the entire clan; they were places to gather in times of trouble or for celebration. English houses, beautiful to look at, shut out all but the privileged few.

The house inside was a typical stately English home, with high-ceilinged rooms, a central elegant staircase, myriad halls, and paintings of two hundred years of the house's inhabitants. As they entered, the butler informed the duchess that the pond was indeed safe for skating. The duchess squealed and clapped her hands like a schoolgirl.

It was the twenty-first of December, Yule, the longest night. They would have a skating party this afternoon, Duchess Mina declared, and then they'd burn the Yule log and have all kinds of festivities that night. The ambassador had said he could join them that evening, and he'd bring Julia's father with him. It would be a fine celebration.

That meant Valentin would come. Mary both wanted him there and feared his presence. His bold offer in the park and her glimpse behind his stoicism had unnerved her deeply.

She wanted him. She might be elderly in Julia's eyes, but Mary was still a strong, healthy woman with a strong, healthy appetite. One reason she'd decided to meet Dougal in London for Christmas this year was because seeing Egan, Zarabeth, and their new baby so happy in Scotland too sharply reminded her of her own loneliness. She was very glad for them and loved her tiny nephew, and Egan never made Mary feel that Castle Macdonald was not her home. But Mary needed more. Her affair last year in Edinburgh had been a desperate need to satisfy bodily desire, but had left her colder than ever.

She knew she'd not find coldness with Valentin. He had a strong, fighting man's body, the muscles she had caressed in the park yesterday hard and formidable. She'd seen him bare, had stood against him, had shared with him the deep kisses of lovers. Mary's body already throbbed with need for him, and what was more—she could love him. She was certain she already did.

Mary tried to distract herself from thoughts of Valentin by watching the duchess. She didn't believe for a moment that Sir John Lincolnbury would deliberately involve himself in spying, but Valentin's speculation made Mary wonder, as well. Why *did* the ambassador and dear Duchess Mina take so much interest in Julia and her father? Simple friendliness? Or something more?

Goodness, she was getting as conspiracy-minded as Valentin.

The duchess roamed the house the rest of the morning, supervising the English servants who decorated with ribbons and greens. No holly yet, Julia told her. It was bad luck to have it in the house before Christmas Day, which Duchess Mina found delightfully superstitious. They ate an informal luncheon, during which Julia and Duchess Mina chattered like old friends. No one mentioned overthrowing Prince Damien or passing secrets to King George or assassinating anyone. All very innocuous.

When the afternoon reached its brightest point, Duchess Mina's skating party went forward.

"Of course you will skate, Mrs. Cameron," Duchess Mina said when Mary expressed the desire to remain on the canvas-covered bench at the pond's edge and watch. "We all must. Do not ruin my fun."

"Skate with me, Aunt Mary," Julia cried, already on the ice. "You must hold my hand so I do not fall too often."

Resigned, Mary let a Nvengarian footman who doubled as a bodyguard help her strap blades to her flat-soled boots. She hoped she'd not end up on her backside every few feet. Her true reason for not wanting to skate was that she hadn't in years, not since Dougal's childhood.

The Nvengarian helped guide her onto the ice, then gave her a slight push when Mary nodded at him to do so. She rocked her body to gain her balance, then tentatively stepped out with her right foot.

The world spun around her, and she sat down sharply on the ice. Julia put her hands over her mouth to hide her giggles. The duchess laughed openly, then glided across the pond with the ease of long practice.

"You will get used to it, Mrs. Cameron. We skate all the time back home."

"I am so pleased to hear it," Mary muttered.

Julia helped Mary to her feet. The girl linked arms with her, and they skated slowly after the more competent duchess. The pond curved to the right, angling behind a thicket of trees, but the butler had indicated that the surface closest to where they'd entered was the safest.

"Oh, look," Duchess Mina cried after they'd skated about a quarter of an hour, the duchess showing off how gracefully she moved on the ice. "Our gentlemen have arrived. How splendid."

She spun with a flourish, finishing with a pose to greet the men heading down the path from the house. *Pride goeth before a fall*, Mary thought in annoyance, but the duchess remained upright.

The train of male figures moved down the snowy, muddy slope: the ambassador, Valentin, and Sir John, followed by more Nvengarian servants. The animal in Valentin was evident as he effortlessly navigated the slippery path. The others picked their way carefully, but Valentin moved with unselfconscious grace.

Julia pulled Mary toward the shore and called out to Valentin: "Do come and skate with Aunt Mary, my lord. She's already fallen once."

Mary flushed. Valentin sent her a little smile, and her heart turned inside out. His rare smile was like a gift just for her.

The gentlemen stopped at the bench to don skates, then came onto the ice. Sir John moved across it remarkably well, but he'd been raised in Westmoreland, which must have plenty of frozen ponds in winter. The ambassador was more awkward, but perhaps his many duties in the Council of Dukes didn't allow him time on the ice.

Valentin glided to Mary and took her arm. She didn't trust herself alone with him, but she didn't have enough confidence in her skating ability to push from him as he skimmed her away from the others.

"You fell?" His breath hung in the air beside her ear. "Are you all right?"

"Fine, if slightly bruised. Both my pride and my backside."

"Perhaps we should go inside, then."

She did not trust herself alone inside with him, either. "No, no. I am of hearty Scottish stock, not a wilting weed. I will survive it."

Mary thought she might not survive his warm body against her side, or the way his thigh brushed hers with every gliding step. She took a long breath, trying to cool herself with the frigid air.

Valentin held her easily as they skated on, his balance

supporting hers. "What have you discovered from the duchess?"

His mission. Of course. "That her favorite English Christmas customs are those that might involve men losing their trousers."

Valentin's half smile returned, and Mary decided she should stop joking. She would melt right through the ice if he kept smiling at her like that. "Jesting aside, she seems harmless. We have unpacked, and Duchess Mina has made plans to skate, light the Yule log, and carry a wassail bowl about to the neighbors. She likes the idea of kissing under the mistletoe, so she has ordered it hung everywhere. Beware of that when you enter the house."

"Hmm." Valentin's brow furrowed, as though he were trying to decipher what sort of code Yule logs, mistletoe, and wassail might mean.

"The duchess has so far not pumped Julia about her father's business, tried to pry English secrets out of her, or confessed a desire to overthrow the Nvengarian government," Mary went on. "Either she is very careful, or she is innocent. I cannot believe she'd know nothing of her husband's involvement in insidious plots."

"Grand Duke Alexander is never wrong."

"Perhaps not, but I do not think the avenue is through the duchess."

"Please, keep watching her."

Mary sighed. "I'm not comfortable spying on my friends. I know you grew up in a country of mad political conspiracies, but I had a fairly normal childhood in a Scottish castle. That is, if you consider being the only girl among a pack of half-crazed Highland men normal. I only had to deal with feuds within my own family, and those weren't secret." She broke off under Valentin's unnerving stare. "What is it?"

"Nothing. I like to watch your lips when you speak."

She flushed from the tips of her toes to the roots of her hair. Very well, perhaps he was not focused only on his mission. The fact that he was happy to see her made her feel like a giddy debutante. "We are skating far away from the others."

"I do not wish them to hear what we are saying."

Because he wanted to talk about his mission, or because he wanted to repeat things he'd said yesterday? *"I want you as my lover. To give you all that the word means."*

Her imagination spun with what he might have in mind. She cleared her throat and tried to speak normally. "It might be dangerous to go too far. The English servants say we should stay near the banks."

Valentin skated her around the bend, then pulled her to a stop. A tangled thicket of trees on the bank above shielded them from the others.

He tapped the ice with his blade. "It is fine here. See, the water is shallow and frozen hard."

"Have you been out here before?" Mary asked. "I presume so, if you are familiar with the depth of the pond."

"I am familiar with ponds in general. We skate quite often in Nvengaria. The winters are cold and long, so we enjoy whatever we can from them."

"When you are trying to convince me to come to Nvengaria with you, you should not mention long, cold winters. Although I confess winters can be bleak in northern Scotland. I spend most of them in Edinburgh. Or London."

"I have decided to stop persuading you to come to Nvengaria."

Mary went cold, though beads of sweat broke out on her brow. "You have, have you?"

"I do not have the gift of persuasion. But I do believe in the magic of my people." Valentin slid his hands under her elbows, holding her steady.

"Magic?" she repeated.

"Today is the winter solstice, the Longest Night. It is said among logosh that the person you stay with on the Longest Night will remain in your life for the next year, perhaps longer."

"Are you saying you wish to spend the night with me?" Her voice cracked. "You know that is a highly improper suggestion, even to a widowed lady."

"It is why I led you from the others." Valentin leaned toward her, his warmth like a blanket. "I want to lie with you, Mary. I have since the day I woke up in Scotland to see you leaning over my bed."

"You were ill. I was tending you."

"Yes." The word expanded, slow and rich. "Your hair was mussed, your dress loose, and you smelled like heaven."

"I am Julia's chaperone. My behavior must be impeccable."

"I am logosh. I know how to come to you without the others knowing."

Mary drew a shaky breath. They both swayed a little on the ice, and Valentin's firm hands moved to her back.

It felt so good to be held. Mary dearly loved her son and her brother, and Zarabeth and the new baby. But that did not mean her loneliness did not make itself felt. Mary wanted to be held, kissed, told she was desirable. She was supposed to admit that her youth was gone, to resign herself to being a widow, a doting mother, a chaperone. No longer wanted by men.

She knew in her heart that this was a lie. She longed for a man's touch, and Valentin, eight years her junior, was gazing at her as though she were the most beautiful woman in the world.

If she let him, he'd pull her into his strange life, take her far away from all she knew. In return she'd get Valentin, with his beautiful eyes, warm voice, and honed body. Hers for always.

"I'm not certain what to do."

Valentin's lips moved from the line of her hair to her cheekbone. "I will come to you, tonight."

Mary touched his face, liking the hardness of his jaw under her glove, the rasp of whiskers catching on the kid leather. He was strong, handsome, and his warmth under her hands made her heart pound.

"Very well."

Valentin kissed her. She balled her hands on his chest, feeling his heart beating beneath them. This wasn't casual for him; he was as lonely as she was.

He tasted raw and wild, like the winter afternoon. Valentin didn't belong in this tame English countryside, with its neat hedgerows and formal gardens that shut out the common people. He'd fit well into the Scottish Highlands, its rugged mountains and cold, dangerous seas. She shivered at she thought of him in bed with her, wondering if he'd be as strong and dangerous as he seemed, and longing to find out.

The quiet was shattered by the sharp sound of shots. Then came the screams of Julia and the duchess, the startled shout of Sir John.

Valentin pushed Mary away from him, and she slid backward across the ice. By the time she stopped herself, Valentin was already off the pond and tearing free from his clothes. Mary skated as fast as she dared to the bank and pulled herself onto firm ground.

Valentin's boots and coat fell empty to the mud beneath the trees. Mary grabbed a branch to steady herself, and watched a huge black wolf sprint across the park toward the woods beyond.

Chapter Five

Julia wouldn't stop screaming. Mary yanked the skates from her boots and hurried around the snowy banks to the path and bench.

Ambassador Rudolfo lay on his back on the ice, a pool of blood under his left shoulder. Sir John had his hands to his mouth, eyes wide in horror, and Julia stood, shrieking, beside him.

The duchess knelt next to her husband, his head in her lap, and was parting his clothes to feel his heart. Mary stopped on the bank, her own heart pounding in fear.

"He's alive," the duchess said crisply. "Wounded only in the shoulder."

Mary sighed in relief, then let her efficient persona take over. She turned to the servants hurrying down from the house and pointed to them one by one.

"You, quickly, carry the ambassador to the house and to his bedroom. *You*, fetch blankets, you, tell Cook to boil water, and find my box of remedies. Tell the butler to fetch the nearest doctor. Hurry." Mary turned back to the pond as the servants, both Nvengarian and English, rushed to obey. "Julia, for heaven's sake, stop screaming. The ambassador is not dead."

"But the bullet," Julia sobbed. "It went right past my cheek."

Mary seethed at Nvengarian politics, which did not care if it hurt innocents in its wake. "Skate to me. I'll take care of you. Everything will be all right."

"Where is Lord Valentin?" Sir John demanded. "He was with you, Mrs. Cameron. Where did he go?"

Mary extemporized. "He ran to find out who was doing the shooting. Do come here, Julia. You are in the way."

As she'd hoped, her sharp tone cut through Julia's hysteria. The girl skated to the bank and climbed off the ice, her eyes wide.

"I thought I saw a wolf, Aunt Mary. An enormous black wolf."

"What absolute nonsense." Mary wrapped her arm around Julia and sat her on the bench to take off her skates. "You saw someone's dog running loose, is all."

"But why would someone shoot at us?" Julia bleated. "Are they trying to kill us?"

Mary quickly unbuckled Julia's skates and pulled them off. "I am certain they were only stray shots from a shooting party. Foolish city folk going after grouse in entirely the wrong place. Lord Valentin will stop them."

Duchess Mina gave Mary a level look as she followed the footmen carrying her husband. She knew quite well that the shots had been deliberate.

What did not make sense to Mary was why the ambassador, suspected by the Grand Duke of plotting against Prince Damien, would be an assassin's target. Perhaps the Grand Duke had sent the assassin himself, not wanting to wait until Valentin finished his investigation. But would even Grand Duke Alexander deliberately endanger Valentin or Mary or innocent Julia in the attempt?

Or perhaps these shooters were in a different plot altogether. The ambassador could have more enemies than Grand Duke Alexander. Nvengaria was rife with plots.

At least Mary knew that Valentin hadn't shot at the ambassador. Her heart pumped faster as she thought of Valentin charging into the woods to hunt the hunters. As a logosh, Valentin possessed strength beyond an ordinary man's, but these men had weapons.

With much fuss, and sobbing from Julia, Duke Rudolfo was carried into the house and up the stairs to his bedroom. He woke halfway through, pressed his hand to his wound, and groaned.

Mary thought she'd have to take charge of his nursing, but Duchess Mina proved unexpectedly competent. Mary helped her put the ambassador to bed and bathe the wound, and then the doctor, a country man round of face and genial of speech, arrived. He gave the ambassador a good dose of laudanum, pried open his shoulder, and probed for the bullet.

The duchess did have to leave then, calling for smelling salts. The rest of the servants turned green and sidled off, and Mary ended up holding the bowl to receive the bloody bullet. She did so without squeamishness. Growing up in a household of rough Scotsmen, Mary had become used to helping set broken bones and patching up wounds, even extracting stray bullets from sheepish men. This was all quite familiar.

She chafed at the delay, however, because she wanted to retrieve Valentin's clothes from the woods before anyone else found them. Valentin himself had not been seen or heard from since the shooting.

"This one is easy," the doctor said cheerfully, as the round bullet clinked into the bowl. "I wrenched out many a ball lodged right into the bone when I was a surgeon on the Peninsula. Sawed off my share of legs, too. This is the most interesting wound I've tended since I became a country doctor, except for the poor lad gored by his oxen two summers ago."

Mary offered no comment. She wiped away blood while the army surgeon-turned-doctor sewed the wound shut, then helped him make the ambassador comfortable.

The sun slid behind the horizon as the doctor packed up and left, the Longest Night beginning. Mary callously handed the bowl and bullet to the nearest footman, suggesting he clean the bullet and offer it to the ambassador as a souvenir. Then she hastened downstairs to see the doctor out, hoping to slip away and fetch Valentin's discarded clothes.

Too late.

The ambassador's valet, a small, fastidious Nvengarian who'd excused himself during the doctor's work, came in the front door, carrying Valentin's clothing and boots.

Mary moved to intercept him. "I will take those."

"Isn't that Lord Valentin's coat?" Julia came charging out of the drawing room with her father on her heels. "Where is Lord Valentin?"

"Where did you find 'em?" Sir John asked. He touched the coat as the valet handed it to Mary.

The valet spoke only broken English. "By the frozen water," he managed.

"Strange place for the fellow to disrobe, eh?"

"He didn't disrobe, Father. The wolf took him." Julia clapped her hands to her cheeks. "Oh dear heaven, the wolf's eaten Lord Valentin!"

Sir John looked shocked, the valet confused. Mary snatched the boots. "Julia, please. If you examine them, you will see that these clothes are quite whole. What wolf undresses his dinner before eating it?"

"Oh." Julia looked doubtful. "But why on earth did Lord Valentin leave his clothes near the pond? How can he run about without them?"

"Perhaps somebody stole 'em," Sir John suggested. "Shoved them down there, planned to fetch them later. Lord Valentin can tell us if he has any missing. Where *is* the fellow, by the way?"

"Still trying to discover who shot at the ambassador, I'd imagine." Mary turned away to the stairs.

"Oh, the chappie wasn't shooting at the ambassador," Sir John said. "He was shooting at me."

Mary turned abruptly. "At you? Why on earth should someone shoot at you?"

"I don't know, my dear. But Duke Rudolfo pushed me out of the way and took the bullet himself." Sir John puffed out his chest. "Damned decent of him, I'd say. Good fellow, that ambassador, even if he's foreign."

The wolf approached the house under cover of darkness, sensing the warmth within. The mansion was a bulk of shadow in deeper darkness, the lower floor black, with only a few lights on the upper floors.

The strange ditch the English called a ha-ha might keep out a wandering tramp, but to a nimble animal it presented no barrier. Valentin easily leapt the ditch and scrambled down the bank to the shadows of the house.

In the back, facing the pond, two square windows showed candlelight. He knew that the window on the far left was the ambassador's bedroom, the one on the far right, Mary's.

Nvengarians considered logosh demons. Logosh regarded themselves as simply logosh—beings that had inhabited the Nvengarian mountains for eons. They were shape-shifters, able to take animal, demon, or human form as they chose.

Valentin was only half logosh, and he'd always found shifting painful. He clenched his teeth as he forced his wolf limbs to change to the demon's. Fur became skin, paws became claws, and his thighs thickened with logosh muscle. All creatures but logosh considered the logosh's demon form hideous, but in it, Valentin could climb.

He moved swiftly and noiselessly up the wall to the lighted window and peered into what must be Mary's dressing room. An open wardrobe showing neat rows of Mary's garments stood next to an armless chaise. At the dressing table, ribbons had been sorted neatly, as had her cosmetics and jewelry. Not one stray glove, hat, or handkerchief rested on the chaise. The pristine neatness of it made him smile.

Mary herself leaned over the washbasin, scooping water from hands to face. Her bodice hung loose at her waist, her corset and chemise spotted with water.

Valentin hooked his claw around the edge of the casement and pulled, surprised when the window opened easily. Mary had left it unlatched, just as she hadn't drawn the curtains.

He'd meant to be silent, but at the window's slight squeak, Mary whirled around. She stood silently, eyes wide, hands dripping, while the logosh climbed into her chamber.

"I do hope that's you, Valentin," she said breathlessly. "Or is there another logosh running about the place?"

Valentin willed his body to become human again. His fingers cracked as they moved from claw to human flesh, his face flattened, his hair grew warm on his head, and his back straightened. He growled, fisting his hands, willing the pain to stop.

Mary stepped past him to close and latch the window. She jerked the heavy drapes across it, and when she turned, he closed his arms around her.

"What happened to you?" Mary whispered. "What did you find out there?"

Not now. He was naked, he hurt, and he needed her. He slanted a kiss across her mouth, tasting the water from the basin on her lips.

Mary made a resisting noise, but then her arms came

around his waist, holding him as tightly as he held her. Valentin unraveled her coiled hair, pulling it loose, burying his hands in it.

This was why Valentin had returned to Britain, to find Mary, to kiss her, to love her. To persuade her to come home with him. This time, he would not leave without her.

He spread kisses down her neck to where her breasts swelled from her stays. Mary cradled him against her bosom, fingers furrowing his hair. He tugged the laces of her stays, loosening them enough to spread open the corset with his broad hand.

Valentin raised his head to kiss her lips again. "Let me love you, Mary."

"Yes." The word was a gasp. "My bedchamber is through there."

Valentin was too impatient to seek a bed. He pulled the laces from her stays, then caught her unfettered breasts in his hands. They were full and round, the breasts of a woman, not a girl. He licked between them, loving their scalding heat.

Mary herself unhooked her skirts and petticoat and pushed them down her hips. Her chemise floated down with them, puddling on the floor. Her stocking-clad calves brushed his legs, but otherwise, she was as bare as he.

She leaned into him as he brushed his hand up the back of her thigh. "I wish I could be young and beautiful for you," she said.

What was she talking about? Valentin turned her around to face her mirror, which put her backside against the swell of his arousal. "You are the most beautiful woman I have ever known. Look at yourself."

The mirror reflected them together, her pale body wrapped in his brown limbs. Valentin's large hand rested on her breast, wisps of her long hair twining his fingers.

He slid his hand down her abdomen to the dark tuft between her thighs, smiling when he found it pleasingly damp.

"Your body is my heaven." Valentin touched each part of her as he spoke. "Your thighs have strength, your hips are soft, your breasts . . ." He returned his hand to the heat beneath them. Her nipples were dark, tight points he wanted to suckle. "I love your breasts."

Mary traced her lower abdomen, which was softly rounded. "I've had a husband and a lover, and I have a grown son."

Valentin rolled her nipple between finger and thumb. "Why should these things make you less beautiful?"

"Because you are young and strong, and . . . heartbreakingly handsome. You should be with a young woman, one who can give you a family. I'm rather past it."

"Past it?" English expressions baffled him.

"You make me feel like a giddy girl, but I know how old I am."

Valentin's blue gaze caught her brown one in the mirror. "My body wants yours; can you not feel?" He shifted the ridge of his arousal until it slid firmly between her buttocks. "I find you desirable, or I would not ache for you so much."

"Lust of the moment is not the same thing."

Valentin lifted her in his arms and deposited her on the narrow chaise, his body pressing Mary's down. Face-to-face, body to body, he hungrily took her in.

"Is 'past it' the English way of saying you have no interest in pleasures of the flesh?" Valentin asked.

"It is the English way of saying I no longer *should* have interest in pleasures of the flesh."

"Do you mean you take no interest in this?" Valentin slid his hand between her legs. He cupped her, fingers brushing her hot, swollen sex. "Or this?" He slid his first two fingers inside her.

She gasped, liquid heat pouring over his hand. "No. No interest at all."

Valentin eased his fingers from her and raised them to his mouth. Mary's pupils dilated as she watched him lick them clean.

Did anything taste better than a woman aroused? Did any woman taste better than Mary? It could not be so. Valentin kissed between her breasts, then down to the indentation of her navel, then at last put his mouth where his fingers had been.

Bliss. He suckled her, surrounded by her incredible scent. *Love you, Mary. Gods, how I love you.*

"Valentin . . ." She was barely coherent.

Now. Valentin sat up on the chaise and lifted Mary onto him. He showed her how to wrap her legs around him—*just like that*—so that he could slide into her warm, pliant body.

She was tight and beautiful, enveloping him with arms and legs, her breasts like pillows against his chest. Mary made warm noises in her throat, her lips on his forehead, his hair, his brow. Valentin gripped her hips and rocked up into her.

The beast in him roared. He'd found his mate, the true match to his soul. He would make her understand that they belonged together, that he was never leaving this place without her.

Mary's teeth latched on to his earlobe, her wanting turning as furious as his own. The sharp little pain made him move faster, sliding in, in, *in*. She was his home, his resting place, the woman who could soothe his hurts. She was a lush armful, her long hair tumbling between them and warming him like a blanket.

"Valentin," she said in a ragged whisper, "I . . ."

He cupped her face in his hands, their bodies moving together. "What?" He willed her to say the words he wanted to hear.

Mary shook her head, her hair brushing his face. "Love me," she pleaded. "Just love me."

Valentin leaned back, pulling her down harder onto him. He wanted to tell her what he felt, how much he needed her, but his command of English fled him. He said the words in Nvengarian, that he loved her, he wanted her, for now, for always.

He felt her body shudder. She opened her eyes in surprise, as though she'd never broken in climax before. Valentin feared for a moment that she'd fight it, Mary who loved control.

Then she laughed. She dropped her head back, her glorious hair tumbling down her back. Her body rocked as she dragged everything from him.

Valentin's excitement tipped over the edge. They moved together, gripping, loving, panting, her sheath so tight on him that he couldn't stop his shout of pleasure.

She opened her eyes and looked into his, the brown of hers coffee-dark. Valentin wanted her to look at him like that for the rest of his life.

"Mary . . ." He spoke a few more words in Nvengarian, then stopped, forcing himself to repeat them in English. "You are mine. Forever. Say it."

Mary closed her eyes. She shook her head as she held him, and Valentin gave up, groaning as he released his seed. He collapsed to the cushions with her tangled around him, breathing like a drowning man who at last finds shore.

Chapter Six

Mary woke in the morning with Valentin in her bed. She opened her eyes to find herself nose to nose with him, his blue irises wide with that *otherness* he had.

Without dismay, Valentin smiled. His face was creased from the pillows, his hair pleasantly rumpled. He was so handsome, warm, and desirable, that Mary tightened in sudden panic.

"Will it come true, do you think?" he asked softly.

"Will what come true? What are you talking about?"

Valentin lifted a curl from her face, his touch gentle but strong. "The legend of the Longest Night. Will the lady I spent it with be with me for the coming year?"

Mary sat up. "Not if someone finds you in bed with me. I'll be utterly disgraced."

"I locked the door. And what if they do discover us? Do you care so much what these English people think of you?"

"Some of the people are Nvengarian. Your people."

"Who would not find it surprising that I want to be with you." Valentin smiled the heart-melting smile that made anything he said sound reasonable. "If you are forced to flee the country, you can always come home with me."

"This is no laughing matter."

"No? Come home with me anyway, Mary. It is nothing to be ashamed of."

"Perhaps not in your world, but it is in mine. I will be

the entertainment of the *ton*—talked about, laughed at. The matron who fell for the young, handsome foreigner with the enticing eyes."

A crease appeared between his brows. "Are you so ashamed, then? Of what we did? Of who I am?"

"No!" Mary's anger rose—both at the easily shocked English and the altogether too-permissive Nvengarians. She was Scottish, neither one, but she felt pinched between the two worlds. She wondered if her brother, Egan, ever felt like this.

No, Egan did as he pleased and damned what everyone else thought. Egan had traveled the world, playing the mad Highlander, entertaining everyone he met. Mary had always wished for Egan's gift of charm. Perhaps then she'd be able to fall into Valentin's arms and let him take her away from her old life and everything she knew.

The trouble was, she didn't hate her old life enough. Her marriage had been a failure, and she was lonely, but she had Dougal, and her family and friends, and her home at Castle Macdonald. There was nothing much better, in her opinion, than the laughter that filled Castle Macdonald to its rafters. Even Sir John and Julia were ties to her childhood, to a friend she'd talked and giggled with; the two of them had once run away to the Edinburgh shops without permission, feeling themselves wicked and daring.

Mary did not want to fling away the happy parts of her life for Valentin, but neither did she want to sacrifice being with Valentin for them. Valentin seemed to think that waltzing off to the eastern edge of Europe at a moment's notice was nothing difficult. But Nvengaria was the end of civilization as far as Mary was concerned.

Valentin was watching her with his intense blue eyes, knowing he hadn't won. "I'll not give up, Mary."

Before she could answer, he slid his hands around her neck and pulled her down to him. Mary went all too willingly. She let him kiss her, let his body warm hers. She never felt so good as when he touched her. Valentin's returning smile told him he knew it, drat him.

Valentin kissed her brow and gently rolled her over into the pillows. Mary wanted to tell him that he really should leave before someone discovered them, but she couldn't speak as he pressed her down with his warm weight and loved her all over again.

Valentin descended to the breakfast room much later to find the rest of the household already at table. Even Duke Rudolfo had risen from his bed, one arm in a sling, and was eating buttered toast with his good hand.

Valentin had made himself leave Mary after their second enjoyment, then stealthily went to his own chamber, to bathe and dress for breakfast. He felt pliant and good, the memory of Mary under him imprinted firmly on his body. He both liked the feeling and knew it would distract him all day, until he could love her again.

The breakfast room was one of light and glass. The floor-to-ceiling windows that faced the frozen pond let in the weak winter sunlight. A fire in the hearth added to the coziness. *Not the best room to sit in,* Valentin reflected as he gathered food from the sideboard, *if one feared sharpshooters.*

Mary had taken little on her plate, but Julia's was piled high, as was her father's. Duchess Mina pushed the remains of her breakfast aside and sipped chocolate from a dainty cup.

"I still believe the shots were fired at me," Sir John

said, as Valentin seated himself across the table from Mary. Valentin smiled at her, but she kept her gaze on her plate. "I make a great deal of money in the City. Perhaps someone wanted to eliminate my wealth by eliminating me." Sir John chortled.

"Oh, Father, do not laugh," Julia cried. "It frightened me so."

Ambassador Rudolfo cleared his throat. "I am not certain, Sir John. I heard the shots and pushed you down to the ice, because you were nearest to me. They must have been firing at me. Nvengarians are notorious for eliminating each other, as you say. Perhaps I have angered a rival."

"It is safer these days in Nvengaria," Duchess Mina pointed out. "Perhaps you should resign your post, Rudolfo, and we will return home, finished with politics."

Rudolfo gave her a smile. "No, my dear, I will not run away because of a few bullets. All will be well."

"There were two men," Valentin said.

Everyone stared at him. Julia and her father stopped chewing, and the duchess peered at him over the rim of her cup. Only Mary would not look at him.

"I investigated the area last night. Two men stood in the trees, on the rise there." Valentin pointed out the window to high ground beyond the pond's icy sheet. "They were gone, but I found evidence of them. They drank whiskey to keep warm and dropped the flask when it was empty. They were English, not Nvengarian."

Sir John gaped. "How the devil d'ye know that?"

Valentin couldn't very well tell him that his wolf had smelled that they were English. The English had their own peculiar scent, as did Nvengarians.

"They wore English boots," he improvised. "The prints are different." That, at least, was true.

"That's clever of you," Sir John said in an admiring

voice. "But how d'ye know it wasn't Nvengarians in English clothes?"

The ambassador answered, "Nvengarians don't like to wear English clothes. And when they assassinate, they stand up and do it. They don't skulk behind trees and shoot when innocent people are about."

"Good heavens, they might have hit *me*," Julia said.

"Is that where you were all night, Valentin?" Duke Rudolfo asked. "Miss Lincolnbury thought you'd been devoured by wolves." He chuckled, then winced as his shoulder moved.

"I told her that was nonsense," Mary said in a firm voice.

"I was investigating," Valentin said. "I did not see a wolf."

The ambassador gingerly touched his coat where the bandage bulged beneath it. "The butler told me another strange tale this morning. He swore that he saw a monstrous creature prowling outside the house late in the night. It had the face of the devil, he said."

Valentin didn't change expression. "I saw nothing of that, either."

The duchess clicked her cup to her saucer. "Do stop pushing at your wound, Rudolfo. You'll open it again. Wolves and monsters notwithstanding, my English country Christmas must continue. We had to postpone the Yule log and the wassail yesterday, but today, we shall do all this."

"Perhaps not the wassail bowl," Mary said. "We will have to ride on open roads, and the men with the guns might try again."

The duchess waved that away. "We will go in a large party with guards and be perfectly well. Rudolfo will stay home, watched over, of course."

Mary at last let her gaze meet Valentin's, her exasperation evident. Valentin gave her a smile, his heartbeat quickening when she gave him a hint of a smile in return.

Her smallest gesture stirred his blood. Valentin wanted to finish with this business quickly so he could turn his attention to convincing Mary to come home with him. His body heated as he remembered the warmth of her skin against his, her sweet cries as he loved her.

Valentin wanted to hear those cries for the rest of his life. His smile turned determined, and Mary looked away, unnerved.

"I am pleased that Baron Valentin stayed behind today," Duchess Mina said, as she rode next to Mary in the rather stuffy traveling coach.

Another carriage, bearing Julia and her father and two English servants with the wassail bowl, followed. Four Nvengarian bodyguards rode nearby, but for some reason Mary did not feel protected. Valentin and two more bodyguards had stayed at the house with Duke Rudolfo while Duchess Mina went resolutely on with her wassailing party.

Mary could not agree that it was good that Valentin had stayed behind; she wanted Valentin beside her, needed him next to her. She'd told him she did not want to leave with him, but her heart knew the lie. Mary craved to stay with him day and night for the rest of her life. Her whole body was loose from their loving this morning, and a warm core burned inside her.

As the carriages wound through the countryside under clear, white-blue skies, Mary sensed eyes watching them. The eerie feeling made her shiver, and the cold wind buffeting the carriage did not help.

Duchess Mina leaned toward Mary, her exotic perfume clogging Mary's nostrils. "I did not like to say so in front of the others, my dear, but I believe it was Valentin himself who fired those shots at my husband."

Mary opened her mouth to explain that Valentin couldn't have—she'd been talking to him at the time, when she remembered that no, she'd been standing in his arms, kissing him. Her face burned, and she quickly looked away.

"I cannot blame him," Duchess Mina said. "Poor Valentin has had a difficult life, and he's never forgiven Rudolfo."

Mary turned back, puzzled. "The ambassador? Forgiven him for what?"

"He did not tell you this? Rudolfo was *there*, my dear. On the day the Imperial Prince called on poor Sophie."

"Was he? Good heavens." Valentin hadn't mentioned this, either.

"Yes, Rudolfo was in the hunting party when it fetched up at Valentin's estate. Everything was in great disrepair, Rudolfo told me, because years before that, Valentin's father had done something to offend the Imperial Prince. I never discovered what. Valentin's father lost all his money and died a broken man." The duchess shook her head and glanced out at the bare, dead trees that lined the fields.

"Please tell me what happened."

"It is so sad a story, Mrs. Cameron. When they arrived at the house and the Imperial Prince ascertained that Sophie was alone, he sent his men off to pen up the servants and do what they liked. Then the Imperial Prince took Sophie into a bedchamber and locked the door. He made Rudolfo stand guard just outside. Rudolfo did not know what to do. He was sick at heart."

Mary's own heart raced in anger. "Well, he ought to have done *something*. Do you mean to say that he kicked his heels in the corridor while his prince ravished Valentin's sister in the next room?"

The duchess furrowed her brow. "'Kicked his heels?' I do not understand."

"An English expression meaning waiting or wasting time. You are avoiding the question. Why did your husband do nothing?"

"Because of me." Duchess Mina sighed. "Rudolfo feared that if he interfered with the prince's wishes it would endanger me and our daughter, who was a debutante at the time. We could not know if the Imperial Prince would mete out the same sentence on our family that he did to Valentin's. He likely would have, unfortunately. It was no idle worry."

Mary balled her gloved fists. "Then Duke Rudolfo ought to have finished off the Imperial Prince then and there. It would not be unusual for Nvengarians; I am told they run each other through with much less provocation. Had I been there, I certainly would have taken up a pistol and shot him."

Duchess Mina smiled suddenly. "Do you know, my dear, I believe you would have. You are a woman of courage. Luckily Grand Duke Alexander saved us all from the Imperial Prince not long after."

"You, too, believe Grand Duke Alexander poisoned the Imperial Prince? Does anyone know that for certain?"

"No, but we all *know*, if you understand me. In any case, Alexander helped drive the prince completely mad, and the man died."

Mary shivered, but she couldn't help feeling glad. Her wild Highlander blood wished she could turn back the clock and rush to Sophie's rescue that day. She'd have told the Imperial Prince what she thought of men like him before she fired her shot.

"But Valentin was not content with the Imperial Prince's death," Duchess Mina continued. "He is obsessed with vengeance. Valentin tried to kill Prince Damien, you know, though he was thwarted from that. He no doubt came with us to England for a chance to punish Rudolfo. Valentin wants revenge on all who were with the Imperial Prince that day."

Mary's head hurt. She remembered what Valentin had told her, that he'd traveled here at the request of Grand Duke Alexander to spy on Duke Rudolfo. She was certain that some of the ambassador's bodyguards and servants were spying on both Valentin and the duke. Spies on the spies, in the mad confusion of Nvengarian politics.

Mary could clear up some confusion, at least. "Valentin did not shoot at your husband, Your Grace," she said in a brisk tone. "When the shots were fired, Valentin was with me. We were talking together, screened from view by the trees."

The duchess looked disbelieving. "Why did he not come out with you? You came right away to see what was the matter, but Valentin disappeared."

"He ran off in the other direction to find the source of the shots."

Duchess Mina smiled archly. "Leaving his clothes behind?"

Mary flushed. "He . . ."

The duchess patted Mary's knee. "My dear, do not bother to explain. I know you are his lover. I know he stayed in your room last night. Oh, yes, I am not as slow-witted as I seem. I know when a woman loves a man. But please be careful, Mrs. Cameron. Lord Valentin might not have fired the shots himself, but others can be hired to do so, you know."

Mary started to argue that in that case, anyone could

have hired them, but Duchess Mina firmly changed the subject. Mary found herself woodenly answering questions about the differences between English and Scottish Christmas customs while they continued to the house of the nearest neighbor.

As they wended down the country lane between cheerful villages, Mary swore she glimpsed a black wolf trailing them, keeping to the fringes of the woods. She watched without drawing attention to the fact, but the wolf never approached, and it disappeared altogether when they finally returned to the ambassador's house late in the winter-dark evening.

Chapter Seven

Valentin scraped the skin off his hands when he helped the footmen position the Yule log in the drawing room's huge fireplace that night. The duchess, Julia, and Mary tied ribbons to the branches, and Julia explained they each had to sit on the log at least once, for luck in the coming year.

Traditionally, the Yule log was to be lit with a piece of the previous year's, but the prior inhabitants of the house apparently hadn't burned one. The duchess made do with a freshly cut piece from the woodpile, and soon she had everyone coaxing the log to burn.

As soon as it caught, Mary said, in her efficient voice, that Valentin needed his hands looked after. She bade him go to the dining room across the hall, where she joined him after fetching her bag of remedies.

Valentin didn't mind her standing so close, never noticed the sting on his palms as she dabbed them. The scent of her filled his nostrils, and her warm body close to his did bad things to his heart.

"I thought you were to stay with the ambassador while we paraded about the countryside," Mary said as she worked. She bent close to his palm, and her hair tickled his nose. "I saw you following us, though I don't think any of the others marked it."

Valentin realized that her hair tickled him because he'd instinctively leaned toward her. But this gave him the opportunity to speak softly into her ear. "I followed because I believe Sir John is correct that he was the intended victim."

Mary jerked her head up, nearly colliding with his. "Truly? Why?"

He liked her face so close. "Perhaps he knows something he should not. Perhaps he is a go-between someone fears, a go-between who needs to be removed."

"Removed?" Her brows arched. "You mean killed. Good grief, Sir John was married to my dearest friend. I can't let him be removed. What would become of Julia?"

"This is why I followed you, today, to keep Sir John safe. Happily I saw no one to put him or you in danger on your outing."

"Thank heavens for that." Mary resumed wiping at his palms. Her ministration was unnecessary—as a logosh, Valentin healed quickly. But he enjoyed how tenderly she nursed him, the light feel of her fingers on his skin.

Mary turned away to her remedy box, and Valentin caught her arm. He'd wanted her all day, could barely contain his patience for the household to go to bed. When the house grew quiet, he'd slip into Mary's room again, splay his hands across her body, ease every bit of worry with his lips.

Mary stepped from his grasp. "The others might come in."

"You fear too much. We have the excuse of mistletoe." He pointed at a gray-green ball hanging from a chandelier.

Mary's stance, her tension, was not about to let him in. She looked up at him with new hardness in her brown eyes, and he sensed all their progress of last night evaporating.

"What is it?" he asked.

She stood silently a moment, looking unhappy. "The duchess told me that Duke Rudolfo accompanied the Imperial Prince to your house that day."

Valentin stifled a growl. Damn Duchess Mina's gossiping tongue. Why the woman wished Mary to know these things, Valentin couldn't understand. But Mary watched Valentin, willing him to be truthful with her, no matter how much it hurt.

"She is correct," Valentin said. "Duke Rudolfo was there that day."

"Why did you not tell me?"

Valentin closed his fingers on her arm again but kept his touch light. "Because I hate to think of that time, that most horrible day of my life. I know Duke Rudolfo could have done nothing to save Sophie. The Imperial Prince would have killed Rudolfo's family in retaliation if he had interfered. I know this. The Imperial Prince was a monster."

"So I have heard. Duchess Mina fears that you have come to kill her husband."

"And I must, if he proves to be working against Prince Damien."

"Is Duchess Mina right, then? That you live for vengeance? Is this why you so eagerly agreed to Grand Duke Alexander's assignment?"

His fingers tightened. "I told you why I so eagerly agreed to this assignment."

"But you had no idea I'd be in London."

"That did not matter. Alexander's task could at least get me to England. I had been saving the money to make the journey alone, but I snatched this opportunity. I planned to make my way to Castle Macdonald when this business with the ambassador was done, for good or for ill."

"Oh. Why?"

Valentin clasped her hands between his, not caring

that his palms still stung. "Because you belong with me, my Mary. I knew it when I first saw you. I need you."

"But do I need you?"

Her breath warmed his fingers. She smelled so good, damp and warm with perspiration, and he wanted to drink her in. "I hope that you do."

"Even if you have no wish to marry me?"

Valentin gripped her hands tighter, but he felt her slipping away. "If marriage is what you want, I will work to make it so. My estate is recovering under Prince Damien's rule. It will take time to make it yield enough for you not to be ashamed to be my wife, but I will work hard to bring it about."

Mary gave him an indignant look, one he'd come to love. "I would never be ashamed to be your wife. But I must understand you. You say you do not blame Duke Rudolfo for not helping your sister, but how can that be true? I'd be enraged at anyone who didn't keep my son, or Egan, or my sister-in-law, or anyone I loved from harm. At anyone who stood by to save his own skin, in fact."

She was stubbornly proud, his Highland lass. The strength of her people flowed through her, and he loved her for it.

Valentin released her hands. He remembered the impossible rage that had filled him when he'd found Sophie in a tight ball on her bed, too stunned and shocked to even cry. Sophie's maid had told Valentin the tale, every detail. The maid herself had been beaten by the Imperial Prince's guards because she'd tried to protect Sophie.

Valentin folded his arms across his chest. "I was angry with Rudolfo, yes, and I still have that anger—I will not lie. Duke Rudolfo should never have let him touch Sophie. If he'd shot the Imperial Prince that day, I doubt the Council of Dukes would have cared."

"Will you try to kill Rudolfo, now?" Mary asked. "For being a spy? How convenient you can take your revenge at the same time. Two birds with one stone?"

"It is complicated. I am angry, yes, but I also have my duty to Damien and Alexander. My personal wishes are no longer important."

"Of course they are important. You likely think it is too Nvengarian for me to understand, and you are right. I don't understand. I am too *Scottish* to understand. In my world, the personal is *far* more important. A clan lord would agree if you had to take care of a personal feud before answering his call to arms. The clan lord might even help you. That way, he'd know you'd be finished with the business and not distracted."

"I am finished," Valentin said in a firm voice.

"Are you? How can I be certain you won't rush off on an unfinished vendetta as soon as you take me home with you? Or that Grand Duke Alexander won't send you to do your 'duty' with another insurrectionist? When will you stop being the dagger hand of Prince Damien and the Grand Duke and just be Valentin? The man I can love?"

"I am not their servant . . ."

"Aren't you?" Her words cut at him. "And yet, every time I've seen you, you've been on some assignment for them. I want *you*, Valentin. Not Valentin the bodyguard or the spy or the hired assassin. Dear heaven, Alexander expects you to murder a man if he turns out to not love your prince."

"You do not understand how dangerous such men can be. If I discover Rudolfo is working to bring down Prince Damien, he will make certain I never report back to Nvengaria. He would not hesitate to kill you, or your Sir John, or even Julia, to stop me. In my world, secrets must be kept secret. At all costs."

"Well, it is a bloody inconvenient world, isn't it?" Mary came close to him, her dark eyes swimming with tears. "I don't think I could live there."

"Mary, let me finish this, and then we will speak."

"No." She gave him a sorrowful look. "I want life and love, not death. I will not marry the man Grand Duke Alexander uses to do his dirty work."

Valentin balled his fists. He'd never been given to demonstrating his rage, always needing to keep the beast inside him at bay. He knew that if he ever gave in to that beast and its basic, volatile emotion, he'd become more of a monster than the Imperial Prince had ever been.

"I did not offer marriage," he said. "I told you I could not."

"I know. You offered me compromises, conveniences even. That is not what I want."

"What do you want, then?"

"I have told you," she said.

She wanted something he couldn't give her. She wanted certainty, and Valentin's entire existence was based on uncertainty. He pressed his lips together, his heart a burning lump in his chest.

When Valentin said nothing, Mary kissed the corner of his mouth and walked away from him. The door opened behind him, and then her light footsteps sounded as she left the room. The click of the door closing was the bleakest thing he'd ever heard in his life.

Mary was ready to run back to London that very evening, but after a bout of agitated pacing in her bedchamber, she decided to make herself stay. Leaving would draw attention to herself and Valentin, and she would not be such a coward. She also could not justify either abandoning Julia or wresting the girl from Hertfordshire when Julia was so enjoying herself. Mary had never seen her this happy.

She arrived at the supper table in time to hear Duchess Mina reveal more plans for her very English Christmas. Mary sank to her place in the richly paneled dining room where she'd ministered to Valentin, both relieved and worried not to see him there. He'd gone out, Duke Rudolfo said, to look for the shooters again. Rudolfo was convinced the gunmen had given up and gone, but Valentin had insisted on checking.

"A mummers play," the duchess interrupted from her end of the table. "As I was saying to the others, Mrs. Cameron. We'll be the mummers ourselves and invite the neighbors 'round to see us."

Mary reflected that the neighbors might well have had enough of their foreign visitors trying to be so English, but she nodded. Julia jiggled in excitement; she *adored* dramatics.

Julia and Duchess Mina conferred on the play in the drawing room after supper, asking for pointers from Mary and Sir John to keep everything traditional. To Mary's dismay, the ambassador announced that he was not needed in London until after Boxing Day, so he and Valentin could stay and take part in the dramatics. Sir John then announced that he'd jolly well take a holiday from business, too. Everyone seemed happy, natural, animated. Everyone, Mary thought grumpily, except herself.

Valentin did not return, and though Mary lay awake most of the night, Valentin never ventured to her room, either as man or logosh. She was angry with him and did not want to see him. So why did she remain awake in the darkness, listening, hoping to hear his step?

Mary regretted now that she'd run away from Scotland and the family celebrations there. She'd told herself she was tired of all the traditions and festivities, and that a Christmas alone with her son in London would be preferable.

She now realized that a warm family Christmas was exactly what she needed. Meeting Valentin here had brought home to her how much she hated being alone.

She wanted Valentin, wanted to be with him in all ways, but the duchess's words had chilled her. Not that she believed Duchess Mina's idea that Valentin lived only for vengeance, but Valentin hid so much from Mary. She saw his pain when he spoke of Sophie, but he'd never volunteered any information about her until Mary pried it from him. She wondered how long he'd have waited before mentioning he'd had a sister at all.

Mary slept finally, and rose, groggy and late for breakfast. In the sunny breakfast room, Duchess Mina passed out the parts for the mummers play and told them to work very hard so they could be ready by the next day, which was Christmas Eve. Mary kept herself from snapping a reply, and again when Valentin strolled into the ballroom where they'd adjourned to rehearse, looking fresh and rested.

The duchess and Julia had decided to improvise a story involving Saint George, sans dragon, very traditional for a mummers play. Duke Rudolfo would be Saint George. Sir John would play a dark knight, and he and Rudolfo would battle it out with swords. Saint George would be slain, but a powerful magician, played by Valentin, would bring him back to life.

Julia would be Saint George's intended bride, ready to weep copiously at the death of her beloved. Mary was to play Athena, goddess of wisdom, who came in at the end to drive the sword of justice into the dark knight.

The duchess, as the playwright, decided to narrate

and direct. "It is a good way to practice my English," she said. "Mary will make a splendid Athena, will she not, Lord Valentin? So stately in her robes, and she will carry my husband's saber."

Valentin gazed at Mary in silence, and she turned away, unable to meet his eyes.

Valentin read his part in a quiet voice. The only time Mary had to be near him was at the end, when she was to point her sword at Valentin and declare that he was the best of them, because he gave life. The duchess had them run through the play a few times before they broke apart to find appropriate costumes. They would have a rehearsal in costume, Duchess Mina said, and then luncheon. Mary obeyed without argument, too tired to fight Duchess Mina's iron-handed enthusiasm.

Upstairs in her room, Mary donned an ivory evening dress, then instructed her skeptical Scots maid to help drape a sheet around her in classical-looking folds. Mary knotted her hair on top of her head and let a few curls fall to her cheeks. Deciding she looked sufficiently Greek, she made her way to the ambassador's rooms to borrow his saber.

Duke Rudolfo was alone in his sitting room, already strapped into Saint George's makeshift armor. The servants had taken apart several real suits of armor from the main hall and fit bits of them to the ambassador. It all looked strange with the swath of white bandage on his shoulder, but Rudolfo had insisted that he was well enough to enact a sword fight; he would use his uninjured arm anyway.

"The English knights must have been uncommonly small," the ambassador complained, adjusting his metal breastplate. "Here is the saber, my dear. I have put on the tip guard so you do not accidentally skewer Sir John."

Mary lifted the saber and examined the intricately etched blade. The sword was a thing of beauty, well made, the hilt bearing small and colorful gemstones.

"A fine piece of work," she said. "I will be careful with it."

"Given to me by the Council of Dukes for my many years of service." The duke looked proud.

"Not a fighting blade, then?"

"It is meant to wear on formal occasions. But the blade is plenty sharp, so be careful you do not cut yourself."

Mary continued to study the saber, a bright and deadly beauty. "Were you wearing this on the day you went to Lord Valentin's?"

"No, as I said, it was ceremonial . . ." Duke Rudolfo trailed off, reddening. "Ah, I see what you mean. No, I did not draw it against the Imperial Prince when he went to Lady Sophie. It was a dreadful day. I am not happy to think of it."

"Valentin doesn't blame you, you know," Mary said. "Nvengarian politics are so very convoluted and bloody. Or at least they used to be. From what I hear, Prince Damien is trying to stop all that."

Rudolfo looked uncomfortable. "Indeed."

"*I* blame you, though."

He jerked his head up in surprise, and then he sighed. "What do you want, Mrs. Cameron?"

"Me? I want nothing. It is Valentin who hurts. You have never spoken of it to him, have you?"

Rudolfo shook his head. "There is nothing to say."

"An apology, if nothing else. Valentin lost everything that day, you know. The sister he loved. His position in your society—though I think he was past caring about that. The Imperial Prince was already a madman, from what I understand, uncontrollable. *He* acted as predicted. You acted to save your own skin."

"And that of my wife and daughter."

"I understand. I might have done the same." Mary paused. "No, I know I would not have. Dougal would never forgive me if he knew I'd let a young woman be hurt in order to protect him. He'd expect me to sail in and try to save her. You are Nvengarian—I'm certain you had some sort of weapon handy, even if not this one." She ran her hand along the saber's polished blade.

Rudolfo's face darkened. "You cannot know, my dear. Since that day I have lived with such shame. It eats at me inside. You are right—I should have killed the Imperial Prince and faced the consequences. But I feared the retaliation of Grand Duke Alexander against my family as much as I did the Imperial Prince. One never knows what Alexander will do."

"Your wife seems to think he would have applauded you."

"Or made an example of me to show the people of Nvengaria that assassination is discouraged. Even if Alexander, too, rejoiced at the death of the Imperial Prince."

"My brother Egan and his wife both speak highly of Grand Duke Alexander, so I cannot believe he would be quite so awful. He wanted to rid your land of the horrible man as much as you did."

"And he did, as rumors say. With poison perhaps."

"And then the crazy old man's son took the throne," Mary said. "I'm certain you weren't pleased about that, either."

"You English have a saying, eh? That the apple does not fall far from the tree."

"I am Scottish, and I think the apple fell very far in this case. I've not met Damien, but my brother is his best friend, and Egan could not love a man if he were anything remotely like the old Imperial Prince. Egan says Damien is a good man. Valentin believes in him, too."

The ambassador looked puzzled. "You are wrong about that, my dear. Valentin tried to assassinate Prince Damien. Sneaked into the palace and attacked him with a knife while Damien and his wife sat down to supper. Even now, Valentin awaits a chance to topple him from the throne."

Duke Rudolfo spoke with certainty. Was he simply pushing his own desires onto Valentin? Or did Rudolfo believe, with his wife, that Valentin was vengeance-mad?

"Do you truly think you were the intended target yesterday?" Mary asked. "Not Sir John, as he believes?"

Duke Rudolfo looked surprised. "Of course it was me. Why would someone want to murder your Sir John? He is harmless."

"Yes, he is, really. Sir John's wife, my girlhood friend, doted on him."

"It could only have been me they wanted to shoot," he said firmly. "I am high in the Council of Dukes, an important man. I imagine all kinds of people wish me dead. Valentin is only one of them."

"I think you should talk to Valentin, Your Grace. Make it right between you."

The ambassador smiled. He was a handsome man when he wasn't trying to be duplicitous. "I will try. However, I will insist that I not meet him alone and that I am allowed to stand well beyond reach of his sword."

"I can arrange that. Thank you for lending me your saber, Your Grace. Now I am to go practice my part with Sir John. Your wife says he needs to die more convincingly."

Duke Rudolfo held out his hand. "Thank you, Mrs. Cameron."

He sounded relieved. Mary nodded as he bowed over

her hand, but she couldn't go without a parting shot. "See that you do it."

Mary left his rooms and returned to her own chamber to re-pin a drape that had fallen from her right shoulder. As she turned from the mirror to snatch up the saber she'd laid on her bed, she glimpsed Sir John walking through the snowy park to the summerhouse at the edge of the garden, near the wood.

"What is he doing?" She was supposed to meet Sir John in the ballroom.

As Mary peered down at him, a woman in white, draped like Mary except for a fold of sheet over her head, emerged from the house and hurried after him. A chance beam of the setting sun caught on the sheathed saber the woman carried, one very similar to the one Mary now held.

Mary straightened in shock. Clutching the sword, she hurried to her door and turned the handle. The door refused to budge. Mary shook it, but it was solidly locked.

She was trapped, while outside, Sir John Lincolnbury trotted happily into the summerhouse, followed, he thought, by Mary as Athena, to practice his death scene.

Chapter Eight

Valentin knew Mary was in danger even before he heard her muffled cries. He discarded the velvet robe that was his magician's costume and fled the ballroom where servants scrambled to render it a makeshift theatre.

He realized as he took the stairs two at a time that no one else had sensed what he had. But the logosh in him screamed at him to find her, protect her. When Valentin reached the upper floor, he heard the unmistakable sounds of Mary pounding on her bedchamber door and shouting for help.

He put his hands on the door, his fingers becoming logosh claws before he could stop them. "Mary," he called.

"Valentin, they've locked me in. Sir John . . ."

Valentin let his hands finish becoming demon. Ugly claws extended from his mottled skin, but his logosh strength was far greater than his human's.

"Stand away," he told Mary. Then he ripped the door from its hinges.

Mary rushed out, swathed like an Athenian goddess, the ambassador's saber in her hand. Valentin reached for her, but Mary jerked away, flinging the folds of her draperies to the floor as she ran.

Valentin caught up to her on the stairs. "What happened? Who did this?"

"She's going to kill him!" Mary dashed the rest of the way down the stairs, racing through the drawing room and out one of the unlocked French doors.

The afternoon had clouded over, and a light snow fell from the darkening sky. Mary ran across the park, bare-armed and bare-headed, wearing only dancing slippers. Valentin ran with her, no longer asking questions. He knew with certainty what was about to happen.

As they approached the summerhouse at the end of the garden, Valentin smelled fear overlaid with rage and triumph. And blood.

He growled. Valentin tossed off his coat, the logosh claws tearing away the rest of his clothes. His vision went dark as the beast in him broke through, changing his shape, bone and muscle.

In moments, Valentin stood on four legs, the world now black and white. His sense of smell revealed in multiple hues and layers what had been hidden to his human eyes. Mary gazed down at him, wide-eyed, but she didn't fear him. She held up the bare blade, her fingers working something from the saber's tip. She was a warrior, preparing to fight, and he loved her.

Valentin broke down the door of the summerhouse. He dodged back as a bullet screamed toward him, then burst all the way inside. Mary came on his heels.

Sir John was slumped on a bench, looking terrified. Duke Rudolfo stood nearby, pistol in hand, acrid smoke hanging in the cold air. His wife, Duchess Mina, held Valentin's ceremonial sword in her hands. She'd draped herself in a costume like Mary's, and she'd pricked Sir John's neck with the point of the saber. The smell of blood lifted Valentin's lips from his long teeth.

Dimly Valentin reasoned that the ambassador had fired his shot, which meant that his pistol was empty. Not a threat. But the duchess was still armed and could run Sir John through at any second. Valentin leapt at her, snarling in animal rage.

The ambassador threw himself between Valentin and

his wife. Valentin fell onto him, Duke Rudolfo's fear filling his nostrils.

This was the coward who'd stepped aside when Sophie had been attacked, a man who'd sacrificed Sophie's virtue and sanity to save his own hide. Valentin hated him. In human form, Valentin could reason that he understood Rudolfo's actions, but the logosh didn't care. This man had let harm come to Valentin's beloved sister, harm that had led to her death.

Valentin wanted to kill. He needed to kill.

Out of the corner of his eye, he saw Duchess Mina raise her saber. The blade came at him, but was met with a clang by Mary's. Mary shouted something. He saw a sword flash through the air, then clatter onto the ground. Then the duchess was on the bench next to Sir John. Mary's dark eyes filled with fury, her sword pointed at Mina's chest.

Under Valentin, the ambassador cried out. Valentin's claws had raked through his clothes to his skin. More blood. *Hot, salty, wet.*

Rudolfo fought, but he was no match for Valentin's strength. *Savage. Kill.*

"Valentin!"

Mary's voice broke through the pounding in Valentin's head. She was afraid, deathly afraid, but she stood straight, her sword unmoving.

"Let him go," Mary said. "Please."

Why? The ambassador was a traitor, a murderer. So was his wife. They should both die.

"Please, Valentin." Mary's voice went soft. "Do not."

The wolf growled in fury, Valentin's need to kill strong. He hadn't forgiven. He wanted blood for blood. It was the way of his people. The cold English did not understand this.

Mary would remind him that she was Scottish. She

knew about blood feuds, and yet she was begging Valentin to have mercy.

Mercy. Had Duke Rudolfo shown mercy to Sophie? No, he'd stepped aside and left her to her fate. Rudolfo was as guilty of her rape as the Imperial Prince was.

Valentin smelled the guilt now in the ambassador's blood. Guilt, shame, sorrow, fear. Did he deserve mercy?

"Valentin," Mary said again.

He heard the tears in her voice. She wanted Valentin to be who she thought he was—a good man, a protector. Mary wanted the man who'd braved a long journey to lead her sister-in-law Zarabeth to safety, the man who'd had compassion enough to forgive Prince Damien for what Damien's father had done.

Mary loved Valentin. She believed in him.

Valentin forced the wolf to leave him. His brain clouded as his limbs stretched and straightened. After what seemed a long time, he found himself panting, on hands and knees, on top of the terrified Rudolfo. Rudolfo's chest was a bloody mess, his face pale with terror.

Valentin climbed painfully to his feet. He was naked, his body covered in sweat and blood, but Mary's eyes shone with relief. Sir John looked on, bewildered; the duchess, furious.

"Get up, Rudolfo," Duchess Mina snapped. "Kill him. You must."

The ambassador shook his head and covered his face with his hands. "No. No more death, my dear. Please."

"Coward! Fool!"

Duchess Mina struggled to her feet, but Mary pushed her back down with the tip of the saber.

"Stay there, if you please," Mary said coldly. "Consider yourself under arrest. Sir John, go back to the house and have someone send for the magistrate. Hurry, please."

Sir John gulped, but under Mary's glare, he got to his feet and rushed out.

"We are diplomats," the duchess hissed. "We do not answer to your magistrate."

"Fine. Then you will be asked to leave the country. You assaulted Sir John and hired people to shoot him. That is highly illegal in England, I must tell you."

"We will fight you."

"No." Rudolfo sat up, his hand to his bandaged shoulder. "We will return to Nvengaria. We must confess and throw ourselves on the mercy of the Grand Duke."

Duchess Mina shrieked in fury. "I will never grovel to Alexander."

"It would be better if you groveled to Prince Damien," Valentin said. "He might actually listen to you."

"I will never speak to that misery of a prince," the duchess said. "The offspring of the horror who destroyed Nvengaria. The Imperial Prince's line must cease. It is the only way Nvengaria will be strong."

"Oh, I see." Mary managed to sound calm. "You consider yourself a patriot. Who will rule your country then, your Council of Dukes? I believe Alexander is the head of that, but you do not much like him, either, do you?"

"Alexander has finished his usefulness. Another Grand Duke must take his place and lead Nvengarian to greatness."

"Let me guess: your husband Rudolfo?"

"A mad idea." Rudolfo sighed. "It is over, Mina. Please see that."

"Fool," the duchess said again, and then she went off into a string of Nvengarian. She called her husband, Valentin, Prince Damien, Alexander, and Mary all manner of things, and Valentin was glad Mary couldn't understand the filth pouring from her mouth.

Valentin's Nvengarian bodyguards burst into the

summerhouse, flanked by curious English footmen, eager for a fight. Valentin gave abrupt orders to the body-guards, who saluted him and moved to take the ambassador and his wife.

Mary finally lowered the sword and stepped away from the duchess. She admonished the man who bound the duchess's hands not to be cruel, then walked past Valentin out into the frigid winter afternoon.

Valentin went after her, but Mary would not stop and wait for him. Still holding the ambassador's saber, she walked with a quick stride to the lighted house, ignoring the servants who boiled down the garden path.

Mary ducked back through the French door from which they'd exited. In the drawing room the Yule log still burned high on the hearth, bathing the chamber in rosy warmth. Mary dropped the saber on a sofa and kept walking.

Julia rushed in from the hall. "Mary, what happened? They will not let me—" She broke off with a squeak when she spotted Valentin standing just inside the French door, still naked.

Mary snapped out of her daze. She clapped a hand over Julia's eyes, turned her around, and gave her a shove back into the hall. "Go tend to your father, Julia. He was hurt. He will need you."

"Yes, Aunt Mary." She rushed away.

"Mary."

Mary turned back, body rigid. "Not yet, Valentin. Please. I need to be alone."

Valentin folded his arms over his bare chest. "Thank you for saving me."

Mary nodded once, her eyes a misery. As she started to turn away, a new voice filled the outer hall, a light baritone with a Scottish lilt.

"Is that you, Mum? Good Lord, what's all the fracas?"

Joy lit Mary's face. She rushed from the room, and Valentin followed in time to see her fling her arms around a young man who'd entered through the front door.

"Dougal," Mary cried. "Oh, my dear, I am so very happy to see you."

Hugging her son was the best thing in the world. Mary kissed Dougal's cheek and hugged him again.

"Everything all right, Mum? I've never seen ye so chuffed to see me before."

Mary pressed his face between her hands. She felt the rough of shaved whiskers—good heavens, when had he become such a man? "Nonsense, darling, I am always glad to see you. Goodness, I think you've grown another inch this term."

"Did ye know that there's a man with no clothes on peering out of th' drawing room? Good lord, is it Baron Valentin?"

Mary couldn't even blush. "It is."

"The pair of ye could be more discreet." Dougal laughed. "What would Uncle Egan say?"

"Valentin and I are going to be married," Mary said.

"Are ye now?" Dougal sounded much like his Uncle Egan as he looked from Mary to Valentin. "Ye could nae wait for the wedding night?"

Mary's face heated. "Do not be so silly. This is not . . ." The feeble words, *what it seems*, stuck in her throat. "Turn your back so the poor man can get upstairs. We shall talk in the library."

Dougal shrugged good-naturedly and turned away. Mary gave Valentin another smile, her heart pounding in both fear and joy, before she hurried after Dougal, and Valentin was lost to sight.

* * *

It was not until late in the night that Mary finally had time to pack her things, alone in her chamber. She would leave on the morrow with Sir John, Julia, and Dougal, making for London.

Duke Rudolfo and his wife had been taken to the magistrate's house for the night, under guard of the Nvengarians and men from the local regiment. They'd begin their journey back to Nvengaria tomorrow. What they'd face, Mary did not want to imagine.

Dougal explained at the hastily prepared supper the stunned cook gave them that he'd come to Hertfordshire straight from Cambridge. He mourned that he'd arrived too late for the fun when Julia and Sir John told him a breathless tale of events. Mary found that she could not speak of it, and Valentin had disappeared, likely to the magistrate's house with the prisoners.

Mary noted distractedly as the other three talked that Julia spoke to Dougal in a friendly, uninhibited way. Julia did not try to preen or be witty; she simply talked to him like she would a friend. Mary found it refreshing, and she could tell that Dougal liked Julia.

Mary breathed a sigh of relief when she finally retreated to her room to pack. She jumped only slightly when Valentin opened the door and walked quietly inside.

"Be thankful that I am used to your abrupt comings and goings," she said. "Or I would have screamed."

"You do not scream," Valentin said in a low voice. "Except on special occasions."

His dark tone made her hands shake. "Is all well?"

She expected him to approach her, but Valentin remained heartbreakingly far away. "Duke Rudolfo has fully surrendered to take his punishment. He seems relieved."

"And the duchess?"

Valentin's smile was wry. "Not so relieved. But she knows she will not win."

"She is a regular Lady Macbeth, isn't she?" Mary moved to the dressing table and folded leather gloves into a box.

"Duchess Mina had many ambitions."

"Funny to think that Sir John was right all along. He *was* the intended target, which is why they enticed him out here in the first place. I recall now what Sir John said when he was introduced to the ambassador at the Hartwell Ball. Remember? He mentioned all the braid that Nvengarians purchased from England and suggested they were for uniforms. I wondered vaguely why Nvengarians did not have their own braid makers, but I had other things on my mind."

"As did I," Valentin said. "Seeing you erased everything else from my thoughts. I paid no attention."

"Well, we should have noticed." Mary shut the lid of the glove box, finding it difficult to breathe for some reason. "The ambassador wanted new uniforms for the army he would raise for the new Nvengaria. But he could not very well order them made in Nvengaria, could he? Sir John did not know why it was important, but they could not risk him inadvertently telling someone who might understand."

No wonder the duchess had been so adamant to get Julia and Sir John out of London and down here, isolated from the rest of the world. They would be far from their friends, and Sir John might "accidentally" fall through the ice or be hit by a stray shot from a winter shooting party. The country was not always a safe place—hadn't the doctor mentioned a boy who'd been gored by an ox?

"They did not seem to mind so much my knowing," Valentin mused. "They thought I was on their side."

Mary shoved the box aside in annoyance. "Duchess Mina filled my head with the nonsense that you still burned for revenge on her husband. So I would believe that you really *did* hire the shooters. If Sir John died, she was ready to push the blame onto you. Bloody woman."

Valentin came to her, his face lined and tired. "She was not wrong. I hated Rudolfo, though I would not admit it. I pretended even to myself that I had forgiven him, but I secretly hoped I would have to kill him." He cupped her cheek with his palm. "You knew that. You stopped me from being a murderer."

Mary's eyes filled. "I couldn't bear the thought of you suffering more because of them. I wanted to keep you free. So you could be with me."

Valentin tipped her head back to make her look into his eyes. She loved his eyes, so deep blue and filled with power, sorrow, and a caring she wanted to reach.

"You told your son we would be married."

"And I meant it." Mary held his gaze, wishing she could project what she felt for him right into his head. "If you'll have me."

"I told you I have nothing to offer you."

"I don't care. I don't want palaces and gold plates and jewels, Valentin. I have a small house in Edinburgh and rooms of my own at Castle Macdonald. You have your estate in Nvengaria. We will always have a home, and that is all I want. A home. And *you*."

Valentin slid his arm around her waist, caught a tear on his thumb. "All I want is you, my Mary. I thought that would not be enough for you."

"'Tis more than enough. 'Tis riches."

"Mary." Valentin put relief into the word. He nuzzled the line of her hair, then moved his warm lips to hers. Mary felt her clothes loosen, his hands on her bare skin. "Enough packing for tonight, I think," he whispered.

"Will you start back to Nvengaria tomorrow? With the ambassador?"

"No." Valentin smiled, his blue eyes warm. "I resigned. The bodyguards were all handpicked by Grand Duke Alexander. They will get the ambassador and his wife back without delay. I have sent a message to Alexander not to expect me with them."

Mary's heart leapt with hope. "Then will you come home with me?"

"To London?"

"No, to Scotland. I have run away long enough. We might miss Christmas Day, but Hogmanay is the bigger celebration anyway."

"I think I would be pleased to see Castle Macdonald again. It holds for me the happiest memories of my life." Valentin's eyes darkened, and he leaned to kiss the curve of her neck. "Except for my memory of this room, two nights ago."

"It is a splendid memory for me, too."

"We will make another memory." Valentin feathered kisses down her throat. "One that will last a lifetime."

"I love you," Mary whispered, her heart in her words.

"I love you, my Highland Mary." Valentin's eyes danced in sudden amusement. "But perhaps I should not allow you to carry my saber."

Mary sent him a wicked look. "You are absurd. A claymore is much more effective."

He laughed, and she twined her hands behind his neck. "May we begin making those memories now?"

"By all means." Valentin swept her into his strong arms and carried her to the bedroom.

"I want to love you all night, Valentin." Mary touched his face as he laid her down, and then his warm weight pressed her into the bed. "And tomorrow, we'll go home."

Epilogue

When they reached Castle Macdonald several days later, Mary insisted that Valentin knock on the door and enter first. Julia and Sir John, a bit breathless from the precarious ride up the hill to the castle perched on top, watched, mystified, as Valentin approached the huge door. Dougal grinned, knowing why Mary had insisted.

The courtyard was strangely deserted, the castle quiet. Valentin pounded on the thick door, but only silence met them when the echoes died away. He tried the door, found it unlocked, and pushed it open.

Cheers and laughter erupted from inside the brightly lit castle. A young Nvengarian woman rushed forward, her arms outstretched, and the tall, massive form of Mary's brother followed her. Egan Macdonald balanced a tiny cloth-wrapped bundle in his great hand.

"Welcome, First Footer!" the young woman cried, hugging Valentin. "Remember, Valentin, you were to have been First Footer last year? And then . . ."

"I got shot," Valentin said. He'd been left to die out in the cold, but Egan had found and rescued him. Then Mary had gone to Valentin's chamber to nurse him, finding him bare in his bed . . .

"I have brought your sister," Valentin said. He drew Mary into the circle of his arm. "And Dougal. And friends."

The band of Highlanders inside cheered again. Egan's cousin Angus roared, "More friends, more whiskey!"

Mary held out her arms for Egan's bundle. Egan relinquished it carefully, and Mary peeled back a blanket to gaze at the next heir to Castle Macdonald. Charlie Olaf Macdonald had been born not long before Mary had departed, and Mary marveled at how much he'd grown in the scant weeks she'd been gone. She remembered wanting to escape the collective joy of the house, a joy she'd not felt part of.

She realized how foolish she'd been. Of course she was part of the happiness, and now she could draw Valentin into it.

Mary handed the baby back to Zarabeth, who hugged Charlie to her as though he were the most precious thing on earth.

"There will be more celebration at Hogmanay," Mary said. "I have asked Valentin to be my husband."

Valentin enfolded Mary from behind. "And I have accepted."

Egan threw back his head and laughed. "That's my sister. Never a demure, soft-spoken creature was she! As laird, let me be the first to say: Welcome to the family. If ye can stand us, that is."

The Macdonald clan behind him yelled at this and pelted Egan with bits of mistletoe. Valentin rested his cheek against Mary's hair, his unshaved whiskers pleasantly rough. "I believe I will be able to stand it," he said. Mary turned and met his lips with hers.

"Och, and there is nae even mistletoe above them," Dougal said in mock disgust.

Egan and Zarabeth led them all into the Great Hall, Valentin with his arm around Mary. Everything was as Mary remembered—the high beams, the huge hearth, the sense of light and happiness. The long tables were laden with food, and fiddlers and drummers waited in the corner. As the family filed back into the hall, the musicians struck up a lively tune.

Dougal seized Julia's hands and danced her into the center of the room. Men and women paired up, and a flame-haired, buxom Macdonald woman even grabbed Sir John to be her partner.

Mary clasped Valentin's hands and spun around and around with him as the fiddlers played faster. Mary was a Highland lass, and this music was in her blood, as was her fighting spirit. She'd not be afraid to leave these shores and travel to far-off Nvengaria, because she knew now that friends awaited her there, too.

It was inevitable that she and Valentin would come back here, always. She was a part of Scotland, as much as he was a part of Nvengaria. And no matter where she and Valentin roamed, it would always be home where they were—together.

Valentin pulled Mary into his arms and held her close as the Highlanders danced around them. Julia was flushed with happiness, and Sir John attempted a mad jig that had everyone hooting with laughter.

"Sophie would have loved this," Valentin said, as he and Mary withdrew into a corner.

"My darling, I am so sorry that I never got to meet her."

Valentin nodded. Sorrow still filled his eyes, but the anguish, the stark grief, had faded. "You would have loved her as I did. But she is with me again, in my heart. When you stopped me from killing the ambassador, she returned to me." Valentin touched his chest. "She is happy for us."

Mary did not know whether he spoke metaphorically

or if Nvengarian magic really did allow him to know what Sophie felt. It did not matter, she realized. Valentin had found his peace.

Mary leaned against his tall strength. "Welcome home, my love." She gestured to the Highlanders spinning to the music. "To all the family you can handle."

"I believe I can handle you best of all," Valentin murmured. He licked the shell of her ear. "I look forward to bed."

"We had better wait, I think, unless you want them all following us upstairs and shouting lewd remarks outside the door."

Valentin looked surprised, but not alarmed. "I am happy to dance with you for now. Tonight, we will begin the rituals of Nvengarian courtship."

"Rituals? What sort of rituals?"

His blue eyes, with their slightly inhuman cast, darkened with promise. "They are numerous, and all very erotic."

Pleasant heat snaked through Mary's body. "I anticipate them with much interest."

"That is my brave Highland girl."

Mary kissed him again, ignoring the whoops from around the room as the kiss turned deep, passionate. Valentin traced Mary's cheek, took her hands, and pulled her back into the dance.

Traditions

Alissa Johnson

For my grandmothers, Patricia Louise Hansen and Violet Jane Johnson.

Chapter One

William Renwick, Earl of Casslebury had a plan.

It was safe to assume that this would have come as a surprise to no one. William Renwick, Earl of Casslebury *always* had a plan. He was, by all accounts, a most organized individual.

Some went so far as to call him a rather charming, but ultimately predictable and even cold individual. William took exception to that. In his estimation, a preference for order over chaos was not the mark of a dispassionate nature but rather that of a man in possession of a modicum (and therefore uncommon amount) of good sense. It was also a fairly reliable sign that the man had spent some portion of his life in uniform.

If forced, William would have described himself as disciplined, responsible, and—again, if forced—perhaps just a touch stubborn.

It was his sense of responsibility that had necessitated his most recently constructed plan. He would marry a young lady of good blood, excellent reputation, pleasant nature, and appealing physical appearance. He was four-and-thirty, and it was time he did his duty to his title by producing an heir. Never mind the fact that he hadn't expected to outlive two cousins and an older brother to inherit the title; it was his now, and he would plan accordingly.

But it was the aforementioned stubborn streak that had him executing his plan by striding down the halls of

Lord Welsing's London town house, peering into rooms and stopping to question any passing staff, while guests danced and laughed in the ballroom. The young lady crucial to his matrimonial campaign had gone missing. Again.

Miss Caroline Meldrin seemed always to go missing. Not in such a way as to invite attention or ridicule, mind you. Rather, she made perfectly reasonable excuses and slipped away from ballrooms and parlors with her friend, Miss Patience Byerly, whenever one attempted conversation, or offered a dance, or looked directly at her for more than five consecutive seconds.

It was damnably irritating.

And he wasn't having any of it tonight. How the devil was he to execute a well-planned courtship of Miss Meldrin if she kept herself hidden away with her friend? Or perhaps Miss Byerly was a paid companion. He didn't think she was a poor relation. Whatever the connection, he was going to find both of them, secure Miss Meldrin for a waltz, and make absolutely clear his intention of courtship. If she didn't care for the idea, she could damn well admit to it. He was quite done with chasing the chit around . . . or would be, after tonight.

After a bit more searching, he found the two women in the library, tucked away in a large window seat while an elderly man snored softly in a chair by the fire.

Miss Meldrin, with her ivory skin, pale blonde hair, and soft blue eyes, looked a very pretty picture with the glow of candlelight casting streaks of gold across her petite form. Her feet were tucked up somewhere under her legs, which in turn were tucked up on the cushions of the window seat. Several wisps of hair had slipped free and curled around a heart-shaped face with a small mouth, high brow, and slender nose lightly dusted with freckles. Seemingly unconcerned with rousing the gentleman in front of the fire, she laughed merrily and pushed a small plate holding a thick slice of cake toward her friend.

"Go on, then. Or I'll not agree."

Miss Byerly scowled. From his position in the darkened hall, William considered Miss Byerly and concluded that she was a rather severe-looking creature, particularly when compared to her friend. She kept her feet on the floor, neatly hidden beneath the blue skirts of her gown, and her hands demurely folded in her lap. Her thick brown hair was pulled into a tight and unadorned knot at the back of her head, revealing an oval face with sharp cheekbones, wide mouth, and thin nose. Her rather plain brown eyes peered out from behind small round spectacles below sharply arched brows.

William thought perhaps it was the hawkish eyebrows that lent her such a disapproving air, as if she were looking down on a man, despite her relatively short stature. One always felt a bit chastised when talking to her.

Which was why Miss Byerly did not feature in his matrimonial plans.

Pity, really, that she wasn't a bit softer. He'd spoken to her once or twice before and she seemed an intelligent sort, with an efficiency of speech and manner he appreciated.

But he wasn't in need of additional efficiency in his house. He was drowning in efficiency. He was in need of a feminine touch. He wanted a gentle woman, with a soft voice and open heart. Someone free with her laugh. Someone who could provide a bit of light in his life. Someone who wouldn't make him feel on his wedding night as if he were bedding the governess.

Confident in his assessment of Miss Byerly, and in his choice of bride-to-be, he straightened his cravat, brushed at his waistcoat, and otherwise readied himself to begin the overdue campaign for Miss Meldrin's affection.

But then, before he could enter the room, Miss Byerly did the most extraordinary thing he had ever had occasion to witness. She picked up the slice of cake with her ungloved hands—which was odd in and of itself—and then, to his supreme astonishment, began to slowly and methodically stuff it into her mouth.

He stood in the shadow of the hallway and watched as she opened wide—tremendously wide—and very carefully wedged the thicker end in first. It caught at the sides of her mouth, leaving behind smudges of chocolate as she pressed the cake in deeper. Next came the center, which required a substantial amount of wiggling of Miss Byerly's jaw, and then finally, with the confidence obviously born of extensive practice, she folded the remainder of the slice in half and neatly mashed it in with the rest.

With her cheeks rounded like a fearful puffer fish, she daintily wiped her fingers on her napkin, and then used the napkin to dab gingerly at the upturned corners of her lips.

It was astonishing. It was appalling. It was, he had to admit, *enormously* impressive. Even his sister, whom William always felt to be in possession of a regrettably large mouth, could not lay claim to such a feat.

Miss Meldrin struggled to speak around fits of laughter. "That . . . must be . . . *must* be the most you have ever managed."

Miss Byerly waggled her finger in disagreement, and then used that finger to spell something in the air.

Miss Meldrin squinted at the invisible word before erupting into more fits of laughter. "Oh, the peas! The bowl of peas! I'd forgotten!"

William couldn't imagine how anyone could possibly forget the day one's friend decided to fit an entire bowl of peas in her mouth. Fascinated by the absurdity of it, he watched as Miss Meldrin once again lost herself to mirth and Miss Byerly chewed with laborious bites.

"There," Miss Byerly pronounced, after her final swallow. "It is done."

Miss Meldrin sighed heavily and wiped tears from her eyes. "Oh, that was brilliant."

"Admiral Nelson's victory at Trafalgar was brilliant," Miss Byerly replied dryly. "This was desperation."

"Effective, though." Miss Meldrin leaned forward to plant a kiss on her friend's cheek before uncurling herself and hopping down from the window seat. "You'll have your dances."

"*Your* dances," Miss Beverly corrected, and stood.

Realizing that his presence would soon be noticed, William cleared his throat and stepped into the room as if he'd only just arrived.

"Miss Meldrin. Miss Byerly." He hid a smile at the guilty start of both women, and moved forward as they curtsied, his gazed transfixed not on his future bride, but on the woman next to her. She of the haughty brows and wide mouth. He stopped in front of them as they straightened, and his eyes caught on a small dab of chocolate Miss Byerly had missed at the corner of her lips. Without warning, he experienced an extraordinary, almost painful urge to lean down and neatly clean away the bit of sweet . . . with the tip of his tongue.

Why he should find food on her lips so irresistible, he couldn't begin to say. His body seemed to react independently of all reason. And he placed the blame of what happened next squarely on that dab of chocolate and his unreasonable reaction. Without thought, without any consideration whatsoever given to his plan, he looked right at the woman and said, "Miss Byerly, would you indulge me in a dance?"

She blinked rapidly for a moment, her eyes rounding

behind her spectacles. "I . . ." She shot a quick glance at Miss Meldrin, who looked as surprised as she, then looked back to him, only to resume her blinking.

Perhaps his earlier assessment of her intelligence had been a trifle premature. "If you'd rather not—"

"No," she cut in quickly. She blinked once more, as if coming to herself. "That is, yes, I would be delighted, of course."

"Excellent. If—"

"Miss Meldrin, there you are."

The group turned toward the door at the sound of a young masculine voice. Mr. Edward Seager stepped into the room, looking impossibly dapper in clothes and hair cut in the latest style. Rumor had it Mr. Seager was soon to accept a living, and William felt a pang of sympathy for his future flock. Dandies did not make for ideal vicars.

Mr. Seager's large brown eyes fell on Miss Meldrin with unabashed adoration. "I've been looking for . . . That is . . ." He tugged at his waistcoat and bowed low. "Would you do me the very great honor of dancing with me?"

Miss Meldrin slid a covert glance at her friend, a small mischievous smile curling her lips. "It would be my pleasure, Mr. Seager."

His face lit with a delighted grin, Mr. Seager held out an arm and led Miss Meldrin from the room. William watched them go and wondered if it was a bad sign that he didn't feel particularly put out by the sight of Miss Meldrin on another man's arm.

Miss Byerly cleared her throat delicately. "Shall we . . . ?" She nodded toward the open door, and fiddled a bit with the waist of her gown.

He found the act of nerves oddly appealing. She'd never before struck him as a woman easily unnerved. "I was thinking perhaps a waltz."

"A waltz," she repeated, and her face took on a blush of pleasure, something else he found appealing. She didn't seem nearly as severe when she was blushing and fiddling with her gown.

As if suddenly becoming aware of the movement, she gripped her fingers tightly at her waist. And then, for several long seconds, the two of them stood in stiff and awkward silence. It occurred to William that he shouldn't have asked for a waltz, but the suggestion had come without thought. It was the dance he'd wanted with Miss Meldrin. There was some time before the orchestra was scheduled to play a waltz, which neatly provided an excuse to draw out his time with the lady. Time he'd imagined filling by engaging Miss Meldrin in conversation on topics he knew, from the discreet questioning of her mother, she found of interest. Miss Meldrin was an avid reader. Spain was her favorite country on the Continent. She was accomplished at both the pianoforte and the flute.

Unfortunately, he hadn't the foggiest idea how to pass the time with Miss Byerly. Her interests were a complete mystery to him. Usually, a circumstance such as this would require him to begin a conversation on a suitably banal topic. Something along the lines of "fine fall weather we're having." In fact, he had a very clear memory of making that exact comment the last time they'd spoken. He'd be damned if he'd have the same discussion tonight.

"This is your first London Season, is it not?" As alternatives went, it left something to be desired, but it was the best he could come up with without planning.

"It is, yes." Her eyes flicked away briefly. "I spent the last year on the Continent with the Meldrins."

Curiosity nagged at him to discover where she'd been in the years preceding. She was six-and-twenty if she was a day. Far too old to be making a coming-out. Why was it that the questions one wasn't supposed to ask were always the questions one most wanted to ask? Like why she'd eaten an entire slice of cake in a single bite.

"Are you enjoying yourself?" he asked instead, fully expecting a polite response hiding her true opinion. Miss Byerly didn't strike him as one to appreciate the social whirl.

She surprised him by smiling brightly, and saying in what appeared to be complete sincerity, "Oh, yes. Very much."

It was his turn to blink. "Really?"

"Yes, really."

"All of it?"

Her expression turned quizzical. "Yes."

"The balls, the dinners, the operas?"

A small laugh escaped her. "Yes."

"Almacks?"

"Oh, well." She faltered a little. "It's the tradition of the thing."

"So it is," he agreed. Growing more fascinated with her by the second, he took her arm and led her to a small settee at the center of the room. "What of the rest? The balls and such? Do you enjoy the stifling crush, the inane talk, the often questionable food and—"

"The crush, yes. The rest is avoidable." She cocked her head at him as he took a seat beside her. "You've a very low opinion of such gatherings. Why ever do you attend?" Her eyes grew round behind her spectacles. "I beg your pardon, that was very rude. I—"

"Seems a reasonable question to me," he replied with a shrug. "And I attend because, as you said, the worst is avoidable. Moreover, if one looks hard enough, and is very lucky, one might find something interesting amid the mindless babble. Something worth the inconvenience."

"*Yes.*" Her smile returned, even brighter, and she shifted excitedly in her seat. "Yes, that is *exactly* what I love about it. It's rather like digging for treasure, isn't it? There's quite a bit of muck to shovel through, but the end result will likely be worth it. And if it's not, there is still enjoyment to be found in the process. The excitement that comes with wondering, with expectations, with possibilities and . . ."

He was having a difficult time concentrating on what she was saying, but not because he considered what she was saying dull. On the contrary, he thought her enthusiasm perfectly charming, for all that it was perfectly unexpected. It was just that he found his attention hopelessly drawn to the excited movement of her lips, and the small, delicious smear of chocolate at the corner. Clearly, if he was to make any sort of reasonable contribution to the conversation, it would need to be removed, immediately.

"Hold still." He drew out his handkerchief and reached for her. "You've a bit of chocolate cake."

She stopped speaking midsentence, and her hand came up to her lips. He caught it, pulled it down gently, and held it as he slowly wiped away the smudge. Far more slowly than was strictly necessary, but he found he wanted to draw out the moment. She had the slightest hint of roses about her, and he wondered if the fresh feminine scent would be stronger if he leaned closer.

Had he really thought her severe and unappealing only a few minutes ago? She didn't look the least bit like either at present. In fact, she made a very pretty sight, sitting there with her lips parted in surprise and her eyes wide with uncertainty. Eyes he suddenly realized weren't a plain brown at all, but an unusually dark green that made him think of deep mountain forests.

Deep mountain forests?

Holy hell, what sort of fanciful babbling was that?

Stunned at the effect her nearness had on him, he withdrew the handkerchief, sat back, and decided to weigh the scales once again in his favor.

"Shall we check your fingers as well?" he asked with a small smile.

"My fingers . . ." Realization dawned on her face, and with it came a bright stain of red on her cheeks. "You *saw*."

"I did, indeed."

"I . . ." She swallowed hard. "I'm certain it must have seemed most odd."

"It did, indeed."

"I . . ." He actually heard her swallow. "Oh, dear."

Chapter Two

To Patience's mind, embarrassment was available in a variety of forms. She'd experienced quite a few of them in her six-and-twenty years. There was the mild discomfort of wearing dated gowns in a room full of stylish ladies. There was the moderate embarrassment of never having learned the art of small talk and therefore never knowing quite what to say, and the more substantial humiliation of having a father who knew less and said more. There was the painful wounding of pride that came from living off the largesse of family friends, and the outright shame of lying about her circumstances.

Where, she wondered, did the mortification of having been caught stuffing an entire slice of cake into her mouth, by the man one had a desperate *tendre* for, fit in?

"Miss Byerly, are you all right?"

Somewhere after her father and before the lying, she decided.

"Miss Byerly?"

"Yes. Yes, I . . ." She swallowed hard and forced herself to meet his eyes. His beautiful dark eyes she'd previously thought of as kind, but which now danced with wicked merriment. "Are you going to tell?"

"About the cake?" He replaced his handkerchief in his pocket. "I rather doubt anyone would believe me."

Of course they would believe him. He was an earl. He could announce to one and all that he had witnessed her trying to eat the drapery, and they'd believe him. Or believe there was enough truth to make life very difficult for her.

"I had reason," she told him.

"I should dearly love to hear it." He glanced down to where her fingers were once again worrying at the material of her gown. "Settle your feathers, Miss Byerly. I'll not betray your secret."

"Oh, *thank you*—"

"But I want something in return." He smiled a little at her wary look. "I want to know how one becomes aware of having such a talent."

She let herself rest against the back cushions of the settee, and blew out a quick breath of both relief and resignation. He wasn't going to shame her, but neither was he going to let the matter drop. "I suppose one is born with an innate awareness of it."

"We're born with an innate awareness of a great many abilities," he pointed out. "Generally, a proper education dissuades us from taking advantage of the most ill-advised."

She gave him what she hoped was a haughty sort of look. "Like eavesdropping on two unsuspecting young women?"

"Nothing ill-advised about eavesdropping. It's a remarkably useful tool. It's getting caught in the act that I'd advise against."

She rather thought the same could be said for her talent. "But you would advise admitting to it?"

"In this case, yes." His eyes darted to her mouth. "It's provided me with the most interesting conversation I've had in some time."

She resisted the sudden urge to lick her lips. "Perhaps you should be more particular with whom you converse."

"Difficult, when those with whom I most wish to

speak are so often nowhere to be found. Miss Meldrin and yourself are deuced elusive creatures."

Patience tried and failed not to feel disappointed at the pointed mention of her friend. It was no secret the Earl of Casslebury was considering taking a wife. Nor was it a secret that men of wealth and position did not make plain women of neither family nor fortune into countesses. They chose pretty young ladies of consequence. Young ladies such as Caroline Meldrin.

No doubt the earl sought information about her friend, or perhaps he hoped to inspire jealousy. Either way, his interest lay elsewhere.

She should have known, should have realized his intentions from the very start. But he'd been standing before her, looking so terribly handsome in his dark evening wear. Handsome, strong, and so wonderfully dependable. How a man could *look* dependable, she couldn't quite say. She might have said it was his self-assured aristocratic bearing, but his features weren't refined quite enough for that. His jaw was too broad, his cheekbones too sharp, and his eyes and hair too dark. Perhaps it was the military carriage of his tall, muscled frame, or his deep commanding voice, or . . . Well, she had no idea; he simply exuded a sense of dependability she found most attractive. Her heart always leapt at the sight of him. When he'd asked her to dance, it had nearly burst from her chest.

Likely it was best that it was now settled uncomfortably at her feet. It wouldn't do to build hopes around such an unlikely prospect. She pushed away her disenchantment and tried to recall what excuse Caroline had given for their latest disappearance.

"Caroline's hem required mending," she said, *relatively* certain that had been the one.

The corner of his mouth hooked up. "Miss Meldrin's

gowns require a great deal of mending, it seems to me. One would think she'd have switched modistes by now."

"Yes . . . well . . ." She fixed her eyes on the wall behind him. "She's quite loyal."

"You must be as well." He caught and held her gaze. "To lie for her."

She narrowed her eyes a fraction. "Are you teasing me, Lord Casslebury?"

"I am, yes."

"I see." She gave that some consideration. "Are you in the habit of teasing ladies you barely know?"

"No." He looked mildly baffled. "I believe you may be the first woman other than my sister I have ever teased."

"Oh, well." She felt a flutter in her chest and wondered how on earth one responded to such an admission. "I . . . Thank you?"

He opened his mouth, closed it, then burst into laughter.

Apparently, that was not how one was supposed to respond to such an admission.

"You surprise me, Miss Byerly," he finally managed to say.

"I imagine I do," she muttered. She wondered how great a surprise she would have been to him a year ago, before she'd had the opportunity to acquire at least a handful of social graces.

"You give a very different impression from the person you seem to truly be," he said.

"There are a great many in the *ton* who do the same," she pointed out.

"Yes, but not quite so much by accident, I think."

Not every false impression she gave was an accident, but she wasn't about to admit to that after less than an hour of the man's acquaintance, even if it was preceded by a much longer fascination on her part. "You make me sound like an ingénue."

"I don't know if I'd call you that, specifically, but there is—"

He broke off when the elderly man in front of the fire suddenly launched to his feet, his substantial weight sending the heavy chair scratching against the floor. "*Aha!* I have it! I have it! *Around* the magnet!" The man bounded toward them, clothes askew, white hair standing on end, blue eyes wide and wild. "It goes around the magnet!" He came to a stop in front of Patience, jabbed a finger toward the ceiling, and spun the index finger of his other hand around the first. "Do you see? *Around!* Ha!"

Patience felt the stirrings of panic. "Yes, I see," she said soothingly, rising slowly from her seat. "Why don't we sit down and you can tell—"

"Around!" He jabbed his finger up again and bolted from the room.

"Oh, dear." *Oh, damn it all to hell.* "I . . ." She gave Lord Casslebury an apologetic smile and edged quickly toward the door. "I have to go."

Apparently under the impression that she was no longer comfortable standing in the library with him now that their chaperone—if the sleeping gentleman could be considered such—had left them, he smiled and followed.

"Of course. Perhaps I can convince the musicians to play that waltz a bit early and . . ."

His voice trailed off as the elderly man, now halfway down the hall, stopped in his tracks to inform a stout, middle-aged maid exiting from a nearby room that "it goes around!" And then, to illustrate his point, grabbed the poor woman about the waist and danced her in a circle.

The maid yelped in surprise. "Good heavens!"

"Oh, no." Patience moved forward, but the man had completed the revolution, deposited the woman on her feet, and bolted down the hall before she'd managed to take more than a few steps. Unwilling to draw more attention to the matter than absolutely necessary, she checked her pace into a brisk walk. When they reached the maid, she was patting her chest and gaping at her sudden and uninvited dance partner as he disappeared around a corner.

"Are you all right?" Lord Casslebury inquired.

"Oh . . . aye." The maid gave a breathless laugh. "Aye. Didn't do me any harm, that one. Don't think he meant to."

"I'm sure he didn't," Patience agreed quickly, and just as quickly resumed her brisk walk down the hall.

"You're in a great hurry," Casslebury commented, as he stepped up to walk beside her. "Are you eager to see what he might do next?"

It was her fondest wish to remain utterly in the dark on the matter of the old man's behavior, but she hadn't that luxury. "Naturally, I'm curious," she responded in what she very much hoped was an offhand manner.

They reached the ballroom just in time to witness the elderly man pushing his way through the tremendous crush. In his rush, he knocked over a footman carrying a tray of champagne flutes, but he seemed not to hear the shattering of glass on the ballroom floor, or the angry shouts of guests at the unexpected shower of wine. He simply continued his advance into the room.

"Oh, no." Giving up all hope of appearing merely curious, Patience dashed forward and began to push her way through the throng of people.

The man stopped suddenly at a small group of matrons, grinned broadly at a dour-looking woman in a bronze turban, grasped her face with both hands, and planted a loud and rather lewd kiss on her lips. He was gone again before the lady could so much as raise a hand to slap at him.

Next to her, Lord Casslebury appeared caught somewhere between amusement and disbelief. "Who the devil *is* that?"

"I . . ." She elbowed her way farther into the room. "I beg your pardon. I believe Mrs. Meldrin is motioning for me for me. I—"

"I don't see her."

She made a very broad, very vague wave in the direction of the front hall. "Over there. I have to go."

"Who is he—?"

Another yelp sounded from somewhere in the room, along with another shattering of glass.

"I'm sorry. I'm terribly sorry. I have to go." Her heart in her throat, she turned away and left him.

She hadn't the faintest idea where Mrs. Meldrin might be, but she found Caroline at the edge of the ballroom, looking rather pale.

"Caroline, did you see—?"

"Yes." Her friend took her hand, gave it a reassuring squeeze, and led her into the front hall. "He's gone upstairs."

"Oh, dear."

"I'm certain he'll be fine. And guests aren't paying him much mind."

"They paid plenty on the other side of the room. He knocked over footmen, broke heaven only knows what, and kissed Mrs. Lindsey on the mouth."

"Oh. Well." Caroline winced sympathetically. "Father's asked for the carriage to be brought 'round immediately. As soon as we find—"

The elderly gentleman suddenly appeared at the top

of the steps. Still grinning, he bounded down with the exuberance of a man half his age. "Bloody enormous place!" he exclaimed cheerfully. "How do I get out?"

The moment he reached them, Patience placed a gentle hand on his arm. "Mr. Meldrin is having the carriage brought to the front. If you would sit for a minute, we'll have you out and—"

"No. No. Don't trouble yourselves." The man shook his head, and danced away from Patience's grasp. "I'd something to do. Something . . . Ah!" He jabbed his finger up as he had in the library. "It goes around! It does! I need my workshop!"

"You'll have it. If you'll just . . ."

But he wasn't listening to her. With a final whoop of excitement, he spun on his heel and dashed out the front door.

They found him twenty minutes later—trotting briskly down the street, grinning broadly and babbling cheerfully about going around the magnet. It took very little effort to convince him to get into the carriage, and it was a simple enough task to bring him home, press a bit of laudanum into him, and tuck him into bed. He was, at least, a congenial sort of madman.

No small blessing, Patience told herself as she took a seat next to his bedside. He liked having someone sit by him at times like this, just as he liked to fiddle with his compass as the medicine settled his overwrought system, pulling him toward sleep.

He tapped at the front of the compass. "Goes 'round, you see. It all goes 'round."

"Mm-hm."

"Explains everything."

He had insisted for years that it explained everything,

but there was little point in reminding him. He'd only forget again, and it gave him such pleasure each time he remembered.

Accustomed to the ritual, Patience pried off her slippers with her toes and settled back in her chair. "I did something very bad tonight," she told him, knowing full well the confession would accomplish nothing. The man before her didn't know her from Eve at present, which meant he'd forget the entire conversation by tomorrow. But the talking seemed to soothe him, as well as her nagging conscience.

"Did you now?" he asked absently.

"I pretended not to know a member of my family."

"Ah, now, that's no good. Important things, families. Important things. I've one of my own."

"I know."

"A daughter." He turned the compass, frowned at it. "Nice girl. Used to bring me tea."

"Would you like some—"

"Always put too much cream in it, though."

That startled a laugh out of her. "Did she? Why didn't you say so?"

"Tea is tea, and you know these young girls. They'll fly off at the slightest provocation." He yawned hugely. "Tell them their gowns are lovely, and they'll think you're insulting their hats."

She took the compass from hands that had grown lax. "I rather doubt she's as sensitive as all that."

"Never know with girls." His eyelids drooped. "Boys are easier. Should have had one of those."

"Boys aren't likely to bring you tea. Overly creamed, or otherwise."

"All the same. Boys are easier."

"I rather wonder if mothers aren't, as well," she said

quietly, and watched as his eyes closed and his breathing evened out in sleep. She stood and bent down to place a gentle kiss on the wrinkled brow of Sir Franklin Byerly. "I'm sorry, Papa."

Patience left her father to sleep and made her way downstairs, where the voices of Mr. and Mrs. Meldrin drifted from the library. It was a nightly ritual for them. Mrs. Meldrin would have her glass of warm milk, Mr. Meldrin his brandy, and the two of them would sit before the fire and share a few quiet moments alone, discussing the events of the day. Patience sometimes left her door open at night, just to hear the murmurs of their conversation. She couldn't make out the words, but her purpose was not to eavesdrop, it was merely to hear the sound. It was soothing, peaceful, and a welcome contrast to the bone-jarring bangs and crashes to which she'd fallen asleep in the years before coming to stay with the Meldrins.

As a child, she hadn't minded the ruckus from her father's workshop so very much. Their house had been old and drafty, and by the time she was twelve, empty of staff. The disruption her father produced gave the house a bit of life, and in a way, kept loneliness at bay.

But by fifteen, financial difficulties had forced them to sell their home and let rooms in London. She grew to dread the sound of her father working. It was inevitably followed by the angry pounding of fists on the thin walls, and the threatening shouts of neighbors. And *that* was eventually followed by the landlord arriving to pound on the door to issue a notice of eviction.

She would find new rooms for them. Her father would promise to take better care. And he might, for a little while. But sooner or later, he would forget. Even when he'd been sane, he'd been forgetful. He'd forget to pay the rent, forget to pay the butcher. Forget not to spend what little income they had on some new scientific instrument, thereby making it impossible to pay the rent and the butcher.

Her stomach twisted in knots at the memory. Then tightened further when she reached the library only to find the doors closed. The last time the Meldrins had closed the doors during their nightly conversations, one of the footmen had been caught stealing coins from Caroline's reticule.

She knocked with hands that wanted to shake, and grimaced when the voices from inside abruptly ceased.

"Come in," came Mr. Meldrin's reply. He turned to frown at her as she pushed through the doors. "Patience, why aren't you in bed?"

"I couldn't sleep." She crossed the room to stand before them, and folded her hands in an effort to keep them from pulling at her skirts. "I want to apologize for what happened, and—"

"Nonsense," Mrs. Meldrin cut in. "Tonight's trouble was not your fault."

But still her responsibility, Patience thought. "I shouldn't have suggested we bring him along. It's only . . . he has so enjoyed going out of late, and I never thought . . . He seemed well just this afternoon. He knew who I was and where—"

"Not your fault," Mr. Meldrin repeated. "We all thought him well enough to attend."

"Still, if I had—"

"Enough," Mr. Meldrin cut in sternly. "You'll not take responsibility for this, Patience. Am I understood?"

She wanted to argue, but knew the effort would be wasted. It wasn't often that Mr. Meldrin put his foot down, but when he did, he became intractable.

She nodded miserably. "Yes."

"Good." He pointed at the door and gentled his tone.

"Now to bed with you. Things won't appear quite so dire after a good night's sleep."

Patience rather doubted that a few hours in bed would cast a more favorable light on her circumstances, but she nodded again and left. She closed the library door softly behind her, and then, after a brief internal battle between manners and dread of the unknown, she leaned her ear against the door and listened.

"Something must be done, Charles," Mrs. Meldrin said. "This cannot go on."

"What would you have me do? Throw them out?"

"Certainly not," came Mrs. Meldrin's indignant reply, "but neither can we have his presence hinder, or even ruin, the girls' prospects—"

"I don't think it will come to that," Mr. Meldrin chided. "We need only do better at keeping him isolated, away from gossip-mongers and the like."

"How? And for how long? Shall we lock the man up every time we've a visitor come to call? Make excuses for every shout and bang that comes from his room?"

"No, I suppose not." There was a long pause in which Patience imagined Mr. Meldrin sighing heavily. "We'll take him to the country with us after Christmas."

And leave him there, Patience finished in her mind. And that meant she would be left there as well. Not at the Meldrins' insistence—they would never be so unkind—but she would remain all the same. She couldn't abandon her father to the care of staff who neither understood nor cared for him.

Exhausted in body and mind, she stepped away from the door and turned toward her room. It mattered little what was said now. The decision was made. To be fair, it was a generous solution, and one the Meldrins were in no way obligated to provide. Mr. Meldrin's debt to an old friendship with her father had long ago been paid. He'd taken in both the man and the daughter over a year ago, bringing them along for a tour about Europe, feeding them, clothing them, treating them as family, and now financing a London Season for her.

Patience had hoped the drastic change in their circumstances would improve her father's health. He never seemed to care overmuch that the roof in whatever rooms they'd been letting was falling down around them, but she had thought that surely regular meals, adequate heating in the winter, and the cessation of the debt collectors hounding them would provide an environment more conducive to healing.

And it had, for a time. He'd gone days, weeks, even a month or two without once forgetting who she was or where they were. He'd been happier and more lucid than she'd seen him in a great while.

Tonight had been a terrible setback, and a heartbreaking sign that no matter how many good days her father might have, there was nothing to be done to make him truly well again.

She stopped at the top of the stairs to scrub her hands tiredly over her face. If there was nothing to be done, then there was nothing to be gained by sorrow and worry. She would set aside the anxiety and disappointment, and make the best of what she had. There was still most of the Little Season left—weeks yet of balls and dinners and operas. It was far more than many young women ever received. She would remember that, find pleasure in the days while they lasted, and be grateful for the memories when they were over.

At the end of those weeks, she would make her own excuses to take her father into the country. There was no reason to stay through the holidays and put the Meldrins in the uncomfortable position of having to inform her that her father could not stay in London. Better if she made the pretense of coming to the decision on her own.

Feeling quite resolute, if not at all better, she gave one determined nod to herself, turned her steps toward her room, and wondered if the memories she took with her would include more of Lord Casslebury. Oh, she *dearly* hoped so, even if he *was* only flattering her to gain Caroline's favor. With only a Little Season at her disposal, she would take whatever she could get. And common sense told her that when it came to the likes of Lord Casslebury, a few happy memories would be the only thing available to her, regardless of how much time she had in London.

As unlikely as it was that a peer of the realm should court a woman of little consequence, it was even less conceivable he would make a serious offer for her if he knew her only living relative was mad. Insanity was not the sort of thing the aristocracy liked to see passed down.

Knowing that despite her exhaustion she'd not be able to sleep with so much weighing on her mind, she passed her own door and knocked on Caroline's. She found her friend in bed but still awake and, not surprisingly, reading. Patience imagined it was the same book she and Mrs. Meldrin had pried from her hands earlier in the day so they might ready her for the ball.

"How is your father?" Caroline asked, as Patience moved to stand at the foot of the bed.

"Asleep and blissfully unaware of the trouble he caused tonight." She found herself plucking at the waist of her gown. "Your parents wouldn't allow me to apologize."

"Of course not. It wasn't your doing." A sparkle of mischief entered her blue eyes. "You're not going to try to apologize to me, are you? Because you know very well I was absolutely delighted with the excuse to leave."

Giving up any hope of having her apology accepted by any member of the Meldrin family, Patience rolled her eyes and walked around the edge of the bed to take a seat on the mattress. "Shall I take that to mean you didn't enjoy your dance with Mr. Seager?"

Caroline returned her attention to her book. "You may."

"Did you at least try?"

"Naturally, I did. That was the bargain we made. I danced, I smiled, I searched high and low for any quality in the man that set him apart from the dozens of other dandies in the room."

"And you found nothing at all?"

"I did, actually." Caroline turned the page of her book. "He smells of cheese."

"I see. Always, or just tonight?"

"I'm sure I don't want to know."

"He's a very nice man," Patience tried.

"He does seem to be."

"And quite handsome," she pointed out.

"In a rather practiced sort of way."

"He's terribly besotted with you."

Caroline paused in her reading to sigh heavily. "It's absurd. We've shared one dance, and no more than a handful of words about the weather, and yet he fancies himself in love. How am I to respect a man capable of such foolishness?"

"Some might consider it romantic," Patience pointed out. "Love at first sight, and all that."

"I suppose it might be romantic," Caroline conceded, and licked her finger to turn the page of her book. "If he didn't smell so much of cheese."

Patience couldn't help laughing. "Your glass is always half empty."

"On the contrary, I find it quite full; else I'd look for more."

"But wouldn't you like to have it overflowing?" *She* certainly would.

Caroline looked up with raised brows. "What good is spilt wine?"

Patience tossed up her hands and rose from the bed. "I give up."

"Probably for the best," Caroline agreed. "Good night, Patience."

"Good night." Patience gave her friend a kiss on the cheek before turning toward the connecting door to her own room.

"Patience?" Caroline waited for Patience to turn around. "I'm very glad you came to live with us."

It was, Patience realized, the closest she would receive to an acceptance of her apology. It surprised her a little to realize how much she had needed it. Her chest tightened, a lump formed in her throat, and tears pressed at the backs of her eyes.

"Thank you," she whispered. "I'm glad as well."

Chapter Three

William stood outside the Meldrin town house with a bouquet of flowers in his hand and wondered what he was doing.

Well, no, that wasn't entirely true—he knew exactly what he was doing. He was about to begin a courtship of Miss Patience Byerly. *Why* he was doing it, however, was still a matter of some confusion.

It hadn't been his plan to woo Miss Byerly. And it wasn't in his nature to change his plans with so little forethought. It wasn't in his nature to change his plans at all.

But he hadn't been able to stop thinking of her. She was such a fascinatingly incongruent woman. Scolding him for eavesdropping one moment, and lying for her friend the moment after. Impossibly stiff and staid at first glance, then eating cake with her fingers in the next. Blushing with pleasure at the invitation to waltz, then disappearing from the hall before they got around to the actual dancing.

Perhaps it was the novelty of having been so utterly wrong about her that had him changing his plans. Or perhaps it was knowing that most of the *ton* continued to have a mistaken impression of her. It was as if he'd discovered a secret. He'd wager there were few others who knew her eyes were a lovely dark green, or that she was fond of the social whirl, or that she was quick to smile and laugh.

And it *had* been his plan to woo and marry a young lady who could make him smile and laugh. Someone who might loosen the tight knot of structure he'd tied about his life. Though he'd not thought her capable of it only the day before, Miss Byerly now appeared quite up to the task . . . Probably, he amended after a little more thought. He couldn't claim to know her well, could he? Which was why he was going to begin a courtship, he reminded himself.

"Holy hell, man. Just do the damn thing."

Unaccountably nervous, he transferred the flowers to his other hand, straightened his shoulders, and knocked on the door. With an efficiency he couldn't help admiring, he was seen in, divested of his coat and gloves, informed that the Meldrins were currently unavailable, but Miss Byerly was home and receiving visitors, and then ushered into the front parlor.

Patience sat alone, looking wistfully out the front window and, at first glance, appearing very much as she had the previous night. Her feet were neatly tucked under her skirts and her hands were once again demurely folded in her lap.

Only she *didn't* look the same. For some reason, she looked vastly different to him today. Perhaps it was because he'd never before seen her in a cheerful yellow day gown, or perhaps it was the way the late-morning sunlight brought out streaks of copper in her dark hair, or perhaps it was simply that he'd not taken the time before to truly look at her. Given a little *more* time, he might have been able to put his finger on what had altered, but he had only a few seconds to watch her unawares before the footman announced his presence and the moment was lost.

Patience rose and curtsied, her face lighting with pleasure a heartbeat before her gaze fell on the bouquet. "I . . . Mr. Seager has taken Caroline out for a drive."

He glanced at the window. "It's a fine day for it. I was thinking perhaps a stroll."

"Yes, well." Her eyes darted away and her hands began

to pluck at her skirts. "I'm sure she'd be delighted to accompany you, if you care to—"

"I'd rather you did," he cut in, and held out the bouquet.

"Oh." Her hands stilled. In fact, except for the widening of her eyes, she went perfectly still for several long seconds. "They're for me," she finally said, sounding rather dumbfounded.

Clearly, he *was* the only gentleman to have discovered the secret Miss Byerly. He found himself both pleased and irritated by the idea. He rather liked the notion of being the only man to recognize her charm. He cared less for the idea that she'd never before received flowers. A woman like Patience shouldn't want for flowers.

Apparently, she was content to want a little longer. She hadn't yet reached for them. "Are you going to make me hold my arm out much longer?" he asked conversationally. "Because eventually I'll have to assume you don't care for—"

"I'm sorry," she cut in, laughing suddenly. "I'm making a terrible fool of myself." She took the bouquet and buried her nose in the blooms. "Oh, they're lovely," she sighed. "They're exquisite. Thank you."

William decided a man couldn't hope for a more gratifying reaction. She made him feel positively heroic, which went a very long way in settling the nerves he'd battled outside the house. "You're quite welcome. Does this mean you'll join me for a stroll in Hyde Park?"

"Hyde Park?" She looked up from the flowers to beam at him. "That sounds wonderful. I'll just fetch my coat and gloves."

William watched her nearly skip from the room and decided it was very much a mark in her favor that she was so readily pleased. What man wouldn't care to have his gifts and ideas met with such enthusiasm?

Nor could he find complaint with the fact that she returned not five minutes later with coat, bonnet, and gloves in place. He did appreciate an attention to promptness.

With a maid trailing discreetly behind, they stepped outside just in time to meet Mrs. Meldrin climbing the front steps.

"Lord Casslebury," she called out in a conspicuously cheerful tone, "what an unexpected surprise. Have you come to take our Patience out?"

"She's agreed to accompany me on a stroll to Hyde Park this morning," he affirmed, and wondered if Mrs. Meldrin was the sort of woman to become miffed at the notion an earl had come to call on someone other than her daughter. But Mrs. Meldrin merely straightened her bonnet, glanced over Patience's shoulder to note the maid, and smiled broadly at William.

"A marvelous idea. There's sure to be a crowd, with everyone taking advantage of this fine weather." Somehow, she managed to smile even more brightly. "Perhaps I can persuade Mr. Meldrin to escort me there as well. Wouldn't that be lovely? Oh, I must see if he can be convinced." With yet another cheery smile, she swept past them and into the house.

William watched as the front door closed behind her. "She looks to be in very fine mood."

"Oh, she's in raptures," Patience confirmed with a small laugh. "She received an invitation this morning for Lord Hartwell's Christmas ball."

"Ah." He turned about and started them on a slow walk in the direction of the park. "It is a popular event."

"Do you attend?"

"Not if I can help it," he admitted. "And I find I generally can."

She looked at him, a small line forming on her brow. "Do you not get on with the marquess?"

"Everyone gets on with the marquess. He's a thoroughly likable gentleman. But I leave London in mid-December." He shrugged. "I don't particularly care for Christmas."

She gave him a skeptical look. "Everyone likes Christmas."

"Most claim to, certainly."

"But you don't? Truly?"

He shook his head as he led her around a puddle on the sidewalk. "It's a deuced inconvenient time of year. Traveling about in the dead of winter. Dragging in boughs of greenery only to have them dry and fall to pieces in your home. Dodging children with sticky fingers and wet heads. Eating—"

"Why should their heads be wet?"

"The children? From playing Bob-Apple, of course."

"Oh." She thought about that. "Does it really require a complete dunking?"

"It does if one has an older sister who takes it upon herself to assist . . . Did you never play as a child?"

"No. I've only ever caught a glimpse of the game. I should like—"

"Why only a glimpse?"

It was her turn to shrug. "My mother passed when I was very young, and my father did not care for celebrations."

"I see." He felt a scowl forming and made a conscious effort to remove it. It was disturbing to think that her father had kept her childhood devoid of parties and games, but he didn't know her well enough yet to make open judgments on a member of her family. Perhaps she approved of the way she'd been reared. He sincerely hoped not. He didn't relish the idea of changing his matrimonial plans yet again.

"A stern man, your father?" he inquired, in what he hoped was a casual tone.

"Stern?" She laughed suddenly. "Oh, no. Nothing of the sort. He simply took no interest in holidays. He wanted . . . His passion has always been his work."

He was still living, then, William mused. He wanted to ask her more, but because her laughter had died when she mentioned her father's work, he let the topic progress in another direction. "You've no Christmas traditions, then? No Yule log, no wassail, no silly games?"

"Not as of yet," she replied, before giving a decisive nod of her head. "But I shall. There are plenty to choose from. Last year in Belgium, Caroline and I met a lovely family who brings an entire tree into their house and covers it with candles. And we met a gentleman from Sweden who said in his village a young woman puts a wreath of candles upon her head and goes about with a procession—"

"Are there any traditions you'd care to try that aren't likely to set home and person aflame?"

"Certainly. I *should* like to try Bob-Apple. And the thirteen desserts I heard about in France. They represent Jesus and the twelve apostles." She pursed her lips thoughtfully. "I'm not sure if that includes Judas. I don't think I care for the idea of eating Judas almonds, really." She considered that a moment longer before turning to study him. "Aren't there any traditions you enjoy?"

He paused before answering. "I'm afraid there is one unavoidable tradition that quite ruins all the others for me . . . the forced proximity and socialization of people who are much happier with a bit of distance between them."

"Your family?" she asked softly.

He nodded, surprised at what he was revealing, but feeling compelled to share a piece of his family history because she had shared a piece of hers. "My parents did not get on well together. My sister did not get on with my brother, and my brother couldn't get on with anyone. Christmas was a . . . disruptive time of year."

"I'm sorry."

He rolled his shoulders in an effort to release the tension at the back of his neck. "Not an uncommon story. These days, I prefer to spend the weeks before and after Christmas surrounded by peace and quiet at my estate in Staffordshire."

"Alone?" she asked.

"If I can manage it."

"Oh. What of your sister?"

He smiled a little. "It is her holiday tradition to insist I visit her brood in Surrey."

"And is she never successful?"

He had to lift his voice a little over the noise of a passing carriage. "As I said, I prefer to spend the holidays in peace."

"Is it not adequately peaceful in Surrey?"

"My sister has children."

"I see." There was a long pause before she spoke again. "I'm quite fond of children."

"As am I, when they're present in reasonable numbers." He waved politely at an acquaintance passing on the other side of the street. "She has twelve."

"*Twelve?*"

"All boys, including two sets of twins from her husband's first wife. And all but two under the age of eighteen."

"Good heavens."

"I believe heaven washed its hands of them some time ago. In fact, I'm fairly certain the three-year-old has a pact with the devil. He tried to eat one of my cravat pins during my last visit. Scampered right into my room, snatched it off my desk in plain sight of me, and popped it in his mouth."

Patience grimaced. "It's fortunate he didn't become ill."

"I pried it out of his mouth before he could swallow."

"Oh, that was—"

"But not before he bit me."

"Oh." Caroline managed to wince and smile at the same time. "I knew a little girl like that once. Her family had rooms above ours. She—" She broke off, looking a bit startled. He imagined she hadn't meant to reveal her family had taken rooms somewhere. "She was a terror," she finished uneasily.

Her fingers lifted to rub at a bit of lace along her neckline for a moment before she gripped her hands tightly at her waist, confirming the suspicion he'd developed the night before. Patience Byerly was not stiff by nature; she merely gave that impression when hiding nerves.

He didn't care for the idea of her being nervous now. What difference did it make that her family was not of great means? As the second son of a second son, he hadn't been a man of great means until his unexpected inheritance of the earldom.

He wanted to tell her he understood, that he didn't care a jot what her circumstances had been, or what they were at present. As a wealthy earl with modest tastes, expenses, and social ambitions, he could well afford to take an undowered bride. Unfortunately, he rather doubted, "I wouldn't mind marrying a poor woman," would serve to make her smile again. And he very much wanted to see her smile again.

"I wager my nephew a worse case than your neighbor," he offered.

"Unlikely," she replied. "It was said even the dogs outside the butcher's door wouldn't go near her."

"Did she ever draw blood?"

"On occasion."

"But did she leave scars?"

She frowned thoughtfully, which he decided was an improvement over frowning with discomfort. "Not that I'm aware of," she replied. "She was a very little girl."

"No excuse." He stopped walking to pull off the glove of his right hand, and held it up to reveal four small white crescents, two on each side of his index finger. "Courtesy of William Grant Higgs, my cannibalistic little namesake."

To his great delight, her mouth fell open, then curved up as she reached out to take his hand and pull it toward her for a closer look. "Good heavens. They're the perfect impressions of little teeth, aren't they?"

Her fingers felt small and warm as they slid down to hold his palm. He had an image of what it would be like to have those small, warm fingers working to untie his cravat, sliding across his chest, his back, down his . . . He cleared his throat and shoved the image aside. They were on a public street, for pity's sake. "Ah, yes, unfortunately. There's no lying about how I got them."

She straightened again, her rediscovered smile firmly in place. It wavered a little when she glanced down to see their hands still joined. He felt a spark of awareness pass between them before she blushed and dropped his hand. "Why . . . why should you want to lie about them?"

If they *hadn't* been on a public street, and if he'd been the sort of man who acted on a whim, he might have recaptured her hand and pulled her in for a kiss. She was nearly irresistible with the hint of rose at her cheeks.

He smiled at her instead. "It's a bit embarrassing, if you must know. Ten years as a soldier, several of them fighting a very bloody war, and I managed to emerge without a lasting physical mark on me." He scowled at his finger. "Five minutes alone with a toddler and I'm scarred for life."

A small laugh escaped her. "Yes, they're quite disfiguring."

"They're a bit new yet," he reminded her, and began to replace his glove. "I'm told scars mellow some with age."

"I believe that's wine."

"Probably," he conceded. "The information did come from the brat's mother." He squinted at a curricle coming toward them at a clipped pace. "Isn't that Miss Meldrin and Mr. Seager? I thought they'd only just left."

"They've been out no more than a half hour," Patience affirmed as the curricle came to stop before them. "Is everything all right, Caroline?"

"Oh, yes." Caroline looked a trifle overheated, with a thick wool blanket wrapped about her knees. "I'm simply not feeling quite the thing, I'm afraid."

"I see," Patience replied slowly. "That was very sudden."

"Yes, well." She pushed at the blanket a bit. "You know how these headaches come on without warning."

"They do, indeed," Patience agreed. "How fortunate for you they resolve themselves just as quickly."

Carolina nudged a little more of the blanket off. "Well, not *always*—"

"And you know there's very little that seems to help so much as a bit of fresh air," Patience continued. "I imagine by the time Mr. Seager turns about and reaches Hyde Park, you'll be feeling remarkably better."

Caroline's face took on a stubborn cast as Mr. Seager reached over to replace the blanket. "I rather doubt it."

"Well, if you're certain." Patience waved her hand in the direction of the Meldrin house. "I'm sure your mother will fix a powder for you, and—"

Caroline's gaze snapped to the direction of her town house. "Mother's returned?"

"She has."

Mr. Seager smiled pleasantly. "That's fortunate, isn't it? I'm sure your mother will know what to do for you."

"She certainly will," Patience said, and gave Caroline a knowing smile. "Are you quite sure you won't give the fresh air a try?"

"Well . . . I . . ." Caroline's gaze shifted from the direction of her home to Mr. Seager, then back again. "Yes. Yes, perhaps I should. Mr. Seager, would it be too much trouble to turn about for a ride in the park?"

He looked momentarily confused. "No trouble at all, if that's what you want."

By Caroline's pained expression, William thought it fairly clear she wanted nothing of the sort.

"I find it the most agreeable option, at present," she fairly grumbled. But by Mr. Seager's elated expression, William assumed the man heard nothing beyond the word "agreeable."

"Excellent. Excellent." Mr. Seager picked up the reins again. "Perhaps we'll see you at the park, then, Lord Casslebury. Miss Byerly."

William waited until Mr. Seager had driven out of earshot before saying, "She doesn't have the headache, I take it?"

Patience did a very poor job of hiding a smile as she watched the curricle roll away. "I'm sure I don't take your meaning."

"I'm surprised Mr. Seager didn't recognize your meaning, or Miss Meldrin's." He shook his head before resuming their leisurely stroll toward the park. "He's not the cleverest of men, is he?"

Patience shrugged. "They say love blinds."

"Is he in love with her, then?"

"I don't know. He's certainly very taken with her."

"The admiration isn't returned," he guessed.

She pushed her spectacles up with her finger. "She's not yet given him a chance."

"It would seem she doesn't care to," he pointed out. "Will she be angry with you for coercing her into spending time with a gentleman who doesn't interest her?"

"It's no more than what Mrs. Meldrin would've done, should Caroline have returned home. Less, really, as I'm not quite so inclined to lecture."

Patience slid a sideways glance at Lord Casslebury and wondered if there was anything behind all his questions about Caroline. It was possible he was simply making idle conversation. It was also possible that her original instincts were correct and he was spending time with her in an effort to better know her friend.

Though she preferred to think he wasn't the sort to be so disingenuous as to bring her flowers when it was Caroline he sought, in truth, she didn't know him well enough to say for certain.

It shouldn't matter. Hadn't she told herself only last night that it didn't matter?

But that had been before he'd brought her flowers and asked her for a stroll in a park she'd yearned to visit, but only seen from a passing carriage. That had been before he'd told her of his family, and she'd admitted to him she'd never played Bob-Apple, or had wassail, or celebrated Christmas with her father. That was before she knew he looked even more handsome in the sun than he did by candlelight and that the mere feel of his hand in hers could send her blood racing.

It had been before the tiny flicker of hope had been lit. It was a rash, premature, and very likely futile light of hope, but she hadn't the heart to put it out. Neither did she have the confidence to fan it higher—not without knowing for certain.

"Are you pursuing me in an effort to gain my friend's attention?"

She wanted to snatch the question back almost before it left her tongue. She hadn't meant to ask so bluntly— she wasn't sure if she'd wanted to ask at all—but then, she never *meant* to be awkward or ill-mannered; it simply happened.

To her immense relief, Lord Casslebury didn't appear to find fault with her inquiry. He simply smiled goodnaturedly and said, "I assure you, Patience, if I were interested in gaining Miss Meldrin's attention, I could manage the feat on my own."

"Then why—?" This time, she literally bit the end of her tongue to silence herself.

"Why am I taking a stroll with you?" he guessed. "For the pleasure of your company, of course."

Her heart skipped a beat, even as she rolled her eyes. "I don't know that anyone has ever described my company as an avenue for joy before."

"I doubt anyone else has witnessed your unique way of eating cake before."

She pulled a face. "I do wish you'd forget that."

"I might consider it. If you could see your way to telling me why you did it."

They turned the corner that signaled the final block before the park. "I did it for Caroline."

"I surmised as much."

"It's always gratifying to have one's suspicions confirmed," she said smartly. "Now, if we could move on to topics of—"

"*Why* did Caroline require you to eat the cake in one bite?" he clarified. "Answer that, and we'll move on to whatever you like."

"Caroline doesn't particularly care for the . . ." She waved her hand a bit as she searched for a way to describe her friend's peculiarities in the best possible light. ". . . the attention of the *ton*. She would prefer to spend her evenings in a quiet room with a good book."

"Are you saying she's shy?"

"No. Not exactly. She's simply . . . less interested in social activities than many young ladies her age."

"I see," he replied, in that way one does when hopelessly confused.

"She made a bargain of a sort with me," Patience explained. "If I could eat the cake in one bite, she would dance two dances. She's always been fond of my ability to . . . well . . ."

"Consume unorthodoxically?"

"Precisely. I think. Is unorthodoxically a word?"

"Absolutely," he replied, just quickly enough to make her suspect he wasn't quite sure. "How did she become aware of that ability?"

"Oh, I don't recall exactly. It came up in a conversation one day, and she asked for a demonstration. I obliged her."

"I would very much have liked to hear that exchange. Have you any other talents?"

After a moment's consideration she said, "I've a passable singing voice."

"Commendable, but I was referring to the unusual."

She slid another covert glance toward him and thought, *I could watch you for hours on end without blinking. Will that do?* But what she said was, "I'm afraid not."

Chapter Four

Crowds of people were, in William's opinion, very much like his sister's children. They were too loud, too disorganized, and too often turning up where they could cause the most inconvenience.

William scanned the droves of people who had come out to Hyde Park to enjoy the fine weather and congratulated himself on having a plan that would allow him and Patience to avoid the most congested areas.

There was a small bench partially hidden by an old oak tree, not far from where they stood. That was where he and Patience would sit and hold a sedate discussion on the genteel topics of art, literature, travel, and at some point, the mysterious elderly gentleman from the previous night.

Patience flatly refused to cooperate with his plan, beginning with her cheerful insistence that they not sit at all. She'd prefer to walk a bit longer.

He rocked on his heels, his jaw tensing just a little, as she looked about, excitement etched into every feature. "Where would you like to go?"

"Oh, I don't know," she replied, before turning to him. "Why?"

Why? She couldn't be serious. "How else do you expect us to get there?"

She shrugged. "By arriving, I suppose."

He gave himself a moment to try to wrap his mind

around that bit of logic. It didn't help. "But one *must* first know where—"

"Have you never gone out for a stroll without having a specific destination in mind?"

"No."

"Oh. How peculiar."

"*I'm* peculiar?"

"Well, no, *you're* not, but the fact that you've never gone walking about for the sake of walking about is. Surely you did so as a child."

"Not that I recall."

She blinked at him, obviously caught between amused and fascinated. "You never once headed out of doors to play without first knowing *where* you were headed?"

He thought about it. "No."

Now she was gaping just a little. "You planned your leisure activities in advance *as a child?*"

"Certainly."

"You *are* peculiar," she teased on a laugh.

He fought back a smile and sniffed in what he hoped was a very peer-of-the-realm sort of way. "There is nothing at all peculiar about desiring a bit of structure in one's life."

"No, of course not," she agreed, with considerable conviction. "Life can be quite difficult without some semblance of order, but when one wishes for a spot of play . . ." She trailed off and tilted her head at him. "*Do you play?*"

"I've been known to indulge in cards and billiards on occasion."

"I see." She pushed her spectacles up. "And do you plan those occasions in advance as well?"

He did, in fact. "Choose a destination, if you would please, Miss Byerly."

She grinned at him. "Since you're so keen on the idea, perhaps I should let you do the honors."

"Very well."

He led her toward the small bench. Halfway there, she pulled him off in another direction so she could sigh over Mr. Brinkly's gray Arabs, and then in another so she could coo over Mrs. Wenthurst's fat and—in William's opinion—*excessively* friendly bulldog, and then in yet *another* so she could seek out pebbles to toss in the water. Willing to compromise, he let her take the lead while he attempted to steer the conversation to the topics of his choice. She met each of those attempts with interest and enthusiasm, before promptly changing the subject to something entirely unrelated.

She was, in short, utterly unpredictable.

After a brief period of bafflement and frustration, William reminded himself that he *wanted* a woman who was not fettered by plans and schedules. And after another brief period of reminding himself *why* he wanted such a thing, he finally allowed himself the simple pleasure of watching Miss Patience Byerly enjoy the day.

And it was a very great pleasure, indeed. She was full of energy and life, obvious in her attempt to take advantage of everything a day in the park had to offer. She laughed a great deal, and smiled a great deal more. And he found himself laughing and smiling alongside her. It was impossible not to find delight in the company of such a remarkable young woman.

Still, he was relieved when she seemed to wear herself out and finally agreed to sit and rest a while.

Patience sighed as they settled on a bench. Her gloves were dirty from picking up rocks, her legs ached from all the walking, her hair was slipping out from her bonnet, and she had a sizable pebble stuck in her boot. She couldn't have been happier. "This has been wonderful, Lord Casslebury. Thank you."

He smiled at her, and for the dozenth time just that day, her heart caught at the sight. He was devilishly handsome when he smiled. Of course, he was devilishly handsome all the time, but no more so, in her opinion, than when his lips were curved in a smile. It was the way his dark eyes crinkled a little at the corners, she decided. It gave him the appearance of being just on the verge of laughter, and made her desperate to know what would send him over the precipice. *Almost* as desperate as she was to know what it would be like to stretch up and feel that smile against her mouth.

It was a lovely, if rather unladylike, daydream, and one she'd had several times in just the last few hours. Ever since she'd taken his hand to peer at his scars. There'd been a moment of . . . of something between them. She dearly wished she had a name for what that something was. It had made her breathless, deliciously anxious, and a bit weak around the knees. She wondered if she might experience it again.

There was certainly some of it about at present—the tingle of nerves when his leg brushed against hers on the bench, the sense of anticipation when his eyes dipped down to her mouth . . . just as they were doing now. Those eyes lingered, then darkened, and she felt a pleasant warmth move across her skin.

"Patience . . ."

"Hmm?"

His gaze snapped up to hers suddenly, and he said something under his breath she thought perhaps was a curse, followed by what sounded rather like, "this isn't the place."

It took a moment for understanding to seep in, but

when it did, the pleasant warmth she'd been experiencing was immediately replaced by the heat of embarrassment. She looked away, and desperate to cover the sudden tension between them, said the first thing that came to mind. "I . . . I don't think it's proper for you to use my given name."

"Did I?" She turned back to see a corner of his mouth curve up briefly. "I suppose I did. You'll have to call me William, then. In the interest of being fair."

That statement was quite effective in distracting her from her from the tension. "I don't think—"

"I insist," he added, in an easy and confident tone that told her he was accustomed to having his orders followed.

Patience opened her mouth, closed it again. It wasn't at all proper to address each other by their given names after so short an acquaintance. But was it more, or less, improper to refuse an insistent earl? She had absolutely no idea. Perhaps they were equally grievous breaches of etiquette. That seemed her sort of luck. "I'm not at all sure—"

"At least when we're alone," he relented.

"We're not alone now."

"When no one else can hear, then. And while we're having a conversation no one else can hear," he continued before she could argue, "why don't you tell me who the elderly gentleman was at the ball last night?"

The mild unease she'd felt earlier was nothing compared to the wave of panic that washed over her now. "I . . ."

"It was impossible to miss your discomfort at his behavior, or that it preceded your premature departure from the ball." He bent his head to catch her eye. "You left before our waltz."

There was a teasing tone in his voice, but she found it

impossible to smile. "Yes. Yes, I know. I'm terribly sorry."

He straightened again. "I'd rather have your reasons than your apology. Who is he, Patience?"

She wanted to tell him. He'd given her a beautiful day—a day of firsts, and quite possibly onlys. Her first flowers, her first stroll with a gentleman, her first visit to Hyde Park.

Before she'd come to live with the Meldrins, she'd been able to do little more than run the occasional errand outside the rooms she and her father shared in London, and never then without worrying what havoc her father might wreak in her absence.

The Meldrins had taken her off to Europe almost immediately after she'd gone to them for help, and since that day, she'd been eager to return and discover everything she had been missing in London. All the things she'd only heard of, or caught glimpses of through grimy windowpanes, or—

William drew her out of her musings by reaching out to gently still the fingers plucking at the lace on her cuffs. She stared down at the large hand covering her own. "I didn't realize I had the habit until Mrs. Meldrin pointed it out," she said quietly.

"We all have our foibles. Like your . . . grandfather?" he guessed.

She shook her head. "If I tell you, will you give me your word to keep it secret?"

"If you like," he said, and cocked his head. "Why do you think it necessary?"

She very nearly gaped at him. *Why was it necessary?* She couldn't possibly have heard him correctly. "His behavior was scandalous. It would be a scandal, if anyone knew he . . . knew who he was."

And her father's behavior not only held the potential

to bring embarrassment on himself, but on the Meldrins as well. He was in London as their guest, after all.

"A scandal?" William looked momentarily perplexed before shaking his head. "You've worried yourself over nothing, Patience. Your . . ." He raised his brows and tilted his head in a prompting manner. ". . . uncle?"

She shook her head.

"Father?"

She was tempted to deny it, almost as tempted as she was to confide in him. In the end, her hesitation answered for her.

"Right." William gave her hand a gentle squeeze. "Your father is hardly the first man of his age to overindulge, fall asleep in front of the fire, and wake up disoriented."

"I . . ." *Overindulge*. Patience felt a tremendous wash of relief, immediately followed by a heavy weight of guilt. William assumed her father had been in his cups . . . and she hadn't enough courage left to enlighten him. She'd used up her meager store of bravery in the first attempt to tell him the truth.

She might have come up with the courage eventually, but Mr. and Mrs. Meldrin chose that moment to arrive and suggest she return home with them for tea.

Worse, as William handed her into the Meldrins' carriage and expressed a hope to see her again soon, she felt more pleasure than she did guilt.

Just a little more time, she told herself as the carriage rolled away. She only wanted a bit more time to keep the truth to herself, to pretend everything was as it should be. Or perhaps more accurately, how it could be . . . if only things were not as they were.

Chapter Five

William straightened his cravat as he strode down the second-floor hall of his town house. The damn thing always went awry on the fifteenth of the month. It was the day he met with his man of business to discuss the running of the estate, a task that often had him pulling at his constricting neckwear.

He'd known very little about the management of an estate before gaining his title, and he couldn't say having spent the last few years educating himself on the matter had done much to improve his opinion of the responsibility. Fortunately for the estate, his good opinion wasn't necessary, just his participation.

He'd been sorely tempted to excuse himself from that participation that morning. There were a thousand other things he'd rather have been doing, and at the top of that list was spending time with Patience Byerly. It was a little unnerving, how much he wanted to spend time with her.

Her laugh, her smile, her quiet wit, and her open heart all pulled at him. It was impossible not to be drawn into her enthusiasm for life—impossible not to be drawn to her.

And his growing admiration was not limited to the merely platonic. He wanted her. Every small aspect of her teased and tempted him—the ivory skin he imagined would feel soft as silk, the thick hair he thought would look delectable spread out on his pillow. He was fascinated by her dark green eyes, intrigued by her haughty brows, and captivated by the soft curves he'd felt a hint of beneath the palm of his hand when he'd helped her into the Meldrins' carriage.

But nothing enthralled and tormented him quite so thoroughly as her lips. He wouldn't have thought it possible to be so utterly undone by a woman's lips. Certainly it was natural for a man to notice and appreciate a well-formed mouth, and there was nothing unusual in wondering what that mouth might be like to taste. But as a rule, a man's attention was eventually drawn elsewhere and, as a rule, that elsewhere was located a bit farther down.

Apparently, he was the exception to that rule, because as much as he noticed, appreciated, and wanted the whole of Patience Byerly, it was her mouth that had kept him up the two nights since Lord Welsing's ball, tossing and turning like a damn green boy.

He hadn't yet decided if he was more irritated by the recent obsession, or intrigued.

He reached the top of the stairs in time to hear a knock on the front door, and he reached the bottom of the steps in time to see, of all people, his sister being ushered inside.

"Virginia."

She looked up from pulling off her gloves, her cherubic face lit with a mischievousness he knew all too well. Those blonde curls, rosy cheeks, and innocent brown eyes were capable of hiding a wealth of trouble. "Hello, William. You look surprised to see me."

"That's delight," he corrected, and crossed the room to place an affectionate kiss on her cheek. "What are you doing here? You're supposed to be in Surrey."

"Change of plans," she said, as he led her into the parlor. "We'll be spending the holidays in London. I'd have sent a note in advance, but this way is so much more fun."

He sent a wary glance over his shoulder at the mention of "we." "The little demons you pass off as my nephews?"

"I left them in Mayfair, plotting to roast their nanny over an open pit. I can't stay long."

"Ah. All is as it should be, then."

"Well, I do like to keep things predictable for you," she replied, taking a seat on the settee.

"I am not predictable," he argued, sitting across from her.

"Not as of late, else I wouldn't have come to London." When his only response was an arched brow, she sighed impatiently. "It has come to my attention that you're in search of a wife."

As there was no point in denying it, he merely said, "Has it, indeed?"

"Yes. It has also come to my attention that you have a particular young lady in mind for the role."

He stifled a groan and leaned back against the cushions of his chair. One bloody day and the woman had already learned of it, packed up her family, and made the hour-long trip to London. "I should have known you'd hear of it. Though I hadn't expected the news to reach you so quickly."

"Not so very quickly," she countered, and gave him a curious look. "Was it meant to be a secret?"

"It isn't meant to be fodder for gossip, though I suppose that was inevitable—" He cut off, noticing for the first time that her expression was one of worry rather than humor. "You don't approve."

She shifted in her seat. "It's not that I don't approve, exactly. It's simply . . . I wonder if the two of you should suit. Physically, she is a lovely girl, and her dowry is most impressive but—"

"Patience has a dowry?" How had he not known of that?

"Patience?" Virginia opened her mouth, closed it, sat very still for several long seconds, and then simply repeated, "Patience?"

"Miss Byerly," he prompted.

Her eyes grew round. "Miss Byerly? *That's* who you are courting?"

He straightened again in his chair. "Who the devil did you think I was courting?"

"Caroline Meldrin, of course."

"Miss Meldrin?" He frowned thoughtfully. "Who gave you that idea?"

"It's been all the talk in London."

"You've only just come to London," he pointed out, struggling with a laugh.

She waved the comment away. "I've loyal correspondents."

"You have ill-informed correspondents." Though not as ill-informed as he would have her believe. Someone had clearly noticed and informed her of his earlier attempts to engage Miss Meldrin's attention. "I am not courting Miss Meldrin, nor have I any—"

"But I don't know anything about Patience Byerly," she broke in, sounding nearly as put out as she did stunned. "I've never met the woman."

"You've never met Miss Meldrin, either," he reminded her.

"Yes, but I've heard all about her, haven't I?"

"Invite Patience for tea, then," he suggested. "I suspect you'll get on well enough. She says she likes children."

Virginia shook her head dismissively. "Much too obvious. I don't want the poor girl to think she's on trial."

"I should think it obvious any way it's done," he commented.

She ignored him completely. "I shall have to give a dinner party." She pursed her lips and tapped her chin thoughtfully. "Night after next, I think. Something with a Christmas theme—or is it too early yet? Perhaps a harvest—"

"You can't be serious." He gave her a pitying look. "A dinner party in two days?"

"I shall keep it small, no more than a dozen guests." She tapped her chin again. "Maybe two dozen."

"Your staff must *abhor* you."

"My staff is exceedingly well compensated for their troubles."

Because he knew it to be true, he merely shrugged. "You may very well find yourself disappointed, if it turns out Miss Byerly has other plans."

Virginia smiled at him pleasantly. "Unless those plans include a single, wealthy, and handsome gentleman who outranks an earl, I imagine she'll find a way to attend."

Patience did not, in fact, have other plans. A circumstance she was still debating the merits of as she rode to the townhouse of Mr. and Mrs. Higgs. The notion of seeing William again was, without doubt, something to look forward to. The notion of meeting his sister, however, was considerably less appealing.

No, that wasn't quite right. She liked the *idea* of meeting William's sister well enough. It was just the *reality* of meeting her that put her stomach in knots.

What if she made some terrible faux pas? What if she bobbled a curtsy, or used the wrong utensil, or addressed someone incorrectly? Or worse, infinitely worse, what if she did everything quite perfectly, and William's sister decided she simply didn't care for her brother's taste in ladies. Perhaps the woman would think her too plain. There wasn't a thing Patience could do to improve the woman's opinion of her in that case. One could practice curtsies and table manners. One could not practice being less plain.

She shifted on the carriage seat, then threw a wary glance at Mrs. Meldrin, who twice already had admonished her for fidgeting. Fortunately, Mrs. Meldrin was too busy fussing with Mr. Meldrin's attire—much to the apparent annoyance of Mr. Meldrin—to notice.

Patience rubbed her fingers against a velvet ribbon at the waist of her gown and turned to Caroline. "Does this gown make me appear plain?" she asked in a nervous whisper. "Or perhaps *plainer* would be a more accurate description."

Caroline rolled her eyes as she dug through her reticule for something. "I've told you no twice already tonight."

"That was for the green gown."

Caroline looked up. "Oh . . . so it was." She gave Patience a thorough if brief inspection. "You look lovely in the blue as well, but out of curiosity, what were you planning on doing if I said you looked dreadful? We're nearly to the party."

Patience had no idea.

A hopeful gleam entered Caroline's eyes. She shot a cautious glance at her parents "Perhaps you've developed the headache?"

It was awfully tempting. "No."

"Pity."

A half hour after their arrival, Patience decided it would have been a much greater pity if she had given in to temptation and returned home. True, there was a moment or two of terrible nerves upon her introduction to

Mrs. Virginia Higgs, but the discomfort was blessedly short-lived. It was difficult to be ill at ease in the company of such an affable woman.

As soon as Patience had arrived, Mrs. Higgs had ushered her to a settee where she, and a good number of her friends, proceeded to ask a long series of friendly questions. Though it put her in the awkward position of having to parry one or two inquiries into her past, Patience felt the amicable interview was preferable to being snubbed. Shame it had the unfortunate side effect of making it impossible for her to *ever* so casually cross the room to where William was speaking to an entirely different group of ladies. It was even more unfortunate that several of those ladies were young, attractive, and unmarried.

"Is something the matter, dear?"

Patience snapped her gaze away from William. On the settee next to her, Mrs. Higgs fluttered her fan below a small, knowing smile. "You look rather . . . distant."

"Oh, no. No, I . . ." Patience scrambled for a plausible excuse for her distraction, only to be handed one by the sight of Caroline motioning for her from across the room. "I believe Miss Meldrin needs me, that's all. Please, do excuse me."

She hurried away quickly, on the slight chance Mrs. Higgs would be so bold as to point out Caroline was standing a significant distance from where Patience had been gazing.

Caroline gave her a rather distracted smile as she approached. "Patience, I seem to have torn my gown. Do you—"

"*Caroline*—"

"I have." Caroline lifted her arm to display a loose seam at the cuff of her gown. She stared at it with a bemused expression. "I've actually torn it."

"Oh." Patience blinked at the loose material. "Well . . . how unexpected."

"Yes, rather . . ." Caroline's brow furrowed further. "I suppose it needs to be mended."

"Yes. I suppose so . . . Did you bring needle and thread?"

Caroline looked up and dropped her arm. "No. Didn't you?"

"No." Amusement tickled the back of her throat. "I never thought we'd truly need them."

Laughing softly, she took Caroline's hand and led her out of the parlor to the ladies' retiring room, some distance down the front hall. She sighed when they discovered the room empty.

"I'd rather hoped to find assistance. No matter. Wait here, and I'll fetch a needle and thread from a maid." She remembered the last occasion in which either of them had attempted to wield thread and needle. Mrs. Meldrin had insisted they practice their stitch work in the creation of a sampler. The results had been grisly. "Perhaps I'll just fetch the maid."

She left Caroline still scowling at her marred gown, and took no more than a dozen steps away from the door before coming knee to face with a small dark-haired boy with enormous brown eyes, drying tear tracks down pink cheeks, and a thin line of blood dripping from his mouth.

Her heart turned over at the sight.

"Oh, you poor dear." She crouched down in front of him. "Darling, are you hurt?"

To her astonishment, he answered by grinning broadly and pointing to a bleeding gap where his front tooth ought to have been. "I've a hole!"

She reared back a solid foot. "Good heavens, that's ghastly."

Apparently well over the pain of his injury and delighted with her assessment of his wound, he giggled and prodded the space with his tongue.

"Oh, dear." Her stomach did a slow, nauseating roll. "Don't do that, I beg you."

"Why?"

She stood up and grimaced. "It's . . . unsightly."

A familiar male voice sounded from behind her. "Unsightly? That's no way to speak about one of my nephews."

The rolling sensation was immediately replaced by a jittery one at the sight of William striding down the hall. He stopped in front of her to smile. "Gruesome is generally a better choice. I've been looking for you."

Oh, the things that smile and those simple words did to her. She hadn't a name for most of them, but thought perhaps bliss summed up the whole rather nicely. She stammered, swallowed, and felt herself blush. "I . . . I was just . . ." William's lips twitched at her reaction, but she thought it best to pretend she didn't notice. She stepped aside to gesture at his nephew.

"He's hurt," she said, sounding rather lame even to her own ears.

"Ah . . . so he is."

Chapter Six

William eyed the little boy before him with something akin to alarm tickling along his skin.

He loved his nephews, each and every one of them, and he would freely admit as much to anyone who might care to listen. He would also admit that, if at all possible, he would prefer to express his devotion from a healthy distance. The younger the nephew, the healthier the distance.

Small children were such unpredictable little blighters—giggling cherubs one moment, with happy smiles and big eyes, and then the next thing a man knew, they were screaming at the top of their lungs, producing vast rivers of tears and demanding you fetch them something called "bwon won," or "gwaba," or another equally incomprehensible object.

This particular nephew had recently outgrown the tendency to babble incoherently, but he remained a very small child and, as a rule, very small children were loud, clingy, sticky, needy, wet, and—perhaps worst of all— terrifyingly breakable.

William glanced down the hall and wondered if there was any way he could shout for his sister without completely unmanning himself in front of Patience.

He rather doubted it.

Resigned to handling the situation, he crouched down, hesitated, then reached up to gently ruffle the boy's hair. "Lose a tooth, did you?"

Patience frowned as the boy nodded. "Isn't he a trifle young to be losing his teeth?"

"I imagine he had assistance." William pointed at the boy's chin. "Did you hit your mouth on something, Will?"

"Felix."

"Felix struck you?"

Will shook his head and patted his elbow.

"Ah. You caught his elbow with your mouth," William translated. "An accident?"

Will nodded, and once again prodded the space with his tongue.

Patience averted her eyes. "Oh, dear."

"Not in front of the lady, if you please," William admonished. He withdrew a handkerchief and used it to stop the small amount of blood that was still oozing from the wound. "Let's find your nanny and get you cleaned up a bit."

"Or a lot," Patience suggested.

William chuckled and stood, then very carefully reached out to pick the boy up, only to have Will back away and point at Patience.

"You want Miss Byerly to accompany you?"

Will nodded.

Excellent plan, young man.

"Me?" Patience took a sudden step back. "Oh, I can't, I'm afraid. Caroline has torn her gown, and—"

William cut her off with a chiding tone. *"Patience."*

"She has," she informed him. "In earnest, for a change. I need to find a maid with thread and needle."

William nodded. "Right. I'll find the maid. You take Will to his nanny."

"I . . ." She bit her bottom lip. "I . . . er . . . Won't they be in the family portion of the house? I don't wish to intrude."

"They're in the orangery at the end of the hall. You won't be intruding," he assured her.

She didn't appear reassured in the least. Her fingers began to rub at a velvet ribbon on her gown. "But . . . couldn't you take him?"

William looked to Will. "Do you want me to take you?"

The boy shook his head.

"It appears I cannot." He smiled at Patience. "He wants you."

"Oh . . . er . . ."

"Is something the matter?"

"No. Yes. I'm not certain. I . . ." She eyed Will a little nervously. "I am fond of children, but to be honest," she leaned toward William and whispered, "I've very little experience with them. I've never been responsible for one."

"I see." Was he going to have to take Will himself, after all? He sincerely hoped not. "I imagine I've not much more experience than you." He leaned toward her and whispered, "I avoid them whenever possible."

"Will is *your* nephew."

"Yes, but you're a woman. Women are born with the instinct to . . ." He waved his hand about, searching for the right word. "To nurture. Or what have you."

She rolled her eyes, but knelt down and smiled at Will. "You are adorable . . . even though you're messy."

Will grinned at her.

William grinned wider. "There you go." He gave her a gentle but bolstering pat on the back. "Just scoop him up and take him down the hall."

Patience straightened and took a step forward. Then a step back. "What if I should drop him?"

William shook his head. "You'll not drop him. A firm grip is part of the womanly instinct."

She sent him a withering look. "And I suppose men are born with a natural urge to toss them about like sacks of flour?"

"We're a stupid lot."

She laughed and offered Will her hand. "We'll walk, if it's all the same to you, Will."

It was all the same to William, as long as she took the child. "Nanny's in the orangery," he reminded her as he began to back away, intending to make good his escape. "End of the hall."

The nanny, Patience soon discovered, was not to be found in the orangery. Oddly enough, neither was a single plant. Apparently, it had been some time since the orangery had been used for its intended purpose. The large stone and glass room was empty, except for one rather harassed-looking maid cleaning up what appeared to have been an exceedingly active game of Bob-Apple. She seemed more than happy to set aside the chore in favor of taking charge of little Will.

"Nanny sent the others to the nursery after the mishap," she explained to Patience, before smiling at Will. "She's been looking for you. Perhaps we'll find her first. Shall we make a game of it?"

In an instant Will let go of Patience's hand and dashed to the maid.

Patience sighed and smiled as the maid led him from the room. She'd worried herself over nothing. The little darling had been no trouble at all. He'd kept his hand in hers, and William's handkerchief in his mouth, for the duration of their walk. And aside from a few garbled comments that hadn't seemed to require any response from her, he'd been quiet as a mouse.

Feeling decidedly smug with her competent handling of Will—*she'd* managed to spend a bit of time with the child without acquiring any bite marks—Patience sighed once more, then glanced about at the remnants of the Bob-Apple game. She noted that one of the barrels had a sizable puddle of water around the base and a number of scraped, nicked, and otherwise mauled-looking apples inside. But the second barrel looked to have gone unused.

The sides were dry, and the handful of floating apples looked free of blemishes. Apparently, the children had all wanted to try their skill on the same apples.

Curious, she reached out to poke at one of the unmarred apples, then watched as it dipped below the water before softly popping back to the surface. *The game couldn't be too difficult,* she mused. *It's not as if the slightest touch would send the apples sloshing about willy-nilly . . .* She poked again just to make sure.

She eyed a stack of drying cloths neatly folded on a nearby chair.

She shouldn't. She *really* shouldn't.

Then again, when was she likely to have the chance ever again? She couldn't very well go home and ask the staff to put apples in a barrel for her. They'd think her as batty as her father.

With a giggle tickling her throat, she took up position in front of the barrel and began to lean forward. She felt wonderfully absurd, and a bubble of laughter escaped before she could help it, then another as she bent farther down. By the time she was in position to actually begin the game, she was laughing hard enough to lose her balance. To steady herself, she reached out to catch the sides of the barrel.

"You're supposed to keep your hands behind your back."

If she *had* been keeping her hands behind her back, she likely would have toppled in at the surprise of William's voice coming from the door.

Still laughing, she straightened and looked up. From his amused tone, she rather thought she'd find him leaning a shoulder against the doorframe, a knowing sort of smirk on his face. Silly of her, really—the military officer in him would never allow for leaning, or smirking for that matter. He stood straight-backed with his hands gripped behind him, a bright twinkle in his dark eyes.

She smiled back at him and wondered a little that she didn't feel foolish at having been caught. Then again, he knew she wanted to try the game. And he *had* witnessed her stuffing an entire slice of cake in her mouth. In comparison to that unfortunate spectacle, a game of Bob-Apple seemed fairly decorous.

She planted her hands on her hips and nodded toward the barrel. "If I don't hold on, I'll fall in."

"Ah." He walked into the room and peered into the barrel. "We can't have that. Go on, then. I'll not tell anyone you cheated."

"Cheated?" She schooled her face into a haughty look—a difficult endeavor when one found it nearly impossible to stop smiling—and pointedly caught her hands behind her back.

"Much better," William informed her. "If you're going to do the thing, you may as well do it properly."

She couldn't help laughing at that. "Any other rules or suggestions you care to impart?"

"No, I believe that's all of it." He motioned at the barrel. "Have at it."

Feeling both silly and delighted, she stepped forward, picked out a nice apple at the edge, and began to lean forward. She straightened again and sent a narrowed-eyed glance at William. "You're not going to play the part of sibling and assist, are you?"

"Assist? Ah, the head dunking." His lips twitched. "Wouldn't you like the full Bob-Apple experience?"

"I'd like to experience it as an only child."

"Suit yourself."

She nodded and returned her attention to the barrel.

Then she sent a wary glance at the door. "What if some-one were to come in?"

Really, she should have considered that earlier, but she'd been so excited at the notion of finally having the opportunity to play . . .

"The polite thing to do would be to issue an invitation to play," William drawled. "Go on, Patience. The door's open and it's just a silly and innocent game. They'd have no cause for censure."

"Right." Of course he was right.

Breathless with amusement, she leaned over the barrel and began her first attempt at Bob-Apple. After a bit of maneuvering, she managed to catch an apple with her chin, and even succeeded in scraping it a little with her two front teeth before the fruit popped free of her grip and bobbed up to smack her in the nose.

"Blast."

Next to her, William chuckled. "You'll never catch one that way."

She wiped her nose and straightened. "Which way would you recommend?"

"Grip the apple at the top and bottom."

"How?"

"Open your mouth wider." He ran his tongue across his teeth. "If anyone can manage that, you can."

She frowned at him. "You agreed to forget that."

"Forget what?"

She snorted and motioned over the barrel opening. "You seem very sure of yourself. Why don't you show me how it's done?"

"I don't think so."

"Why not? You said it was an innocent game."

"I also said it was silly."

She felt her brows rise. "Are you above being silly?"

"Naturally. I'm an earl." He eyed the barrel, his jaw

tensing a little. She was beginning to suspect that occurred whenever one of his plans threatened to go awry. As if to confirm that suspicion, he said, "I'd planned to watch, not play."

"Well then, change your plans so you may provide me with a bit of instruction."

"Thank you, no."

"Very well." She shrugged and bit the inside of her cheek. "If you wish to be stodgy about it."

"I am *not* stodgy."

"My apologies. Can't imagine what I was thinking." She turned her back and said in a barely perceptible voice. "Except that you won't play an innocent—"

"Step aside."

He moved to stand in front of the barrel, casting her a warning glance.

"There will be no dunking."

"I wouldn't *dare*." Not now, anyway.

"And no laughing."

"What?" She gaped at him. "You can't possibly be serious."

"I am merely providing you with a lesson in the most effective method—"

"Lesson or not, you'll be an earl with his head stuck in a barrel of water."

He considered that, then the barrel, and then her. Suddenly, his face lit with a grin. "There is that. I can't believe you talked me into this."

William truly couldn't believe it. Even as he leaned over, he found it difficult to grasp that he was actually putting his head into a barrel of water to demonstrate how best to go about catching a floating apple with one's teeth. It was beyond his scope. He was a grown man, an *earl*, engaged in a ridiculous child's game. And, he was forced to admit as the first apple bobbed out of his reach, he was enjoying it immensely.

He'd forgotten the fun of it, the challenge, and yes, the sheer ridiculousness of it. He'd also forgotten what it was like to take a spot of water up the nose, but he didn't let that unwelcome reminder ruin his fun, or his concentration.

To his satisfaction, considerable pride, and what he rather hoped was Patience's impressed amazement, he caught the next apple he went after.

Stodgy, was he? He'd like to see her find success so quickly. He took the apple out of his mouth, set it aside, and used one of the cloths to dry his face. "There you are. Nothing to it."

There appeared to be a great deal to it for Patience. She was nearly doubled over with laughter.

"Oh, heavens," she gasped, pushing her spectacles up. "Heavens, that was *enormously* silly."

"Delighted to have amused you." He motioned to the barrel. "If you would be so kind as to return the favor?"

William listened to the sound of Patience's continued laughter as she took her turn at the barrel and decided that "silly" did not accurately describe the scene before him. Charming, endearing, and oddly arousing were a far better fit.

Watching Patience Byerly try to catch an apple with her mouth was, without doubt, one of the most delightful things he'd ever witnessed, and not only because the game required her to spend a considerable amount of time bent at the waist. Although that did, naturally, capture a substantial portion of his attention.

It was her obvious determination to enjoy herself, however, that captured his heart. It was the same eagerness he'd seen at Hyde Park and heard in her voice every time she spoke of trying something new, or going somewhere different, or meeting someone she didn't know. The woman seemed to have a boundless supply of enthusiasm.

A supply she drew on now as she followed her apple moving about in the barrel, shuffled her feet, and stretched her form across the water. She angled her head one way and then another, tried a variety of tactics, and then finally succeeded in biting into her apple.

"Ha!" She straightened, took a hardy bite out of the apple, and grinned at him. "I did it."

"So you did," he said, or at least that's what he thought he said. He wasn't really paying attention to what came out of his mouth. It was *her* mouth that suddenly held his interest. That wide mouth now damp with water and juice from the apple. It was an unholy temptation. *She* was an unholy temptation. He couldn't look away as she chewed, swallowed, and reached up to wipe away a small drop of apple juice from the corner of her lips.

Without thought, he stepped forward and took the apple from her hand. He caught the flash of nerves and excitement in her eyes. Fearing the nerves might get the better of her, he tossed the apple aside, closed the remaining distance between them, and pulled her into his arms.

She made a small feminine sound he sincerely hoped was surprise and not protest, and then he bent his head and took his first taste of Patience Byerly.

He meant to keep the kiss sweet and light, a gentle meeting of lips. A woman's first kiss should be gentle and sweet, shouldn't it? And that it *was* her first kiss, there could be no doubt. She was the very picture of innocence. Her face tilted straight up, her eyes squeezed tight, and her lips firmly clamped together. She looked nearly as naive as she did charming.

She didn't taste like either. She tasted like sin.

He should have expected it. Hadn't the majority of his

decidedly sinful fantasies over the last week been centered on that incredible mouth?

But even as he berated himself for being unprepared, he realized that the reality of kissing Patience Byerly was far more vivid than anything his imagination could have created. Nothing could have prepared him for his body's reaction to her taste—the wave of heat, the sharp stab of desire. He wanted more. He wanted everything. And absolutely nothing that could be reasonably described as sweet and light.

As her mouth relaxed and began to move beneath his, his hands began to explore of their own accord—up her back, across her shoulders, down to mold her waist. She made a soft sound and arched closer, her fingers flittering along the back of his neck and into his hair.

The sound, the movement, the feel of her body molded to his was overwhelming. Dimly, he wondered how something so simple as a kiss could feel so monumental, how it could stir a desire in him more powerful than any he'd ever known. He marveled at it, reveled in it, even as he—the most disciplined of men—felt his control begin to slip. Though it took an enormous act of will—and, in truth, more than one attempt—eventually he succeeded in pulling away before he lost himself completely.

For several long moments he could do little more than stare at her as their breath mingled. When he was certain he could touch her without pulling her close and starting the kiss all over again, he lifted his hand to gently cup her face. "Perhaps—" He had to pause and clear the gruffness from his voice. "Perhaps there is one holiday tradition I wouldn't mind adhering to."

She blinked very slowly. "Bob-Apple?"

Laughing softly, he pressed his lips to her forehead. "Kissing you."

Chapter Seven

The morning following Virginia Higgs's dinner party, Patience woke, dressed, sat down for a spot of early breakfast, and came to the sudden and rather disturbing realization that she had no clear memory of what had happened at the party after she had kissed William in the orangery.

How very odd.

Vaguely, she recalled returning to the ladies' retiring room and then being accompanied by Caroline back to the parlor. She knew she had eaten, drunk, and spoke with the other guests during the dinner, but for the life of her, she couldn't remember what she'd dined on, to whom she'd spoken, or what she had said.

Her mind had remained utterly fixed on William and that one spectacular kiss. At least, she *assumed* it was spectacular. Having never before kissed a gentleman, she couldn't claim to be an expert on the matter, but it had certainly *felt* wonderful. It had left her lighthearted, light-headed, and decidedly over-warm.

The only remaining portion of the party she could recall with any clarity was the few parting words she'd had with William, when he mentioned seeing her again at the Meldrins' dinner the following night. *Tonight,* Patience thought with a sigh. She smiled around a mouthful of scone. Only a few more hours and then . . .

And then what? Would he kiss her again? Would she let him? Probably, she *shouldn't* let him.

Probably, it mattered very little what she did.

Scowling, she set down her scone. Whether she never let William kiss her again, or she let him kiss her at every opportunity, it changed nothing. She was still the daughter of a madman.

At best, she had the remaining weeks of the Little Season to indulge in a bit of flirtation before going to the country with her father. At worst, William would offer for her. She nearly groaned at the idea. If he proposed, she'd have to tell him the truth about her father. He would no doubt retract his offer, likely become angry with her for the deception, and *then* she would go to the country with her father.

Perhaps it would be best to avoid any further contact with him and save them both from future heartache. Then again, heartache appeared inevitable at this point, and every moment she spent with him was another memory to take with her when she left. Those memories would be all she had soon. How could she bear to give up even one?

She decided she couldn't. She wouldn't. Furthermore, she wasn't going to merely allow William to kiss her at every opportunity; she was going to put a concerted effort into seeing that he did.

William made his way across the Meldrins' crowded parlor in a manner he sincerely hoped looked casual, but was, in reality, a well-planned route to Patience on the other side of the room. It was a slow process, requiring he do something for which he had no affinity—meandering. He moved from one group of guests to the next, exchanging a few pleasantries and then strategically slipping away before he could be drawn into a conversation. He paused in front of the fire to warm hands that weren't cold, and then paused again to accept a glass of spirits he had no interest in drinking.

The ruse wasn't necessary, really. He wasn't doing anything untoward. But his sister had made a comment that morning on the amount of time he'd spent with Patience the night before, and he didn't wish to make Patience the center of gossip, any more than he wanted to be the center himself.

He'd made a point not to arrive until dinner was nearly served, and he'd been equally careful not to glance too often in Patience's direction during the meal. And now, heaven help him, he was meandering.

At last he reached a spot he felt was close enough for Patience to come to him without appearing bold. He stopped to peer at a small watercolor that looked as if it had been rendered with all the skill of a five-year-old, and none of the charm. Upon very close inspection he thought it was meant to be a mountain range, or perhaps a series of very pointed waves. Whatever it was, it was awful. He very much hoped Patience hadn't had a hand in its creation, its purchase, or the decision to hang it in the parlor.

He felt rather than saw Patience step up from behind him. "Dreadful, isn't it?"

He wanted to shift his feet. Insulting the Meldrin family's taste in artwork was not how he had imagined beginning their conversation. "Ahh . . ."

"It was a gift from Caroline to her father when she was eight." She pulled a face at the painting. "Mr. Meldrin insists on keeping it in the room."

"I see. He's fond of it, then."

"Heavens, no—other than that it was a gift from his daughter. He says it's a test of his guests' tastes."

"Did I pass?"

"Difficult to know for certain. He also says it's a test of good manners, depending on whether or not he likes his guest. I think he keeps it in here for the sole purpose of embarrassing Caroline."

He looked at the painting a moment longer. "That would certainly do it."

"The . . . uh . . . the Meldrins do have some very fine art in the house. I . . ." Her hands went to her waist briefly, before she tucked them behind her back. "I could give you a tour of those in the hall, if you like."

He stifled a startled grin. It was rather forward of her to offer. Not so forward as to be improper, as the hall was in full view of anyone who cared to step outside the parlor, but the area was separate enough from the other guests to make her suggestion just a little bit bold . . . and therefore all the more irresistible.

"I should enjoy that." Very much, he added silently.

This time, they meandered through the room together. Avoiding stares and whispers wasn't feasible, but a casual stroll toward the door was less likely to cause a stir than a brisk walk out of the room. And in the end, it was just as effective in getting Patience alone.

Upon entering the hall, Patience gestured to a mid-sized watercolor in which he had absolutely no interest. "Mrs. Meldrin purchased this piece in Rome. The artist is of no renown, but the colors are lovely."

He motioned farther down the hall. "What of that one?"

"Which one?"

"That one." He walked away from the parlor doors and hid a smile when the sound of her footsteps followed. "The large one in the ornate frame."

In which he also had no interest.

They stopped in front of the frame. She peered at it while he peered at her. It was nice to finally be able to really look at her without worrying over the stares of others.

"It's a portrait in oil, William."

He loved the way her lips pursed when she used the letter *p*. "Of course it is."

She opened her mouth, closed it. He enjoyed watching that as well. "Of Mrs. Meldrin," she said slowly. "Commissioned only last year."

"I . . ." He tore his eyes away from Patience to take his first real look at the painting before him. It was indeed a very clear rendering of Mrs. Meldrin. "Ah. So it is."

She tilted her head at him. "Are you all right?"

"Yes, quite." He decided he also liked the way the furrow of concern in her forehead made her sharp brows appear even haughtier. "Why is it I always feel as if you're looking down at me?"

She started a little at the sudden change of subject. "I'm sure I couldn't say. I don't mean to give the impression."

He lifted a hand to very briefly trace a brow with the pad of his thumb. "They're always lifted, as if you're mildly intrigued, but mostly just annoyed."

Even in the dim candlelight he could see a blush rise to her cheeks. "I'm not annoyed . . . Perhaps it is my height."

"Your height," he repeated on a chuckle. "I must admit, that logic fails me."

"Well, when one looks up to a great height, one's brows tend to raise."

"I hardly think I qualify as a great height."

She used her finger to push up her spectacles. "The principle remains unchanged."

He frowned down at her; her brows had lifted higher when she'd adjusted her spectacles. "It's your spectacles, isn't it? They're too small."

"They're not."

"They are." He reached up and slid them off.

"What are you doing?" She grasped for them but he held them out of reach. "Give them back."

"You see? Your brows have lowered."

They lowered even farther. "Because I'm squinting."

"No. Well, yes, you are a little," he conceded. "But that's not it. You're not trying to see above the bottom wire. Why are you wearing ill-fitting spectacles?"

"They're perfectly adequate."

"For another woman, perhaps. Not you. Why don't you procure a pair that fits?"

"I shall, when I want them."

He was quiet a moment before he said softly, "If you'd rather not discuss it, you need only say so."

Patience glanced to where the sound of laughter drifted from the open doors of the parlor. Someone could step into the hallway and interrupt them at any minute, and she wasn't sure if she hoped or feared that would happen. With an uneasy tightness squeezing at her chest—a tightness she recognized as humiliation—she swallowed hard, bent her head to stare at a spot on the floor, and decided if she couldn't tell William the whole truth of her circumstances, she could at least find the courage to tell him this one part.

"I . . . I haven't the funds for it."

She looked up long enough to see him nod slightly. "I see. Is your father ungenerous? Or have you no head for money?"

"I've a fine head for money," she replied, feeling a little indignant at the implication. A silly time for indignation, perhaps, but it was preferable to embarrassment. "There simply isn't any available. My father and I are . . . we are dependent on the generosity of the Meldrin family."

"Ah." He dipped his head in an effort to catch her eyes. "Your circumstances are hardly unique, Patience."

"No, but I haven't been entirely truthful about them, have I?"

His lips twisted. "Very few in the *ton* are honest about their circumstances."

"That hardly excuses my behavior."

"Your behavior?" This time, it was his brows that lifted. "Have you claimed to have a dowry that doesn't exist?"

"No, of course not."

"Have you told anyone that your father is flush?"

"Certainly not."

"Then I fail to see the cause of your guilt."

"I wear these gowns," she replied, plucking at her silk sleeve. "And these fine gloves and lovely jewelry. I go from dinner parties to balls and the opera as if I belong and—"

He reached out to gently still her fidgeting hands. "Of course you belong."

"I don't," she said quietly. "I truly don't. I am the daughter of a commoner. These gowns are Caroline's castoffs. Only the fact we've been on the Continent keeps them from being recognized as such. I've very little education in skills appropriate for a lady. I play no instruments. I've no talent for art. I speak no more than a word or two of French. I haven't the faintest idea how to manage a household with staff. I—"

"You sing," he interrupted. "You told me you've a passable singing voice."

"Only by luck." She found herself staring at the floor again. "I've never received instruction."

"Patience, look at me." He tilted her chin up with his knuckle. "You belong and for better reasons than most in the *ton* can claim. You're an intelligent, charming, loyal, kindhearted woman—"

"You haven't known me long enough to know I'm kindhearted," she interrupted.

"I didn't need long," he said gently. "You spend your evenings in libraries and the backs of parlors rather than out dancing as you'd prefer, just so your friend won't have to sit alone."

"I owe her. My father and I—"

"No, you owe Mr. Meldrin."

"And Mrs. Meldrin. I'd not be able to go out into society without embarrassing myself if not for her. She tutored me extensively."

He was quiet for a moment before saying, "It's rather important to you, to be out in society."

He didn't phrase it as a question, or even a guess, and so she didn't offer a direct answer. Instead she wandered over to a portrait of a past Mr. Meldrin and stared at it without seeing it at all.

"All my life," she began quietly, "I stayed at home, stayed inside while the world outside worked and played and . . . lived. I wanted a chance to do the same. The Meldrins gave me that."

She heard him step up behind her, and knew that to anyone looking out from the parlor, they would appear to be simply discussing the portrait. "How did you come to know the Meldrins?"

"Years ago, my father and Mr. Meldrin met through a mutual acquaintance in The Royal Society. They shared a love of all things pertaining to magnetism, and Mr. Meldrin, who is quite a bit younger than my father, looked to my father as a mentor for a number of years. He often came to visit us in Kent."

"Then you moved away," William prompted softly.

"Yes, and my father grew . . . ill. We lost touch for a long time."

"But not forever."

"I sought out Mr. Meldrin in London." He'd been kind to her as a child, often bringing her a special treat of candy when he came to visit her father in his workshop. Later, he'd substituted coins for the candy. Out of funds, evicted once again, and with nowhere to turn but the poorhouse, she'd called on him with the hope he'd not outgrown his generosity. "I went to ask for a loan."

"He offered something else."

"Yes, he took us in . . . I'll never be able to repay him for that, and I'll not ask for more."

William nodded and she expected words of understanding from him, but instead he stepped around her to brush the back of his knuckles along her cheek, his expression unreadable. "You're a beautiful woman, Patience."

"I . . ." Flustered, she attempted to make light of the compliment. "Without my spectacles, you mean."

With exquisite gentleness, he slid her spectacles back into place. "You're a beautiful woman," he repeated.

"I . . . thank you."

He took her hand, and after glancing down the hall at the parlor doors, drew her into the shadow of a small alcove. Before she could even think to utter a word of protest as she should have, or encouragement as she *would* have, he pulled her into his arms and covered her mouth with his.

The kiss was brief. She only had time to register the taste of him, and the way her skin came alive at the feel of his lips moving across hers, and then he was pulling away from her, and pulling them both back into the hall.

"My apologies," he said hoarsely. "I should not have done that."

She could barely hear him over the pounding of her heart and the rush of blood in her ears. "I don't mind kissing you."

"I'm not apologizing for the kiss, Patience. I'm apologizing for being careless with your reputation."

"Oh." Though she knew he was right, it somehow seemed terribly wrong to be receiving an apology in that moment. "I . . . it's all right. I could have—"

"Patience!" The sound of Caroline calling her name made her take a guilty step back from William. Silly of her, really. She wasn't standing improperly close—not now, at any rate—and Caroline would have been the last person to notice and comment if she had been. The girl simply didn't pay attention to those sorts of things.

True to form, Caroline strode quickly down the hall and came to a stop before them, a little breathless and clearly oblivious to the fact that she'd interrupted a private conversation. "Patience, I've been looking for you. Your father is asking for you."

"My father?"

Caroline nodded. "He is . . . quite insistent."

"Insistent." Patience blinked to clear her head. And then she heard it—the distant pounding from upstairs. She hadn't noticed it over the sound of her own heartbeat. "Oh, dear."

She turned to William. "I'm sorry, I have to go."

He caught her arm gently before she could leave. "Patience. Your father is still unwell?"

"Yes. I have—"

"He seemed fit enough at Lord Welsing's ball."

"His illness is unpredictable." She pulled away. "I have to go."

For the first time since coming to live with the Meldrins, Patience had the fervent wish that the family weren't quite so well off. Their town house may not have been unusually large by *ton* standards, but for a young woman trying to reach a father in the midst of a madman's rant, the house seemed perfectly enormous.

She and Caroline moved as swiftly as their skirts, and

the possibility of any wandering guests seeing them, allowed, which wasn't nearly as quickly as Patience would have preferred.

"What's happened, Caroline?"

"I don't know for certain. It was only minutes ago. The footmen say he came out of his room, livid about the party downstairs. They've locked him in again, but not before he ran down the back steps, went down the side hall, and then . . . then plowed directly into Mr. Seager. He's a little put out over the matter."

"Who, Mr. Seager or my father?"

"Both, I imagine."

"Oh, *blast*. What the devil was Mr. Seager doing in the side hall?"

"He said he was looking for an absent partygoer."

Patience glanced at her friend as they hurried up the stairs. "Where were you, Caroline?"

"I'd gone to my room to fix my hair." Caroline swallowed audibly. "I may have stayed longer than strictly necessary. I'm sorry, Patience."

Patience shook her head and took the last step. "This isn't your fault."

They reached her father's room to find three footmen, the housekeeper, Mr. Seager, and several maids standing outside the door. Their argument nearly drowned out the sound of her father pounding on the door. Nearly.

Patience pushed her way to the front of the melee. "Mr. Seager. If you would step aside, please."

The young man jabbed a finger at the door. "That man accosted me."

"He didn't mean you any harm, I'm sure."

"He's mad. He very nearly killed me."

Mrs. Keesnip, the housekeeper, snorted derisively.

"Sir Franklin Byerly, hurt *you*? The man's seventy years of age and harmless as a new babe."

"Harmless . . ." Mr. Seager's eyes shot to Patience. "Byerly? That . . . that *man* is a relative of yours?"

"Mr. Seager, please—" She broke off at the sound of Mr. Meldrin's voice sounding from behind her.

"I'll handle this, Patience." He laid a gentle hand on her shoulder. "See to your father."

Patience felt her heart sink further as Mr. Meldrin and Caroline steered a stammering Mr. Seager down the hall. Unless Mr. Meldrin could convince Mr. Seager to keep quiet, her secret would be out before the night was over and all the talk by morning. And included in the gossip would be the Meldrins.

She felt like screaming, and crying, and washing her hands of the whole horrible mess. Instead she took a deep breath and held her hand out to the housekeeper. "The key please, Mrs. Keesnip."

Her father kicked at the door. "Devil take it, where's *my* key?"

"Calm yourself." She jingled the housekeeper's immense key ring. "I've the key right—"

"Why do you have it? I'm the one locked in the room." He resumed his pounding on the door. "Why the devil am I locked in this room?"

Patience stepped up and pounded right back. "Sir Franklin Byerly, you will take four steps back from the door or I shall instruct the footman to swallow the key!"

She heard a grumble and a shuffle. The outline of his shoes disappeared from the space between the door and the floor. With a heavy sigh of both relief and misery, she turned the key in the lock and let herself in.

She found him standing in the center of his room, his

arms folded across his chest and his face set in a childish pout. "There's a party. Why am I not at the party?"

Frustrated, she tossed the key on a side table. "You don't like parties."

He seemed to consider that a moment before shaking his head. "Everyone likes parties."

"No, not everyone. You . . ." Oh, what did it matter? She wasn't going to convince him of anything. She threw her hands up and searched for a way around the argument. "It's . . . it's a rehearsal . . . for your birthday party. It's to be a surprise."

He uncrossed his arms. "Is it my birthday?"

Not for months and months. "It will be. And you shall have a grand—"

"Who's ever heard of a party rehearsal?"

"It's a new fashion. The very latest."

"Is it? How odd." In an instant, his features went from baffled to delighted. "How marvelous. Is the rehearsal going well?"

"Like clockwork, although I suspect the guests would be very disappointed to learn you've been sneaking about trying to catch a glimpse of the surprise rather than sleeping."

"Sleeping, yes. It is late, isn't it?" He glanced at the locked metal box where she kept the laudanum and scowled a bit. "Shall I take my medicine?"

She shook her head. The laudanum was only useful as a last resort to calm him down—it certainly wasn't effective in making him more lucid—and since he appeared to be calming down well enough on his own, she saw no reason for further sedation. "Not if you let Simmons dress you for bed without complaint."

"Who's Simmons?"

"The nice footman waiting outside the door."

"Ah." He made an inviting motion with his hand.

"Bring him in. Bring him in, then. The sooner I fall asleep, the sooner it will be tomorrow."

"Yes, that's true."

"And tomorrow is my birthday."

"Well . . ." Oh, there was no point in arguing with him. It wasn't as if he would wake up tomorrow and be disappointed. "I'll just go fetch Simmons."

She ushered in the footman, then wandered about the room tidying up while Simmons patiently readied Sir Franklin for bed. It took a bit of doing, but eventually, her father was cozily tucked up in bed with his compass in hand and the very beginnings of exhaustion tugging at his face.

Patience took the seat next to the bed and toed off her shoes. She watched him fiddle with his compass for a minute before leaning forward to gently brush away a lock of hair that had fallen into his eyes. She wished he'd sit still long enough for a decent trim. "Would you like me to fetch you anything? A cup of tea, perhaps?"

"Tea," he repeated slowly. He went very still all of a sudden, and then turned clear blue eyes up to hers. "You're a good girl, Patience." He reached up to take her hand in his. "A good daughter. Have I told you that?"

She squeezed his hand as a pain swelled in her chest and tears burned at the back of her eyes. "No," she whispered. "You haven't." He'd never told her that. Not once had he said anything close to it.

In the past, before his infirmity had become apparent, she'd often felt wounded by his lack of open affection, and what sometimes even amounted to a failure to acknowledge her very existence.

That he should choose to acknowledge and praise her now was almost cruel.

She wasn't a good girl, and she certainly wasn't being a good daughter. Since the night of Lord Welsing's ball, she'd allowed the staff to keep, even lock, her father in his room in the evenings so she could enjoy herself without worrying what trouble he might get into while she was out. She'd left him isolated and alone while she flirted and danced and indulged in dreams of a future that included her happiness, but not necessarily his.

She'd been horribly selfish.

"A good girl," her father repeated. And then as quickly as his moment of lucidity had arrived, it was gone. His eyes clouded again and he released her hand to tap at the compass. "Goes 'round," he murmured.

"Yes." She sniffled and pulled away. "Yes, it goes around. You were very clever to discover it."

And she was very late in discovering her conscience. Closing her eyes, she let out a long shaky breath and sorted through her options. Perhaps, with a little bit of luck, she could still make a few things right.

But to do so, she needed to speak with the Meldrins, and then, though it would break her heart, she needed to say good-bye to William.

"Things will be better now, Papa. I promise."

Chapter Eight

William waited impatiently in the small study off the hall. No doubt it made him look a pathetic fool to be pacing about the little room while guests were gathered in the front parlor. But he couldn't bring himself to rejoin the festivities. Worry for Patience ate at him. She'd looked so stricken, so panicked as she'd pulled away. How was he to go about making frivolous conversation after seeing her like that?

It had taken every ounce of his will not to follow her and Caroline into the family wing of the house. Only the knowledge that he'd be escorted right back out again had kept him from trying. If Patience had wished for his assistance, she'd have asked for it.

He had to remind himself of that fact after a quarter of an hour had passed without any word of her, and then again after half an hour. After three quarters of an hour, he was ready to seek out and assist the stubborn woman whether she liked it or not.

He was nearly to the door when it opened and Patience stepped into the room. He wouldn't have thought it possible, but she looked even more distraught than she had been in the hall. Her face was drawn and tired, her green eyes glassy. It broke his heart.

"Patience, what is it? What's happened?"

In a move too subtle to be an intentional insult, she turned away to softly close the door behind her. "Mrs.

Meldrin said you were in here. It wasn't necessary for you to wait."

"Yes, it was."

"I . . ." She pressed her lips together and nodded. "Thank you."

He took a small, careful step back from her. If she wanted space, he could give her that. At the moment, if she wanted the moon in her hands, he'd find a way to give her that, too. "How is your father?"

"He's asleep."

That didn't quite answer his question, but he decided not to press the matter. Not if it was going to prolong the sadness in her eyes.

"Would you like me to escort you back to the parlor?"

She shook her head. "I can't . . . I need to pack."

"Pack," he repeated dully.

"Yes. I'm leaving. First thing in the morning."

"Leaving? For where? How long?"

"Hertfordshire. Indefinitely."

He couldn't have heard her properly. "I beg your pardon?"

"I'm going to Hertfordshire. To the country."

"The Little Season isn't over yet."

"It is for me, I'm afraid."

He leaned down in an effort to catch her eyes, but she kept her gaze studiously on the floor. "What is this about, Patience? Is it your father? Has his illness taken a turn for the worse?"

"No, he is the same."

"Is it . . . Patience . . . it's not catching, is it?" Surely it wasn't something she could have caught. He'd never once considered the possibility. The Meldrins had more sense than that, didn't they? "You're not . . ."

She glanced up at him for the first time. "No. No, I'm quite well."

The rush of relief nearly made him dizzy. "Then what is it? Have you had a falling-out with Caroline or Mrs. Meldrin?"

She shook her head, but still couldn't meet his eyes. "No. Leaving is entirely my decision."

"I see." He scowled at her. "No, I don't. Tell me why."

"I . . . I've reasons."

"What are they?"

"They're complicated."

His mouth hooked up in a humorless smile. "That's a very uncreative way of saying you'll not tell me."

She tossed her hands up in frustration. "We . . . we're a burden to them here. We'll be a burden to them in the country as well, but less so than in London."

"The Meldrins can well afford the burden of keeping you and your father in London for another fortnight."

"What burdens Mr. Meldrin *can* afford and what burdens he should have to carry are two separate matters."

He hated that she made a sound point. Hated more that he could think of nothing to say that might change her mind . . . except perhaps an offer of marriage. She couldn't leave him if they were bound by an engagement. And he bloody well didn't want her leaving.

The words "marry me" hovered on the tip of his tongue. He bit them back.

Only a rash fool would propose marriage to a woman after such a brief courtship. These sorts of things took time, and thought, and planning.

He had a plan, damn it.

Another fortnight of coming to know each other, a visit to the Meldrin estate after the holidays, a conversation with Mr. Meldrin, or her father if he were well enough. And if those steps in his plan went well, then, and only then, would it be appropriate to extend an offer of marriage.

"Is there nothing I can do to convince you to stay?"

She shook her head.

"Then there is nothing left to be said." He stared at her for several long moments, and though he wasn't aware of it at the time, later he would realize he used those moments to memorize every detail of her face.

She dropped her gaze again and turned away. "I have to go."

"Safe journey, Patience."

He watched her move quickly to the door. And then she was gone. A tickle of something that felt uncomfortably like panic skittered along his spine. Just like that, the woman had walked out of his life. She hadn't even offered a proper good-bye. Then again, neither had he.

"Bloody hell."

They should have a proper good-bye, damn it. He headed for the door, determined to remedy the oversight. He knew it was irrational, perhaps even a little desperate. But he bloody well didn't care.

He'd taken no more than a step when the door swung open again, admitting Mr. Meldrin. The older man took one look at William and shook his head. "It won't do you any good to go after her right now."

"I'm not . . ." William swore under his breath and fisted his hands at his sides. "You're certain?"

Mr. Meldrin nodded as he closed the door behind him. "Girl's as stubborn as they come."

"Stubborn," William repeated. The panic had begun to dull into a sick empty feeling.

"As her father."

He wouldn't have guessed it until that night. "I'd have learned that for myself, with a little more time."

"And she'll learn to trust you, with a little more time."

"Time we no longer have." He turned and looked at Mr. Meldrin. "Trust me with what? What is she hiding?"

"Nothing so terrible, in my opinion." Mr. Meldrin shook his head. "But then, our own troubles always seem more consequential than they do to those around us." He walked to a sideboard and poured a finger of brandy. "Just last week, Mrs. Meldrin refused to attend a dinner party because of a facial blemish. Damned if Caroline or I could see a single thing wrong with her, not so much as a bit of red. But she refused to budge, absolutely refused to believe she had anything but a mountain perched on the end of her nose."

"Are you . . . are you telling me Patience left because of a pimple?"

Mr. Meldrin handed him the drink and poured one for himself. "You're not much for riddles, are you?"

"I'm a bit distracted." William swallowed the liquid down, not caring that he generally avoided spirits. He was already working on a plan that would allow him to be completely foxed before the night was out.

"The pimple is something of a metaphor," Mr. Meldrin said. "Patience's blemish is not quite so imaginary as my wife's, but neither is it quite the mountain she believes it to be. Or perhaps, more importantly, the mountain she is certain others believe it to be."

"Mountains out of molehills. Yes, I get it." He couldn't quite grasp the fact that, on top of everything else, he was having a conversation about pimples. "The difference here is that your wife told you about her blemish."

"At length."

"I can't tell Patience she's overreacting if I don't know what she's reacting to."

"As I said, she needs time. Time," Mr. Meldrin emphasized before William could interrupt with an argument, "you could make at Lord Hartwell's Christmas ball next month."

"The Christmas ball."

"Indeed. My wife and daughter were able to gain a promise of attendance from Patience. Our estate is but a half-day's ride from London. She'll be returning on the eighteenth, the day before the ball, and leaving again the day after."

"May I ask how they managed that?"

"Patience is remarkably susceptible to guilt, and my wife and daughter entirely too accomplished at providing it. They made something of a fuss at Caroline being left without her friend for the remainder of the Little Season." Mr. Meldrin ran the back of his hand across his jaw. "It's not a method I normally condone, but in this instance, I allowed it."

Because he appreciated the result more than he disapproved of the method, William chose not to comment.

Mr. Meldrin swirled the liquid in his glass. "Do you know the odd thing about pimples, Lord Casslebury?"

"I . . ." They were back to pimples? He ran a tired hand down his face. "I'm sure I don't."

"The odd thing is that there's no telling who will make mountains out of them. Nor is there any way of knowing who will point those mountains out to all and sundry." He looked at William over his glass. "Mr. Seager saw something tonight. Something Patience would have preferred he had not."

Bloody hell, Mr. Seager knew her secret, but not him? "I see. Any idea where I might find Mr. Seager?"

"His home, I imagine."

"Right." William set his drink down. "You'll excuse me?"

"By all means, but a final piece of advice before you go? When Patience does confide in you, you might wish to avoid using the word 'overreacting.' It seems to have an adverse effect on women."

William did indeed find Mr. Seager at home—a slightly less than fashionable town house on the very edge of fashionable Mayfair, where he was seated at a very small table, in his very small study, with a very large decanter of brandy within grasping distance.

William took a seat across from him and said a quick prayer of thanks that the decanter retained most of its contents. Mr. Seager was a trifle thick even when sober. Though William had never seen the man in his cups, he'd wager a considerable sum the condition wouldn't enhance the man's powers of perception.

Mr. Seager tipped his glass at him. "Thought you'd be at the dinner yet, my lord. Or were you run off as well?"

William decided to ignore the question in favor of one of his own. "You've had an interesting night, I'm told."

Mr. Seager made some sort of scoffing noise in the back of his throat. "Nothing interesting about it. Horrifying, that's what it was. To think of the attention I've devoted to Miss Meldrin, only to find her family hasn't the sense to toss Miss Byerly's father in an asylum where he belongs. Wager you weren't aware they kept a madman in the house, either."

While Mr. Seager slurped at his drink, William let that bit of information sink in. There it was, then—the reason Patience had left him. Her father hadn't been in his cups the night of Lord Welsing's ball, and he wasn't suffering from a physical ailment now. He was mad.

The revelation prompted several emotions at once—sorrow for Patience, hurt that she hadn't trusted him enough to share her burden, and most prevalent at present, anger at the man who would so carelessly spill Patience's most guarded secret.

Realizing his hands were curling into fists, William made a conscious effort to relax them. "It's bad form to gossip about a family whose table you've only just come from, don't you think? Bad form to gossip about a lady at all, really."

Mr. Seager blinked slowly, as if trying to wrap his mind around a rather complicated puzzle. "Beg pardon?"

William resisted the urge to take hold of the man and shake some sense into him. Instead, he tried a more direct approach. "I believe you're expecting a living from Viscount Wentwise in the near future?"

"Er, yes." The man frowned and lifted his glass again.

William reached out, snatched it out of his hand, and set it out of reach. "Do I have your full attention, Mr. Seager? Because I should like to make myself absolutely clear on a particular matter."

"I'm listening." Mr. Seager's voice came out perilously close to a whine. It was just irritating enough that when he reached out to reclaim his glass, William took some pleasure in slapping back his hand.

"Ouch! What the devil—?"

"If I hear a word," William said slowly and, lest the oaf try to claim a misunderstanding, very clearly, "a single whispered word of what you witnessed tonight, from anyone, you will lose your living. In fact, I'll make it my life's work to see there is not a vicarage available to you in all of Britain. Do you understand?"

Mr. Seager gaped at him. "You can't do that."

"Really? Shall we put it to the test?"

"You . . . I . . . my grandfather is the Marquess of Bruckhaven."

"I imagine if the marquess had the inclination to support the third son of his second daughter, you wouldn't be in search of a living. But I could be mistaken."

"This is an outrage."

"I prefer to think of it as coming to an understanding." He held Mr. Seager's gaze for a moment. "*Do* we have an understanding?"

The younger man dropped his eyes and nodded miserably.

"Excellent."

With that ugly bit of business concluded, William returned Mr. Seager's glass and took his leave. He walked out the front door feeling both grimly satisfied by the visit, and still painfully deflated by Patience's news of an early departure.

It was the latter that prompted him to follow through with his idea of becoming foxed. Well, *that* and for the satisfaction of knowing he was still capable, if he really put his mind to it, of seeing at least one of his plans come to fruition.

His attempt was met with great success, much to his regret the following morning. He woke and dressed, battling a tremendous headache, and lurched his way to the breakfast room determined to conquer the rebellion in his stomach with a proper meal. He fought his way through his first cup of coffee while contemplating the notion that his problem was not so much a recent inability to follow through with his plans, but the far more worrisome inability to devise a plan that did not lead to disaster.

Had he really expressed a desire for less order in his life? How did people *stand* it? Never knowing what to expect, what to do, what to *feel?* The uncertainty of it all was so damn . . . aggravating. The disorder was maddening. The disappointment was heartbreaking.

He paused in the act of reaching for his cup again.

Was he heartbroken? That seemed a trifle melodramatic. He rubbed the heel of his hand against the hollow ache in his chest. Bruised, he decided, perhaps a bit scuffed up, but surely not broken.

Which led to the question—did he plan for his usual, peaceful holiday at his estate in Staffordshire, where the heart Patience had managed to bruise, but not break, could heal in peace . . . or did he plan for a Christmas in London and hand her the opportunity to finish the job?

Chapter Nine

One month later.

Lord and Lady Hartwell's Christmas ball was, by all appearances, a tremendous success. The house was filled with beautiful music, savory refreshments, and best of all, the laughter of a hundred delighted guests. Patience did not number among them. She was in attendance, certainly; she just wasn't delighted.

What she *was*, was weary from the trip, still heartbroken from when she'd last been in London, and now worried about her father. She shouldn't have come to town without him. He'd overheard her discussing her trip to Hartwell House for the Christmas ball, and he'd been agitated before she'd gone—arguing with the staff, complaining bitterly of being left out of the holiday festivities.

What if something happened while she was away? What if she was needed and couldn't be reached in time?

What if Mr. Seager appeared at the ball and made a fuss about her father? The Meldrins had assured her that he'd left town without saying a word to anyone, but what if—

"This isn't at all like you—to be so resolute not to enjoy yourself." Caroline handed her a glass of lemonade. "It's really more like me. Have we decided I'm fashionable?"

"I'm not miserable. I'm concerned."

"Well, you look miserable."

Patience turned and blinked at her friend. "Was that comment meant to improve my mood?"

"It was meant to alter it, at the very least." Caroline scrutinized her face. "It worked as well. Your lips are twitching."

For the first time in too long, Patience felt the beginnings of a real smile. "I missed you, Caroline."

"And I you. So much, in fact, that after your departure, I danced at every ball I attended, simply because I knew you'd want me to."

"Did you really?"

Caroline nodded. "At least twice at each."

"That's wonderful. Did you enjoy yourself?"

"No. I was quite miserable." Caroline shrugged and took a sip of her drink. "But I did dance."

Patience laughed and winced simultaneously. "I do wish you could find a gentleman who appealed to you."

"As it happens, I did. Just not while dancing."

The sound of Virginia Higgs's cheerful voice kept Patience from responding. "Miss Meldrin, Miss Byerly, how lovely to see you both again."

Patience turned, swallowing past a dry lump in her throat. She hadn't expected to see Mrs. Higgs at Hartwell House. She'd hoped, very much, not to see anyone or anything that reminded her of William, which was a hopeless wish, really. *Everything* reminded her of William. Even the trees outside the house made her think of the day she'd spent with him in the park.

But the appearance of his sister was more than she could have prepared for, as was the realization of just how much the woman resembled her brother. They had the same shaped eyes. Patience couldn't stop herself from staring as Caroline and Mrs. Higgs exchanged polite greetings.

She'd thought of William's eyes for weeks, along with his smile, his laugh, the sound of his voice, the way he rocked on his heels when he was thoughtful, and the way his jaw tensed just a hair when she'd upset one of his plans. She thought of the way his gaze so often dipped to her mouth, the feel of his strong hands as they gently pulled her close, and the heat of his body pressed against hers as they kissed.

Oh, how she missed him. She'd never known it was possible to actually hurt with missing someone, and hurt even more knowing she had only herself to blame. What a hypocrite she'd been, pushing herself and Caroline to enjoy everything life had to offer, and then cowering away when life offered the greatest experience of all: the chance to love.

If only she could go back and do things differently. She'd tell him the truth. Surely the pain of being jilted could be no worse than what she felt now. She rather doubted it was any better, but at least it wouldn't have the added weight of cowardice attached.

Perhaps there was still a chance to fix things now. Perhaps she could write him a letter. On second thought, that seemed terribly impersonal, and it would be far too easy for him to dismiss her. Perhaps she could sneak away someday soon and visit his estate in person. It would be scandalous behavior, but she ached enough to simply not care. If scandalous would garner her a chance to win him back, scandalous she would be.

As long as she could be that way without getting caught. There were still the Meldrins to consider, after all.

"Miss Byerly? Miss Byerly."

Patience blinked, the sound of Mrs. Higgs's insistent voice pulling her from her musings. "I beg your pardon?"

"I asked if you might accompany me for a brief tour of the house."

"Oh. I . . ." A tour of someone else's home? What was one to say to such an odd request? "Of course . . . um . . . you've visited before?"

Virginia took her arm and led her away at a brisk pace, before Caroline could comment. "Oh, yes, many times." She threw a glance over her shoulder as they exited the ballroom. "And I don't really mean to give you a tour. There is something in one of the rooms I should think you'd like to see."

"Like to see? At Hartwell House?" She felt a small bubble of laughter form in her throat as they moved quickly down the hall. "What is it?"

"A surprise."

Patience rather thought that was a given, but she held her tongue until she was led into the private family portion of the house. "I must say, Mrs. Higgs, this seems rather—"

"Do call me Virginia."

"If you like, but—"

"Here we are." Virginia stopped suddenly and motioned to a wide set of doors.

Bewildered, Patience pushed through one and stepped into a spacious room with a few bookcases, a large fireplace giving off a warm glow, and a scattering of comfortable seating arrangements. A family parlor, or an outsized study, Patience mused. She moved inside, fully expecting Virginia to follow. Instead, the woman paused in the open door and smiled at her. "Do you know, I believe I neglected to inform my poor Edward where I was going. Do excuse me. I shan't be long."

"But . . ." Patience stared, wide-eyed and open-mouthed, as Virginia briskly stepped out of the room and closed the door behind her.

"What on earth?"

Reeling, she gaped at the door for a moment, then tossed up her hands in utter disbelief and turned to seek a place to sit and wait. She'd taken no more than three steps into the room before the astonishment of being left alone in a strange room in the middle of a ball was replaced by the shock of discovering she wasn't alone at all.

William was there.

She didn't quite believe it at first, *couldn't* believe that it was really him stepping out from the shadow of a bookcase near the fire. She was overtired, heartbroken, dreaming. She closed her eyes slowly and opened them again, fully expecting to find him gone.

"Hello, Patience."

Her heart pounded painfully in her chest. He was real. He was there. "You . . . I . . ."

"You're well, I hope?"

She wanted to run into his arms. She wanted to run away. She wanted to cry and laugh and demand to know what he was doing there. Most of all, she wanted the courage to do the things she'd thought of only minutes ago in the ballroom.

William watched the play of emotions on Patience's face. Even from afar he could see the shock, the delight, and the hurt.

The need to touch her, to comfort, to breathe her in was nearly overpowering. He'd never missed another human being so much in his life. Every hour, every bloody hour, had felt like an eternity. The emptiness in his chest he had felt the night she'd left him had become a heavy weight soon after. And it had grown in size with each passing day.

Regret, that was what the heaviness was. Regret that he'd let her go, that he hadn't set aside his need to follow his bloody plans long enough to admit his need for her.

He pushed aside instinct honed by years of training and admitted it now. "I've missed you, Patience . . . I need you."

He walked toward her, slowly at first, terrified she would turn and leave. But when she stepped toward him instead of away, he closed the remaining distance between them in three long strides and pulled her into his arms.

"I missed you." He bent his head and kissed her forehead, her cheeks, her brows. "I missed you."

His lips wandered restlessly over her face. He couldn't keep still, couldn't stop himself from tasting her jaw, her chin, the tip of her nose. "Missed you."

He wanted to cover every inch of the face that had haunted his dreams, night after night, for the last four weeks. He wanted to kiss her until her body recognized, as his did, that they were made for each other. And he wanted to do it before she pulled away. He waited for that, for the painful moment when doubt and fear overtook her once more and she pushed him away.

That moment never came.

She trembled and sighed, clutching at his shoulders. "If we're caught . . . I haven't told you—"

"Shhh. Door's locked." Virginia had seen to that, and to a maid keeping watch down the hall, expecting her impossibly reserved brother to do little more than talk to Patience.

But William wasn't at all inclined to be reserved at present, and his interests went beyond talking. Taking gentle hold of Patience's face, he silenced her with his mouth. She was just as she'd been in the orangery—an intoxicating mix of sin and innocence. He wasn't sure which he craved more, but he ached to take his fill of both.

His mouth moved hungrily over hers, even as his mind told him to stop, to pull away before it was too late. The plan he'd outlined had involved kissing, a marriage proposal, and a promise from her never to leave him again. It did not involve taking her virtue.

But there was nothing virtuous in the way Patience kissed him back—untutored perhaps, but not virtuous. Her mouth moved eagerly over his. Her arms wrapped around his neck in an almost desperate move to bring him even closer.

His hands moved of their own accord to unbutton her gown, pausing just long enough to brush along the satin skin of her back. She shivered and moaned as the silk of her bodice loosened and slid down, exposing the ivory swell of her breasts.

He allowed himself only one intoxicating moment to indulge in the exquisite softness of them before lifting her into his arms. Still kissing her mouth, her throat, her lovely bare shoulders, he carried her to a settee in a darkened corner of the room. He would have preferred—he certainly would have planned—to take the time to explore every part of her, to linger over every curve and plane. But he hadn't the luxury of time, and suddenly, surprisingly, he found he didn't *want* to plan or orchestrate anything. Suddenly, he wanted nothing more than to follow his heart and trust in the wonder of what unfolded before him.

And, truth be told, a small, selfish part of him was grateful for the excuse to hurry. Desire was rushing through his blood with increasing force. It clawed at his skin, inflamed his senses, and demanded fulfillment.

Their kisses became more urgent, their embrace more feverish. Clothing was pulled and shoved out of the way.

Her glasses disappeared, his waistcoat was removed, his trousers slid down his hips. Someone said, "Hurry." He sincerely hoped it was her.

His palm trailed up the tight muscles of her calf and the soft skin of her thigh to find the heated flesh between her legs. She started at the touch, though whether from fear or pleasure it was impossible to tell.

"Shh. Darling, let me." He used deft fingers to soothe and arouse, until her whimpers became moans and her soft form tightened and strained beneath him.

The sound and feel of her pleasure tore at his control.

He pushed into her, regretting the pain he knew he caused, even as his body shuddered with pleasure. "I'm sorry. Darling. I'm sorry."

He kissed her tenderly then, until the fingers digging into the skin of his back relaxed and she let out a long, unsteady sigh.

"Hurry."

This time, he was certain it was she who said it. It was all the urging he needed. With his jaw clamped tight with the effort to retain control, he began to move. Slowly at first, determined to be careful and their limited time be damned. But when she arched against him impatiently, her breath hitting his cheek in sharp pants, he quickened the pace.

He lost all track of time after that, lost track of everything but the exquisite pleasure of Patience Byerly reaching for completion in his arms. When she found it, when she bucked and cried out softly, he reached for and found his own.

Though he knew he was crushing her with his weight, it was several moments before he amassed the coordination needed to shift their positions. And in the confines of a small settee, the movement took some doing, but eventually he succeeded in pulling her atop him, her head nestled against his chest.

He stroked a hand down her back. "Are you all right?"

She nodded rather than answered, which made him a little nervous.

"I hurt you," he whispered. "I'm sorry."

She tilted her chin up to blink at him, her green eyes squinting adorably. "I'd rather you not apologize for anything at present."

"I should have waited. Given you a bed." *And a ring.*

"I didn't want that." She laid her palm against his cheek. "I wanted you. I hadn't realized how much until . . ."

"Until you left," he finished for her. He took her hand to press a kiss to her palm. "Does that mean you missed me as well?"

"Yes." She laughed softly. "Every second of every day."

"You shouldn't have gone." He pressed another kiss to her hand. "Don't leave again. Stay with me. Marry me."

A long, shaking sigh escaped from her lips. "I want to," she whispered, closing her eyes. "I want to."

The weight in his chest began to grow once again. Was he too late? Had he missed his only chance? "Want to, or will?"

There was a long moment before she opened her eyes and spoke again. "I will. I will marry you *if,*" she said quickly, "*if* you still want me . . . after I explain why I left London." She swallowed hard.

It was tempting to tell her he'd already learned of her secret, but he knew it would be better for her, for both of them, if she found the courage to tell him herself. "All right." He bent down to press another kiss to her forehead. "I'm listening."

She opened her mouth, closed it, and shifted a bit.

"Could we do this dressed? It might take a bit of time, and if someone were to find us—"

"You'd have to marry me," he finished for her. Not a terrible plan, really. Maybe he should have taken his time after all. Then again, that might have only resulted in the pair of them being discovered before he was ready to be caught.

She laughed a little and shoved at his shoulder when he refused to loosen his hold of her. "William."

"Yes, all right."

He let go of her reluctantly, rose from the settee after she did, and helped put her gown to rights. He made an attempt to assist with her hair as well but found he couldn't keep his fingers from running through the silky tresses. It added a certain level of difficulty to the endeavor.

He wanted to take out the remaining pins and watch the locks fall to her shoulders. He wanted to see her hair spread out before him on a pillow. He wanted to know what it looked like wild and mussed after a night of passion. He wanted, he was *tempted* to—

As if she could sense the tenor of his thoughts, Patience batted his hands away with a laugh. "Keep your plans to yourself for the time being, if you please."

He heaved a disappointed sigh and turned his attention to straightening his own attire. He ran into a spot of difficulty with his cravat.

"Here, allow me." Patience pushed one last pin into her hair and stepped forward to knot his cravat with the efficiency of an experienced valet.

"Where did you learn to do that?"

"From my father." She gave her work a soft pat and stepped away. "Because of my father might be more accurate."

He tilted his head to catch her eye. "Part of what you need to explain?"

"Yes, I . . ." She bit her bottom lip. "Oh, dear, I don't know how to start."

"I believe the usual response to that is to start at the beginning."

She smiled a little, but there was no humor in it. "It might be easiest for me to tell you the worst of it first and be done with it."

He reached for her fidgeting hands. "Whatever it is, Patience, we'll find a way—"

The doors swung open before he had the chance to respond.

"Patience?" Virginia rushed inside, noticeably out of breath. "I'm sorry. Mr. Meldrin is looking for you. I had my maid keep watch and—" She shook her head and crossed the room to grasp Patience's hand and draw her to a trio of chairs near the light of the fire. "No time. Come here. William, sit there."

They'd only just arranged themselves in their seats when Mr. Meldrin arrived, a handful of footmen and maids trailing behind him. William had an unpleasant image of the man coming after him, glove in hand, to demand a duel, but it was short-lived. Mr. Meldrin spared him a brief nod, but he didn't appear angry, merely worried. And the concern in his eyes was directed solely at Patience.

She saw it as well, and rose unsteadily from her chair. "Mr. Meldrin?"

"A message just arrived by special courier." He crossed the room to place a hand on her shoulder. "Your father's gone missing."

Chapter Ten

Patience had known fear before. She was no stranger to guilt and regret. But until Mr. Meldrin had uttered the words, "Your father's gone missing," she'd never known true panic.

The force of it was disorienting. It sucked the air from her lungs and tore a great hole in her chest. She felt her world spin and whirl while her mind leapt erratically from one thought to the next.

What was she supposed to do now? She'd encountered a thousand difficulties with her father in the past, but he'd never just disappeared from his own house. It simply wasn't something he did.

She found herself looking helplessly from William to Mr. Meldrin. "I don't know what to do."

Mr. Meldrin gave her arm a comforting squeeze. "We'll find him, Patience. Lord Hartwell has offered whatever assistance is needed. But the staff and stables are overrun at present. It will take a bit of doing to ready the horses and bring them around."

She felt herself nod. "Yes, all right."

"I'll see what I can do to hurry things along."

"Thank you."

She only half heard Mr. Meldrin leave with Virginia, and was only distantly aware that William continued to issue orders to the staff who came in and out of the room. But it was impossible not to notice when he stepped in front of her to tilt her chin up with his hand.

"Now, would you like to tell me why I'm about to head off into the dead of a winter's night to search for a grown man?"

She dearly wished the question were rhetorical. It would be so much easier to answer truthfully if that were the case. *No. No, I would not like to tell you.* Instead, she pushed past the dizziness and fear and said in a voice so small she hardly recognized it as her own, "He's mad. My father is mad."

To her amazement, he nodded once and lifted a hand to brush the backs of his fingers across her cheek. "Is he a danger?"

"What? *No.*" She shook her head adamantly, then rather wished she hadn't. It made the room spin unpleasantly. "No, he's perfectly harmless. He is, I swear it. He's just ... he's unable to take proper care of himself. He ... why aren't you shocked?"

"I had a discussion with Mr. Seager."

"You knew?" He'd known and still come for her? A pressure built behind her eyes. She tried to push it away. What good could possibly come from falling apart now? But the harder she grasped at control, the quicker it slipped away.

"I'm sorry." She felt the first tears spill over. "I'm sorry."

His strong arms wrapped around her, pulling her against the warmth of his chest. "It's all right." His hand stroked her hair, across her back. "Darling, don't. Don't cry. We'll find him."

"That's not ..." Well, yes, it was a very large part of why she was crying; it just wasn't the only part. "You're not angry. You should be angry."

He pulled back a little and used the pad of his thumb to wipe away a tear. "Why should I be angry?"

"For not telling you." She hiccuped and swallowed back a new round of tears. "About my father."

He pulled a handkerchief from his pocket and handed it to her. "I'd rather you had, to be honest. It could have saved us weeks of torment."

"I—"

"We can discuss it later. For now, we'll concentrate on finding your father." He tipped her chin up with his finger. "All right?"

She took a shuddering breath and nodded.

He stroked her hair once more before stepping back. "It's nearly Christmas. Where might he think to go this time of year?"

"Nowhere." She wiped away the remainder of her tears. "He doesn't like Christmas. He's never wanted to celebrate it before. Not even when Mother was alive."

"Your mother," he said thoughtfully. "Would he go somewhere that holds memories of her? Your childhood home?"

"No, I don't think so. It was not a love match. He took little interest in her, I think. In us. In everything but his work."

"I'm sorry."

She shook her head. "He wasn't unkind, just . . . distracted." She sighed in frustration. "I don't know where he'd go. I don't know *him*. Not the man he was, or the man he is now. I know he's changed. He never cared for company before, and now he can't abide being isolated. He wants parties and attention. He gave me a birthday present last month, a book of his. I could scarcely believe it."

If she hadn't been working herself into a rant, she might not have missed his startled expression, or heard the wince in his voice. "Birthday?"

"It's in June, but that's not the point. He's never given me a present before. He's never remembered my birthday. The week before that, he handed me an old fob and told me to pay the butcher." She threw up her hands. "Do you know what I would have given for him to take an interest in our finances two years ago? He paid no heed to the limits of his income. He spent every penny on his workshop. I had to sell off our lives in bits and pieces just to put food on the table, and then resort to accepting charity from old friends. And suddenly, years too late, he's willing to sacrifice his precious science?"

"You're angry."

"I'm not. I'm . . ." She trailed off, noticing for the first time that there were tears burning at the backs of her eyes again. "I am. I hadn't realized."

"You've a right, if you were struggling and he refused to help."

"No. No, he'd just forget. I'd explain that we couldn't afford some new bit of equipment and he'd agree. And then he'd forget. He was always forgetting. Perhaps . . ." She blew out a long breath. "Perhaps he's always been a little mad, and I hadn't wanted to see it."

William wasn't given a chance to respond. A maid appeared at the door. "My lord, the horses are ready."

Already exhausted, she followed William from the room and found Mr. Meldrin and several grooms waiting at a side door to the house.

"Take the east and west roads," William instructed two of the grooms as they stepped out into the night air. "Mr. Meldrin, if you'll go south, I'll search north. Any sign of—"

"Beggin' pardon, milord," one of the grooms interrupted. He pointed into the darkness. "Rider coming."

Patience squinted into the darkness and saw the dark figure galloping toward them.

"Another messenger?" someone ventured.

It wasn't another messenger. Patience's breath quickened. Even with distance and darkness between them, she knew her father.

"Papa!"

She raced forward and had hold of the horse's reins the moment her father reached her. "Papa, are you well? Are you hurt?"

"Hurt?" Sir Franklin Byerly hopped down from his horse with a surprising agility. "Why should I be hurt?"

She gripped his face in her hands and searched for signs of injury. Other than being red-nosed and out of breath, he appeared in perfect health. "You left . . . it's cold. We didn't know where you were and—"

"Should've been here," he grumbled and handed the reins over to a groom. "Left without me, don't you know. The lot of them left without me."

She clung to him, even as she pulled him toward the house. "I know. I'm sorry. I'm so sorry."

"Ah, now, don't trouble yourself. Found my own way, didn't I?" He turned to blink out at the darkness behind him. "Might have gotten a bit lost along the way."

The idea of that, of her father lost and confused on some desolate road or in London, sent a chill of horror along her spine. "What were you thinking, riding out by yourself?"

"Grown man, aren't I?" He looked up and smiled cheerfully at the group of men still standing at the door. "Are we all here, then?"

William discreetly took hold of her father's elbow and helped usher him inside. "Mr. Byerly, you're well?"

"Sir Franklin Byerly, my good man," her father corrected.

He slanted a questioning look at Patience, but it was Mr. Meldrin who answered. "Knighted for his work in magnetism."

"Goes 'round," her father informed William.

"Does it, indeed?" William smiled at her father as if his comment made complete sense. "I hadn't realized . . . Mr. Meldrin, I believe Lord Hartwell won't mind the continued use of our private little room, but would you be so kind as to—?"

"I'll see to it."

While William continued to issue orders to the staff, Patience bustled her father into the room they'd just vacated, wrapped him in blankets, and set him in front of the fire. He turned to look at her as she fussed over him, and his face suddenly showed surprise, as if he'd quite forgotten she'd been at his side since he arrived. "Ah, Patience! Wonderful to see you, child. Wonderful to see you." He patted her cheek. "Be a dear and fetch your father a cup of tea."

She nodded toward a maid who had just arrived with a tray. "Just a dollop of cream, please."

While the maid served her father, William took her arm and gently pulled her a few steps away.

"So, this is the man who's kept us apart," he said quietly. "The reason you thought I might reconsider my offer of marriage."

The mention of their earlier discussion had her eyes darting to the settee in the darkened corner of the room and the heat rushing to her cheeks. Had that really happened just a short time ago?

She pulled her eyes away to look to William. "They say madness is a result of weak blood, that it shouldn't be passed on, and that men like my father should be kept in an asylum."

He made a noise that sounded suspiciously like a snort. "They also say high foreheads are a sign of intelligence, and that taking the water at Bath is good for the constitution."

"Aren't they? Isn't it?"

"I've met many a twit with a high forehead, and I don't know that I've ever felt particularly well after drinking the water at Bath." He took her hand in his. "What I do know, Patience, is that I love you. I adore you. I cannot imagine spending one more day without you." He waited a beat before smiling wryly. "It's generally preferable to have one's proclamation of love met with a similar declaration."

She couldn't help laughing just a little. "I *do* love you." She took a quick glance to be certain her father wasn't watching, then stood on her toes to press a kiss to William's mouth. "I've loved you from the very start."

The breath he took was a trifle shaky, but there wasn't even a whisper of hesitation to his smile. "Bit rash, that."

"Yes." She laughed. "It was, rather."

"I'm glad for it."

"I am as well."

Her father chose that moment to remind them of his presence. "Where the devil is the Yule log?"

"Papa?"

"Can't have Christmas without a Yule log."

"It's several days yet before—"

"And some wassail." He pulled a face. "Can't abide the stuff, myself, but it is tradition, after all."

"The thing is, Papa . . . the thing is . . ." She looked to William, who proved to be no help at all.

"You're absolutely right, Sir Franklin." William nodded. "We should indeed have a Yule log."

Patience started and blinked. "William—"

"And wassail." He stepped over to the bell pull and gave it a decisive tug. "Any other requests?"

"William, this really isn't necessary."

"It is," he told her in a resolute tone. "You told me once you've always wanted a Christmas tradition."

"Yes, but—"

"Traditions have to begin somewhere." He grinned suddenly and swept her into her arms, ignoring her small noise of protest and struggle to free herself before someone walked in or her father made a fuss. "We'll start our traditions here. An early Christmas celebration every year. With all the trimmings. I'll even bring in a bucket of water and apples for you, if you like."

"I don't need—"

"We'll exchange gifts." He tapped the edge of her spectacles gently. "A new pair of these to begin with . . ."

Keeping hold of her with one arm, he reached inside his pocket and pulled out a small box. He flipped open the lid with his thumb to reveal frames for a new pair of spectacles. "It wasn't possible to include the lenses, I'm afraid," he told her. "But I hoped the sentiment . . ."

"They're perfect," she whispered. "As is the sentiment."

"You can have whatever you desire for Christmas when you're Lady Casslebury." He bent his head a bit to look down at her. "You will be Lady Casslebury?"

Patience ceased caring if they were seen embracing. What did it matter now? She took the box from him, grinned, and stood on tiptoe to press a kiss against his mouth. "There's nothing I desire more."

He drew the kiss out a bit longer before pulling away. "When the wassail arrives, we'll toast to our first family Christmas."

"Family Christmas!" Sir Franklin Byerly said suddenly. He took a long sip of his tea, settled himself more comfortably in his chair, and smiled into the fire. "Important things, families. Important things."

William looked down into the green eyes of the woman he planned on spending every day of his life falling more in love with. "I couldn't agree more."

DAWN MACTAVISH

"...An enthralling, non-stop read. 4 ½ Stars!"
—*RT Book Reviews* on *Prisoner of the Flames*

Counterfeit Lady

"NO, MY LADY, I COULDN'T—"

But Alice could—and did. Against her better judgment, she allowed herself one night at a masquerade ball, playing the role of her mistress. When else might she, daughter of an austere Methodist minister and a servant, sample the pleasures of the ton? She had but one obligation: deter the coxcomb and would-be suitor, Nigel Farnham.

"WHEN HAS 'NO' EVER STOPPED ME?"

She vanished in a swish of buttery silk and left behind the scent of sweet clover and violets. Mischievous and bold, Lady Clara Langly was a chit who desperately needed to be taken in hand—but she had left Nigel abruptly, fled into the night, and he'd had no chance to see her pretty face unmasked. If he was right, and dancing was nothing but making love to music, their quadrille was just the beginning. . . .

ISBN 13: 978-0-8439-6321-2

INTERACT WITH DORCHESTER ONLINE!

Want to learn more about your favorite books and authors?
Want to talk with other readers that like to read the same books as you?
Want to see up-to-the-minute Dorchester news?

VISIT DORCHESTER AT:
DorchesterPub.com
Twitter.com/DorchesterPub
Facebook.com (Search Pages)

DISCUSS DORCHESTER'S NOVELS AT:
Dorchester Forums at DorchesterPub.com
GoodReads.com
LibraryThing.com
Myspace.com/books
Shelfari.com
WeRead.com

☐ **YES!**

Sign me up for the Historical Romance Book Club and send my FREE BOOKS! If I choose to stay in the club, I will pay only $8.50* each month, a savings of $6.48!

NAME: _____

ADDRESS: _____

TELEPHONE: _____

EMAIL: _____

☐ I want to pay by credit card.

☐ VISA   ☐ MasterCard   ☐ DISCOVER

ACCOUNT #: _____

EXPIRATION DATE: _____

SIGNATURE: _____

Mail this page along with $2.00 shipping and handling to:
Historical Romance Book Club
PO Box 6640
Wayne, PA 19087
Or fax (must include credit card information) to:
610-995-9274
You can also sign up online at **www.dorchesterpub.com**.
*Plus $2.00 for shipping. Offer open to residents of the U.S. and Canada only.
Canadian residents please call 1-800-481-9191 for pricing information.
If under 18, a parent or guardian must sign. Terms, prices and conditions subject to change. Subscription subject to acceptance. Dorchester Publishing reserves the right to reject any order or cancel any subscription.

Get Free Books!

You can have the best romance delivered to your door for less than what you'd pay in a bookstore or online. Sign up for one of our book clubs today, and we'll send you *FREE* BOOKS* just for trying it out... **with no obligation to buy, ever!**

Travel from the Scottish Highlands to the American West, the decadent ballrooms of Regency England to the blazing sands of Egypt. Your shipments will include authors such as **JENNIFER ASHLEY, CASSIE EDWARDS, SHIRL HENKE, BONNIE VANAK**, and many more.

As a book club member you also receive the following special benefits:
- **30% off all orders!**
- **Exclusive access to special discounts!**
- **Convenient home delivery and 10 days to return any books you don't want to keep.**

Visit www.dorchesterpub.com or call 1-800-481-9191

There is no minimum number of books to buy, and you may cancel membership at any time.
*Please include $2.00 for shipping and handling.